DARK LIGHT

Shattered Light

2

DARK LIGHT

Chelsea Quinn Yarbro

POCKET BOOKS
New York   London   Toronto   Sydney   Tokyo   Singapore

This book is a work of fiction. Names, characters, places and
incidents are products of the author's imagination or are used
fictitiously. Any resemblance to actual events or locales or per-
sons, living or dead, is entirely coincidental.

An *Original* Publication of POCKET BOOKS

 POCKET BOOKS, a division of Simon & Schuster Inc.
1230 Avenue of the Americas, New York, NY 10020

Copyright © 1999 by Chelsea Quinn Yarbro

ISBN: 0-671-03267-4

First Pocket Books printing March 1999

10 9 8 7 6 5 4 3 2 1

POCKET and colophon are registered trademarks of
Simon & Schuster Inc.

Cover art by David A. Cherry

Printed in the U.S.A.

For

Maureen Kelly
why not?
and Pimpernel, ancestor to mrem

Chapter 1

THIS TIME HE CAME FROM THE BADLANDS
where seven of the Ten Cities had once been. He
was in the robes of a mage that were as much
illusion as reality. He made himself noticed by
the arms he carried—a sword with a jeweled hilt
and a throwing axe stuck through his wide belt.
He did not look like the nomads of the wastes
who sometimes stumbled into the place, but he
did not appear to come from Dismas, either, so
no one hindered him. Men in the streets of the
village watched him warily, knowing that he
represented something they might not want to
confront, as strangers so often did. He ignored
them and the occasional stray dwarf mrem that
wandered the empty places and villages of
Delos, too small to be useful to their ferocious,
larger cousins.

Ahead was Fuego, the city Wladex had been
searching for, the place he intended to find his
next paladin. He adjusted his spell to make his
appearance more convincing, then stopped at the

well in the middle of the village and took a drink from the community cup.

"This is very sweet water," he said loudly enough to attract the attention of those standing about the little square. "No wonder your village has survived. I suppose you had a fine market here, in the Great Age." It was too insignificant a place for memorial monoliths, or any other structures where the history of the place could be recorded.

One of the men—small and wizened, as those on the edge of the badlands tended to be—stepped forward. "The stories say so." He studied Wladex a short while. "You are a fire mage, are you not?"

"I am," Wladex lied, his eyes glittering, "as you see."

The man became a bit more curious. "Bound for Fuego?"

"Of course," said Wladex, telling the truth this time. "Where else would a fire mage go? I have been traveling a long way, and have had to battle many times. I am tired. Do let me stop here for a while. I have gold to pay for a place to rest."

The villager shrugged. "Fuego is not far. You can walk there in six or seven hours without using spells to speed your travel. But if you are truly weary, you may rest here." He glanced at his companions. "What do you think?"

"He can stay," announced a more senior version of the villager who had spoken to Wladex. "There is a rest-house." He pointed to a building that was indistinguishable from the others. "Go in. The keeper will show you to a sleeping chamber."

The first villager added a warning. "We have no food to spare. You cannot buy it, for there is hardly enough for us."

Wladex chuckled. "No matter. I will fend for myself. You are good to a mage alone in the wastes." He made a ritual gesture and produced four little flames on the tips of his fingers. "I thank you for your hospitality." He noticed a dwarf mrem nosing about his feet and he shooed it away before he recited the usual phrase of good intentions: "May the Laria not touch your lives."

This pious wish gained supportive murmurs from the men. The youngest of their numbers said, "The Laria has no use for people like us." He was immediately hushed by his elders.

"Never think that," Wladex warned. "The Laria can turn anything to its own purpose, and that purpose is always destruction."

"Destruction." The oldest man said it emphatically. "The youngster is a fool."

Wladex did not want to get drawn into an argument. "May he grow wiser with age," he said as he went toward the rest-house. The building was squat, cobbled together with mud and straw. There were two windows, small, with rickety shutters to keep out the constant light of the suns that blazed over Delos. There was a dry, dusty smell to the place.

The keeper answered Wladex's summons with a look of surprise—travelers were rare in this place, even mages usually kept to the established roads. He looked his guest up and down. "Two gold craters for five hours in the dark."

"Done," said Wladex, and handed over the ensorcelled coins. Their illusion would last long enough for Wladex's purposes. "Darkness is a luxury for travelers."

"That it is," said the keeper smugly, and pointed Wladex to a chamber not much larger than a coffin. "There. Close the door and you will be in darkness." He tossed the magical coins in the air, unaware of their worthlessness.

"Wake me when my time is up," said Wladex, as he went into the chamber. Once he secured the door, he released his spell. He no longer appeared to be a mage—fire or otherwise—he was now himself, a vampire lord. The constant light that flooded Delos was exhausting to him, and he welcomed the darkness the chamber provided. He lay back on the pile of straw that served for a bed and told himself that in places like this he could not be picky; the keeper and one or two of the villagers would be blood enough to sustain him until he reached Fuego. With that comforting thought, he lapsed into the stupor that passed for sleep among his kind.

The keeper was prompt, striking the door with a sharp blow the instant Wladex's five hours were up. "Rise, mage."

Wladex got to his feet. "If you would assist me?" he called out in a weak voice. "I fear I am ill."

"A mage? Ill?" The keeper was astonished and suspicious.

"There must have been a spell cast while I slept," he said in quavering tones.

As Wladex intended, the keeper came through the door, and he fell upon him at once, famished for what the keeper provided. He sank in his teeth greedily, taking as much blood as the man contained. Fortified, he reactivated his illusion spell, once again taking on the appearance and manner of a fire mage. He let the body of the keeper fall behind the door of the chamber he had occupied. Then he went out into the continuous, blazing sunlight.

"You are resuming your travels?" one of the villagers asked. Wladex did not know if he had spoken to the fellow before, or if he was someone new.

"I must." He blinked and silently began a summoning spell. "I will be glad of company. These empty places are most troubling when one is alone." He glanced at the villagers and saw two of the men lose all expression. These would be the ones to come with him.

"I will come," said the two, almost in unison.

"How good of you. Fuego is a fine place to visit." Though neither of them would live to see it. "Bring your packs and come with me."

A few of the unaffected villagers exchanged uneasy glances, for the ways of mages were powerful and strange. No one made any effort to deter the two from leaving. In a very little time, the three were on the road, all walking briskly in the effulgent light.

"Your village is an old one," Wladex said companionably as they went along after going an hour or so in silence. "It has the look of age." *And neglect*, he added to himself.

"Some say it goes back to the one sun," said the taller of the two. "There was a great city in the plains. One of the Ten Cities. Our village was near it." To their right the blue sun was sinking at the horizon, casting long orange shadows along their right, and the red sun was halfway up the morning sky, lending them short green shadows on their left. The green sun was hidden by the bulk of the world but would be shining above them by the time the red sun was setting.

"One of the Ten Cities," the shorter villager confirmed. "It was supposed to be the most wonderful place. Our village was not far beyond its gates, or so the stories say."

"A most unfortunate fate, the fall of the cities," said Wladex, who decided to use the tall one first, in case the man would be foolish enough to fight him. "So long ago."

"Such days will not come again in our lifetimes," said the shorter man.

"No," said Wladex, knowing how little time the two villagers had left. He picked up the pace of their travels, and the brisker pace stopped all conversation.

By the time the red sun was directly overhead—the only sun in the sky—there was a scruffy sort of oasis not far ahead, just off the line of the road. "Let us get out of the light for a short while, and refresh ourselves. There is shelter in those tall bushes," he suggested, knowing the villagers would agree to a halt, for he had pressed them most of their time traveling.

The taller villager spoke up. "When we return the rest of the villagers will envy us."

"That they will," said Wladex, an evil smile playing at the corners of his mouth. "When you return."

The shorter villager grinned. "We will see Fuego. No one in our village has done that. We will have much to boast of."

Wladex kept his thoughts to himself, for he knew they would never return. "There is something in the oasis," he said, making it a warning.

"It is probably a swarm of brown nits," said the taller villager. "We often hear travelers complain of them."

"Brown nits. Merely a nuisance," said Wladex. Just in case it was more than that, he drew his ruby-hilted sword—it was actually onyx-hilted, but the spell made it look like a ruby—as they approached.

The shorter villager looked about apprehensively. "I . . . I don't know how to fight."

"Don't worry," said Wladex. "I do."

"You mean you will do a spell?" asked the taller. They were very near the oasis now, and the two men were becoming edgy.

"I can do that, but why bother using magical power for nothing more than brown nits?" Truth to tell, he was eager for the fight. He had not battled anything but open spaces and desolation for six red sun days; his longing for destruction, for the consumption of life was a living hunger within him that the keeper had only sharpened. He swung his sword suggestively. "Nits make good fighting practice. Keep back if you are frightened."

The villagers were only too willing to follow that order. They fell a step or two behind. Wladex was secretly pleased they were so nervous, for he did not want to try to fight and maintain his own illusion spell as well as their summoning spell at the same time. He strode purposefully through the scrub and into the heart of the oasis.

The oasis was alive with grey and brown nits. There were easily fifty of the pesky reptilian creatures who were vaguely man-like. The tallest stood no higher than Wladex's waist, the smallest came up to his knee. Most of them rushed him, chittering with rage and hunger as they streamed toward him. A few of them were so excited that they were unable to attack, but ran in circles after their scaly tails; at another time Wladex might have found such antics amusing, but now he was too depleted to see any value in them beyond what they could feed him.

Relishing the chance at easy kills, Wladex raised his sword and brought it scything down, scattering nits in all directions, a half dozen of them in severed pieces. "Ah!" he exclaimed as the dying energy of the nits flowed into him. They were hardly more than a snack, but they stimulated him as he swung again, taking delight in the chaos of their dying. Again he swung, and another rush of life went from nits to Wladex in a splendid tide.

One persistent grey nit managed to jump onto his back. Wladex tried to shake him off, and when that didn't work, he took his sword, swung it over his head and down. The nit gave a high, inhuman cry and fell away. Wladex did not pause, but rushed toward the nits, hacking at them without artistry, chopping off limbs and heads with every stroke. He was almost disappointed when the last of the horrid little beasts fled.

Wladex stood still for a long moment, taking in the last residue of energy. It would have been better had there been blood to drink, but he knew the villagers would provide that, so he did not feel too disappointed.

"Is it safe? It's quiet," called one of the villagers as the two men tiptoed through the brush around the oasis.

"See for yourself," said Wladex, indicating the dead nits with the sweep of his sword before he returned it to its scabbard.

"So many," marveled the taller villager.

The shorter man kicked at one of the ugly little carcasses. "I hate these things. They're mean and mindless."

"That they are," Wladex agreed, showing his teeth in what could be a smile.

The taller villager went to the old well in the middle of the oasis. Water trickled over ancient stones, a few of which had ancient script carved

into them—writing that was now nearly obliter-
ated by sand and wind and time. Perhaps this
had once been the heart of one of the Ten Cities,
Wladex thought as he watched his companions
prepare to drink. The well might have been at
the foot of a city monolith, such as those still
standing in Fuego and Terris and Astra. And
Dismas. The taller villager bent down to the
fountain, smacking his lips as he did. "Very
good."

"No doubt," said Wladex. "Nits often gather
in places with water."

The shorter villager went to take his turn
drinking. The water seemed to rise up to meet
him, which should have alerted him to danger,
but unaware he bent and slurped the crystal
stream.

Wladex took advantage of the moment to cast
a spell of immobility over the shorter villager,
and when that man froze in place, Wladex
swung around to the taller and threw himself
upon the man, pinning him to the ground before
draining him of blood. When he was finished
and much restored, he cloaked the body in a
vanishing spell, and released the shorter villager
from his immobility spell.

The villager blinked. "I'm sorry, great mage. I
think the journey has tired me more than I knew.
I just . . . nodded off." He looked around, his
expression perplexed. "Didn't we . . . wasn't
there someone else with us?"

The brief annoyance Wladex felt at the villager
faded quickly and he managed an affable smile.

"Why, no," he said. "But you have been regaling me with stories of your village, and that may account for your feeling." He smiled engagingly. "Tales often make the people in them seem real, do they not?"

"Oh." The villager rubbed his eyes. "Well."

"Your village has many interesting stories," said Wladex as he indicated the man should drink his fill.

"But mage, are you not thirsty?" He seemed unsure of himself, and ill at ease.

"I drank while you were napping," said Wladex. "Have all you need. It is still three hours to Fuego, and the green sun will be in the sky by then." He pointed toward the road. "When you are done, we will move on, and you will tell me more about your village."

The man drank rapidly, as if he feared Wladex would change his mind. "There," he said as he wiped his mouth with the back of his hand. "I will last until Fuego."

"Very good," Wladex approved, and led the way out of the oasis.

"I can't rid myself of the feeling we were not alone earlier," the villager said when they had left the oasis behind.

By now Wladex had an easy answer to offer. "I have a guardian spell to keep us from any of the dangers we might find on this remote road," he explained glibly.

"Oh." The villager thought about the answer. "I should have thought of that."

"So you should," said Wladex. Now that his

hunger was satisfied, he could feel his own illusion spell growing stronger, making his disguise complete. "These badlands are home to all manner of creatures."

"Yes, I know," said the villager in a tone that told much more than his words about how familiar he was with ogres, gargoyles, Lizcanth, and ghouls.

Wladex let the matter drop, allowing the villager to believe himself safe as they went on toward Fuego.

Chapter 2

THE GREAT GATE OF FUEGO WAS A BUSY
place with traders and armed men at odds about
admission. The long red shadows of the dawning
green sun contrasted with the short green shadows of the westering red sun. Where the two
shadows crossed there was a darkness greater
than any in the fabled ruby mines of Fuego. In
these stark contrasts the massive red walls
seemed sinister, as if the opposition of colors revealed some hidden danger within.

Finally Wladex and the villager made it to the
gate where an armed reaver with a ruby badge
on his breastplate scowled at the two. "Your
purpose?"

"I am a fire mage," Wladex said, pointing to
himself. "My companion is a villager from out
in the wastes. He was good enough to give me
company on my journey."

"Yes," the villager chimed in. "We have come
here together."

The reaver glowered at the two of them and

signaled to one of his companions. "How much should we charge them?"

The second reaver—a grizzled old veteran of many battles—rubbed his stubbled chin. "No good trying to tax mages. They only pay in magic coins, anyway. Let them pass and see they are taxed on the way out." He pointed to Wladex. "You haven't stated your purpose for coming."

"I should think it obvious. I am a fire mage and this is Fuego, the city of fire. But if you must know," he went on with exaggerated patience, "I am searching for a paladin with whom to join forces. This seemed a good place to find one."

The veteran reaver laughed cynically. "The only thing paladins are good for is impossible fights. Stay with a knight, or join one of our reaver companies. You'll do better if you don't throw in your lot with a paladin." He winked. "Still, you have come on a good day."

"That may be," said Wladex, not wanting to betray his knowledge. "But I do not wish to do better than to find a worthy paladin. As all fire mages must, I wish to bring down the Laria." He did not add that he intended to take its place.

The old reaver shrugged. "If you must be mad," he said as he stood aside to permit Wladex and the villager to pass.

Inside the gate the city was crowded. Tall, old buildings leaned together as if to make it easier for those living within them to shout and babble across the narrow streets. Vendors of all sorts huddled against the walls offering everything from trinkets to spells, from food to assassination to those who made their way toward the center of the city. Wladex ignored them all, but the villager was enthralled by everything and often paused to gawk at the amazing sights. The people of Fuego were restless this day, and more of them poured into the streets swelling the throng bound for the main square.

Wladex could sense something of the cause of this excitement, and he let himself be carried along, for a contest between the knights of the Houses Cladius and Capulet would draw all the champions in the city, and Wladex hoped he would find the paladin he sought amid those come to watch. He all but dragged the villager after him, not wanting to be separated from his next meal. In this jumble and confusion he had to work to maintain his illusion spell, and he found this tiring. He would have to feed before the green sun was overhead or he would have trouble sustaining his illusion.

The square was already jammed except for the open part between the monoliths, and it took a minor spell for Wladex to push forward to the front ranks of the audience. He quickly took stock of all he saw.

Beneath the third monolith the three knights and a paladin of House Capulet were gathered together, selecting their weapons and testing them carefully—this was to be a contest without the aid of magic. No spells, no enchanted weapons would be allowed—only old-fashioned skill at arms would make it possible for a champion to prevail. The knights would fight together against the knights of House Cladius, and the paladins would engage in single combat when the knights were done. The prizes were jewels and gold, as well as glory and reputation. Across the open area, the Cladian knights were making their selection of weapons, but the paladin was performing ritualistic exercises, no weapon in his hands. Wladex watched him with interest, for this was either a superior fighter or an utter fool.

An official in wide-shouldered red robes came to the center of the open area and raised his hands for silence. The crowd obeyed, with only a few catcalls to inject a kind of derisive humor into the occasion. As soon as there was silence, the official began his announcement: "This is a fight to capitulation or the incapacity to continue without magical intervention. The Houses Capulet and Cladius have brought their champions to this place to show their prowess. Knights fighting for Capulet are Hornos of the Tall Gates, Guelm Long-Eyes, and Dusho the Fist. The paladin for Capulet is Left-Handed Ninnian. For Cladius, the knights are Brior the Scarred, Moidun of the Old Spurs, and Lykal of the Bridgehead. The paladin for Cladius is Stariat the Questor." The official lowered his hands, permitting the crowd to cheer and shout to their favorites. "When the red sun sinks behind the western tower, the conflict of the knights will be at an end. Any use of magic, deliberate or otherwise, will disqualify the fighter using it. To monitor all magic, the mentor Albiates, whose rulings shall be final." He made a sign to the crowd and they bowed in respect.

Albiates stepped forward, a formidable figure in billowing robes of pale gold. He was old, but straight as a lance, with a clever face and the strength of presence of a ruler. He carried a staff which he held out to each of the combatants in turn as if taking their measure, then he stepped back to his place under the second monolith.

"The monitor of the fighting will be Photin of House Gaius. House Gaius is neutral in this contest." The official pointed to the tenth monolith where Photin stood; he was a much-revered leader of fighters and the crowd cheered for him. As he took his seat on a raised dais, there was another hush.

The official made the traditional summoning gesture, and the various knights came to him in the center of the area between the monoliths. "Each of you is allowed three weapons and two shields beyond your standard armor. Any more will be a breach of conduct and will exclude you from the fighting. You are to follow the rules of chivalry and the code of honor. If any one of you fails to do so, he will be disqualified and disgraced in Fuego. Do you understand?"

The six knights indicated that they did.

The betting in the crowd was frantic, for all wagers had to be laid before the first blow was struck. Everyone seemed to have a bet to make, and the odds shifted mercurially. Wladex listened to the hasty cries around him, and toyed with the notion of betting on the fight himself, but knew that would appear odd in a fire mage.

"Then retire to your appointed places and be ready to fight at my signal." The official frowned as if to give weight to his orders.

From his place at the side of the central area, Wladex watched avidly as the villager at his side held his breath.

As soon as the knights were in their positions, they all checked their weapons and made their last-minute adjustments. Then they signaled their readiness.

"Champions of Cladius, champions of Capulet," the official boomed out in stentorian tones, "Have at it!" He jumped nimbly back as the two groups of knights rushed together in a thundering attack.

Guelm Long-Eyes was the first to raise his weapon—it was a nasty, double-headed battle-axe—and swing it at Brior the Scarred, who parried it handily with a stout round shield. The sound of the impact shuddered in the air, and was at once replaced with the clang of the long swords of Lykal of the Bridgehead and Dusho the Fist. They disengaged and struck again. Moidun of the Old Spurs and Hornos of the Tall Gates fought hammer against mace, their shields ringing like ill-tuned gongs as they clashed.

Brior pulled his shield free of the edge of Guelm's battle-axe and drove his three-pronged trident toward his opponent. Guelm was quick to duck and to slam his axe toward Brior's legs, missing by less than a fingerwidth.

Dusho made another feint at Lykal and succeeded in striking his armored shoulder. Lykal brought his sword around in a deadly arc aimed at Dusho's hip. Dusho managed to side-step the blow but stumbled against Guelm. The two knights teetered together and struggled to remain upright. Lykal held his sword up, but Brior took advantage of the situation and used his wedge-shaped sword to try to penetrate Guelm's armor.

Photin was on his feet at once, shouting that Brior had pressed his advantage unfairly. "Go back to your station and wait for my signal to rejoin the fight."

"But that puts Cladius at a disadvantage," Brior protested.

"And that is your fault!" Photin accused, unmoved by Brior's complaint.

"What do you think?" Brior appealed to the crowd. The fighting stopped while the audience bawled out conflicting opinions.

"Enough!" Photin roared. The people went silent. "Continue," he ordered the five knights permitted to fight.

Hornos at once swung his hammer at Moidun, and the battle resumed. With the numbers so uneven, Capulet had the advantage and the three knights took ruthless advantage of it until Photin signaled to Brior that he could rejoin the fray, and then the fighting became more equal, and the knights clashed in the center of the open area.

While most of the crowd watched with exuberant attention, yelling encouragement to favorites and condemnation to the others, Wladex gave more attention to the two paladins, who watched the fight with scholarly detachment. Until there was blood to be seen, neither the paladins nor Wladex would be caught up in this conflict that was more entertainment than battle.

A blow from Moidun's mace clanged off Guelm's helmet and Guelm stood, stunned by the impact. This time all the knights stopped fighting until Photin was satisfied that Guelm could go on.

Wladex sighed in disappointment and went back to studying the paladins, trying to decide which would make the better tool to his purposes. Left-Handed Ninnian was tall and angular with a somber look of great purpose on his weathered features. He carried a long sword in a scabbard across his back and throwing starknives rimmed his helmet like the points on a crown. The man had a formidable bearing, his dark armor shining dully in the red light.

By contrast, Stariat the Questor seemed unimpressive. He wore only a simple breastplate of light-colored metal, the rest of his body was protected with heavy padding. In real war, the padding would be reinforced with spells, but here it offered little protection against the weapons Ninnian held. Wladex decided that Stariat was either very capable or very arrogant.

A shout from the crowd, and then a moan announced that Moidun was out cold. The fighting

stopped as he was carried off the fighting area
and given to the care of the Cladian retainers.

The possibility of injuries meant also the possi
bility of blood. Wladex found his interest in the
battle growing and he turned his attention from
the paladins back to the knights.

Chapter 3

Chapter 3

THE VILLAGER AT WLADEX'S SIDE WAS fascinated by what he saw as the fighting surged back and forth across the open area between the monoliths. The knights shifted opponents and weapons with the ease of experience and mastery, all of them seeming to enjoy the contest and the opportunity to display their valor as well as their expertise at arms. The villager had never seen anything like it. He stood with his mouth gaping open and his eyes wide as reavers' buttons as the fight went on. Wladex was more excited now, and when Hornos was struck a glancing blow that left a red furrow down his arm, it was all Wladex could do not to leap into the open area and drink down the blood as it flowed.

The red sun was nearing the tops of the western tower. The fight was more than half over.

When it became apparent that Hornos could not fight on without magic to aid him, Photin ordered Hornos taken out of the melee and the battle went on. The knights were growing tired and their skirmishing was growing more purposeful, for none of them had energy to waste. Without magical support, they had to rely solely on their physical strength, and it was beginning to ebb. There was a change in the rhythm of their fighting, as well. No more flashy thrusts, no more elaborate footwork. Now the remaining four knights did their fighting with the singular concentration of men approaching their limits.

Lykal and Dusho had cast their major shields aside and were fighting each with short sword and dagger, their expressions as irate as their movements were swift. They stood less than an arm's length apart as they slashed, parried, and slashed again. Brior and Guelm were using their spears and bucklers, each seeking an opening in the other's defenses. Suddenly Guelm got lucky and his spear nicked Brior's ear and cheek, and slipped down to cut into his throat, not deeply, but enough to cause heavy bleeding.

Wladex stared as if caught in the power of a spell. The blood was so hot! He was sure he could see it steaming. He licked his lips and watched while Photin stopped the fight again, evaluated Brior's injuries, and wrapped a length of cloth around Brior's neck. It was tempting to volunteer to heal Brior's wounds with a mage's spell, but Wladex knew that would be unwise; discovery here would lead to another death and he was still recovering from his last one. He remained where he was, trying to concentrate on the paladins.

"He can continue, for now," Photin announced, and the fight resumed. But it was quickly apparent that Brior was losing strength as rapidly as he was losing blood. He was sweating heavily and his movements were slowing down. After a quick passage of arms, Guelm dropped the point of his spear to show he would not fight so badly injured a man.

"I can go on!" Brior insisted, poking his spear in Guelm's direction. His effort was so poor that Guelm had only to step to the side to avoid it. "I will not capitulate."

"Guelm is right," Photin declared. "Brior cannot continue."

Brior began to argue, but the representative of House Cladius came into the open area and examined Brior, saying finally that he was ordering the knight to withdraw, leaving Lykal to fight for Cladius alone.

Photin made a quick inspection of the remaining knights and ordered the fight to go on, although he remained in the fighting zone, watching the combat closely so that no one would be seriously hurt. Once he called a brief halt when he saw the strap on Dusho's wristguard had come loose, and once he stopped the fighting in order to remove a lady's token that had been thrown onto the open area.

Dusho was growing over-confident, and, with Guelm fighting well against the beleagured Lykal, he became reckless and made a fancy lunge at Lykal, trying to injure his knee. But Lykal was ready for him, and as Dusho thrust his short sword, Lykal spun and caught Dusho in the shoulder with his dagger. Astonished, Dusho dropped to his knees, his face going pale as Photin intervened, calling for Capuletine supporters to get Dusho off the field.

Lykal and Guelm remained standing, facing each other. Both kept the weapons they had been using, and so spear and buckler faced short sword and dagger. It was a precarious match, and the two knights knew it. Several times Lykal tried to use his short sword to break the shaft of Guelm's spear, and each time Guelm managed to thwart his efforts. Lykal watched for that one instant of inattention when he could use his short sword or his dagger and Guelm would not be able stop him in time. The two knights continued their clash and made themselves exhausted, neither willing to give in, and both completely enervated without magic to shore them up.

Then the sun sank behind the western tower and Photin rose to declare the fight at an end. "Very good. Done to a draw," he approved, and signaled all the knights to come receive their awards for the fighting. The four knights who had not finished the melee had been restored with healing spells and now came to accept the tokens of esteem given by Fuego to all those who fought in the central area between the monoliths.

Wladex made sounds of approval as the knights stood to receive the acclaim of the crowd. He was eager to see the paladins fight, for their battle promised more than the knights had given.

The official directed the knights to the dais of

honor and went on with his announcement. "The fight between these paladins is to be to capitulation, the rising of the green sun over the eastern tower, or to incapacity to continue without magical intervention. There is no limit on the weapons to be used so long as they are not projectile weapons. No slingshots, no explosives, no energy-beams of any kind. The paladins will follow the rules established and stand by the code of honor. Any failure to observe the terms of combat will result in automatic victory for the opponent." He nodded to the representatives of House Capulet and House Cladius. "This is the wish of your Houses."

Both men made a formal gesture to show their acquiescence, and Photin stepped into position to referee the fight.

Stariat the Questor had three weapons now—his long sword, a short pike, and a poignard. Left-Handed Ninnian had four weapons—a broadsword, a battle-axe, a double-pronged dagger, and the little throwing stars in his helmet. The two paladins came to the center of the fighting ground and began the ritual salutes. Then Ninnian drew his sword, Stariat swung up his pike, and the fight began.

From the first move it was plain to see that Ninnian had the advantage of height and weight. He swung his broadsword in vicious sweeps, driving Stariat back until it seemed that Stariat would be driven off the field. Then Stariat nimbly leaped into the air, performed a somersault over Ninnian's head and landed lightly, his pike in position to chop at Ninnian's legs.

"Magic!" someone in the crowd shouted angrily. "Foul!"

The crowd took up the complaint in loud calls until the mentor Albiates stepped down from his place and said, "There is no magic being used. Stariat the Questor has done nothing prohibited by the rules of combat." With this somber announcement he returned to his seat.

Wladex leaned forward. Stariat was far more interesting than he had first supposed. He waited for the fight to begin again while the villager babbled his excitement.

Ninnian had taken advantage of the examination for magic to turn around, and once again he faced Stariat. He swung his big sword again but did not force Stariat to give ground as he had done before. It was quickly apparent that he intended to exhaust Stariat before he began closer fighting.

"This might work with reavers and gargoyles, but I am neither," said Stariat.

"Save your breath," Ninnian recommended. "You'll need it."

Stariat performed another gymnastic feat, taking a long leap, then bouncing to land on Ninnian's shoulders, legs around Ninnian's neck. He tapped Ninnian on the helmet with the pommel of his pike as Ninnian tried to slash his legs, then scrambled off and crouched, ready to receive the onslaught he knew must come.

Wladex nodded his approval as Stariat side-stepped the furious rush Ninnian made. He decided that no matter how the fight turned out, he would seek to ally himself with Stariat, who was so inventive. The Laria had defeated all opposition sent against it so far. Clearly traditional attack would not succeed. But an inventive paladin like Stariat just might be able to find a way around the Laria's defenses, for it was not possible to go through them.

The two paladins were exchanging blows, the broadsword catching again and again on the hook of the pike. The sound was as loud as mallets on bells, making a predatory music as the fight raged on. It was apparent that Ninnian was truly angry, and his anger made him rash. He made a swipe with his broadsword and managed to clip Stariat's padded thigh. Stariat hopped backward, landing unevenly. His leg must have been badly bruised, for Stariat was visibly limping.

Photin held up his hand. "Are you able to continue?"

Stariat shook his leg and tested it. "Yes," he said.

"Very well," said Photin skeptically as he signaled for the fight to recommence.

"He's a fool," said the villager as Stariat nearly tripped in his haste to get out of the way of Ninnian's relentless pursuit.

"I don't think so," said Wladex, who was fairly certain that Ninnian was being led into a trap. This was more exciting than any mock-battle he had seen in his last three lives and he reveled in it.

On the dais of honor, the knights were watching the battle with critical eyes. Wladex could see that Dusho and Brior suspected the trap, too, though the others were less certain about it.

The double shadows of red and green suns cast the fighting ground into black shadow, making the action hard to follow. Many of the spectators shouted out their disappointment, though neither paladin seemed to hear them.

"Look!" the villager cried out to Wladex as Ninnian made what looked to be a deadly thrust.

Stariat used the shaft of his pike to vault over Ninnian's shoulder, this time landing a fair distance from Ninnian so that Ninnian had to turn to face him and then walk half a dozen strides to catch him. In those few heartbeats, Stariat planted himself as if his toes could grow roots, and when Ninnian reached for one of his star-knives, Stariat was in position to bat the lethal little weapon out of the air, and did so with ease. As Ninnian came within striking distance again, Stariat drew his long sword from the scabbard across his back and took advantage of its unusual length to hold Ninnian at sufficient distance to keep him from striking.

"The green sun will be over the eastern tower soon," said the villager, all but wheezing with excitement.

"So it is," said Wladex, a little disappointed that this fight, too, would end in a draw. He had such hopes of seeing Stariat deliver a final comeuppance to the more soldier-like Ninnian.

Wladex heard a few of the odds-makers shout their rates to one another and that annoyed him. He folded his arms and watched the battle.

Ninnian's frustration was obvious as he slammed his sword into Stariat's, cursing aloud as he did. He battered Stariat's sword three more times, then flung his own away in total disgust. He drew his battle-axe with one hand and his double-pronged dagger with the other as he whirled around to confront Stariat, who still held his long sword. In a sudden rush, Ninnian tried to force Stariat into retreat again, but this time Stariat would give no ground. In a skillful move, he side-stepped Ninnian's rush at the last moment, turning with Ninnian so he was still facing his opponent when Ninnian realized he had been duped again.

"Very adept," Wladex approved.

Stariat readied himself for another passage of arms when the mentor Albiates raised his hands to stop the fight. "Left-Handed Ninnian is using his powers to make his weapons more potent," he announced.

A hush fell over the crowd, for a paladin was supposed to be above such trickery. Photin stared at Ninnian even as he asked Albiates, "Are you sure?"

"If Ninnian is not doing it himself, he knows it is being done. He does not refuse the spell cast in his favor." Albiates frowned portentously. "This is a discredit to House Capulet." He glanced up at the sky. "The green sun has almost risen."

"Do you want to complete the fight?" Photin asked, expecting Stariat to refuse because of the disgrace of his opponent.

"If Ninnian is minded to continue, I will fight on," said Stariat, making a gesture of compliance to Photin and then to Ninnian.

"You insufferable—" Ninnian shouted as he ran at Stariat, his arms extended with weapons in each hand.

Stariat avoided the assault with such ease that the crowd realized his apparent fatigue had been a ruse. An uneven cheer arose from the crowd as Photin went to stop the fight again.

"This fellow is formidable," said Wladex to the villager. "He is a most capable fighter."

The villager blinked. "I have never seen anyone so skillful."

"You have never seen paladins fight," Wladex pointed out. He nodded to the open area. "These two are both very good, but that Stariat is more talented than Ninnian. Ninnian is probably the stronger man, but he is not as clever, and in paladins, cleverness means a great deal."

The nail-shaving edge of the green sun was just rising over the eastern tower, marking the end of the fighting. The crowd hooted their displeasure at so inconclusive an ending. A few of the odds-makers demanded the fight go on.

Taking those protests for encouragement, Ninnian dropped his dagger and pulled two of his star-knives from his helmet and threw them expertly at Stariat, who ducked swiftly as the knives passed overhead. One lodged in Photin's chest.

The crowd let out a loud bellow of disapproval, and for three heartbeats it seemed that the spectators would charge the two paladins, determined to exact recompense for this most unfair action. Everyone was appalled at Ninnian's unforgivable impudence, and some of them said so loudly. Gradually the people became dissatisfied. The restless milling of the crowd was alarming. Then Photin himself raised his hand. "Mentor Albiates himself will heal me with his spells," he proclaimed, and let Stariat help him from the central area. The representatives of the Cladian and Capuletine Houses followed, their concern delineated by every aspect of their demeanor. Albiates left the fighting place to tend to Photin.

In the crowd, a flurry of paying off bets began, many of the gamblers grumbling at the lack of a decisive victory, and the knights came down from their dais of honor. The air hummed with celebration and commiserations at once. No one seemed to notice that the paladins had been given no recognition for their contest.

Wladex turned to the villager. "You have had a rare opportunity today. What did you think of it?" In this amiable manner, he was able to draw the villager away from the heart of the crowd. He found a narrow alleyway where the light of the green sun did not penetrate. He muttered something about a very good inn being at the end of the alley. The villager accompanied him readily, too delighted with what he had just seen to question Wladex's recommendation.

When they were at the most deeply shadowed part of the alley, Wladex caught the villager in a powerful grip and bit out his throat, drinking the blood and excitement together as if it were the headiest wine, making the most of the heightened state of the villager as he sated himself on the poor man's life.

Chapter 4

INVIGORATED BY THE LIFE-BLOOD OF THE villager, Wladex emerged from the alley with his illusion spell brilliantly in place. He strode through the roiling crowd toward the dais of honor, certain that the formalities of the occasion would still be going on. He arrived just as Photin was finishing his summing up of the fighting. Standing to the side of the dais, he heard Photin say, "That last display of Ninnian's is beneath comment. I would have thought I was watching a rogue than a paladin." The green sun was now blazing down on the central area, making deep red shadows everywhere it did not touch. The walls of the red city glowed as if bleeding.

This condemnation drew murmurs from the men still near enough to the platform to hear, for coming from such a distinguished paladin as Photin, this censure carried more blame than the disapproval of any other fighting man in Fuego.

"You would have done the same," Ninnian

said, sulking. "He was enough to drive a real paladin mad."

"But he is a real paladin," Photin said patiently. "You are the one who has conducted himself as if he were not." He paced in front of the knights and paladins. "What say you, Hornos?"

Surprised by this sudden question, Hornos coughed to show his discomfort. "I was not pleased with how Ninnian fought," he admitted reluctantly.

"You see?" Photin said, almost pleading with Ninnian. "Honorable fighting men do not behave as you have done." He saw that Ninnian was not paying attention to him, and he shook his head. "I hope House Capulet will not commend you for your fighting this day. I am going to recommend that your token of battle be withheld."

This was a drastic step to take, and the knights and paladins all knew it. Worried glances were exchanged as those who had fought felt the weight of disapprobation descend.

Stariat spoke up. "I do not require disgrace of Left-Handed Ninnian. He knows that he acquitted himself poorly. That is comeuppance enough for me." He looked at Ninnian who sat at the other end of the dais of honor. "Shall we declare our contest a show of poor judgment?"

There was a slim chance that Ninnian might have accepted this had no one said anything more, but unfortunately Lykal added, "It was a bad decision. Who among us has not made a bad decision from time to time? There is no reason to disgrace Ninnian because he was impetuous."

This dispute was more interesting to Wladex than the display of fighting prowess had been. He moved a little nearer, listening intently.

Ninnian rose from his seat, his severe features flushed with emotion. "I need pity from no one!" he shouted, leveling his hand and sweeping it past the other fighters, making them partners in his wrath. "You are wrong!"

Photin was now seriously alarmed. He tried to approach Ninnian only to have the paladin draw his two-pronged dagger to fend him off. "Left-Handed Ninnian," he began, his tone of voice reproachful. "Do not add to our discontent, I beseech you."

"I will not," he said as he turned on his heel, trod down the steps, and marched into the open area between the monoliths, defiance in every line of his body. He walked to the nearest one—the fourth monolith—and mockingly read what was written on it. " 'Here lies the body of the greatest of heroes. His deeds in the first days of our city are so legendary that none will ever forget him.' You notice they did not put his name on his monolith." He cracked a laugh and walked away without looking back.

"How are we to . . .?" Guelm stared after Ninnian, his expression showing his dismay. "Do you think he will . . . change?"

"Do you mean do I think he will become a rogue, an anti-paladin?" Photin asked with a heavy sigh. "I fear that has already happened."

The silence that followed this dread pronouncement was more eloquent than words would have been.

Wladex took advantage of it, coming to the foot of the dais of honor and bowing in good form to Stariat. "Good paladin," he said melifluously, "allow me a moment of your time."

Stariat blinked in astonishment. "Fire mage?" he said.

"I know this is an inopportune moment to approach you, but I fear that if I do not, I will lose all opportunity to speak with you." He did his best to look at a disadvantage. "You have impressed me greatly, not only as a warrior of ingenuity and courage, but as a model of how paladins are behaved." He hitched his shoulder in the direction Ninnian had gone. "That was inauspicious, but I ask you not to consider my presence as part of his renunciation."

Three of the knights were staring at Wladex, openly curious. They were glad of the distraction his presence provided, and were all the more alert for that reason.

"Say what you have come to say," Stariat told him, using the proper form of response.

Wladex bowed again, a show of deference that was not lost on those watching him. "I am Ossato, the fire mage, and I have vowed to put my skills at the service of a paladin willing to go directly against the forces of the Laria." Except for his name and identity, he told the truth, which struck him as ironically funny. "Your valor and your benignancy have impressed me so much that I felt moved to propose an alliance between us, so that we might, together, set out to end the power of the Laria." He said nothing of his intention of usurping the Laria's place and dominance. That, along with his real name and nature, he would keep to himself, as befitted a vampire lord.

"Ossato," Stariat said thoughtfully. "What makes you hope that you can overcome the Laria with nothing more than one paladin to support you?"

It was the question Wladex had been expecting. He answered readily, "I believe that if we can show the weaknesses of the Laria's forces, we would not have to fight alone for very long. Others—paladins, knights, mages, and mentors, perhaps even reavers—would join with us to bring an end to the Laria's rule."

These were huge sentiments, and the men on the dais of honor listened in growing awe. Finally Photin spoke up. "Fire mage Ossato, I only wish I were still young enough to go with you on so worthy a campaign. It does my old heart good to know that there are still those on Delos willing to undertake such an arduous mission."

Wladex did his best to look humble. "It is not my intention to be admired for doing that which will preserve the existence of my world." He looked directly at Stariat. "Well? If you would like some time to consider this venture, I will gladly wait for your answer."

Dusho grinned. "If he does not want to go, I

do. There is merit and influence to be gained, and what knight can refuse that?"

Two of the others—Brior and Guelm—gestured their agreement. "Yes," said Guelm. "I would be glad of joining such an undertaking."

Not to be outdone, Brior said, "I will accompany you, as well. There is bound to be wealth and honor at the end of this when the Laria is no more."

Wladex smiled. "You give me hope, knights."

Moidun regarded Wladex skeptically. "One can always make massive promises; that does not mean anything will come of it."

Before Wladex could speak, Photin said, "This is not some merchant from Terris, or a reaver out for money. Ossato is a fire mage, and therefore a man of utmost probity. You cannot question him without questioning everything in Delos."

"Maybe it would be wiser to question," said Moidun, unconvinced. "There have been many times that we have heard of men with great magic and greater ambition declare that they will find a way to defeat the Laria, but so far no one has done it." He rested his hand on the hilt of his ceremonial dagger. "Why should you succeed where others have failed?"

Wladex managed a philosophical smile. "I understand your reservations. I can even share in them. I have pondered long on what would be needed to defeat the Laria. I am aware it is as if I proposed to fight a storm or defeat an earthquake. The Laria is a foe of imposing might and enigmatic nature. Anyone seeking to destroy it would have to plan very carefully, and with contingencies in the event the first strategy did not work." He saw that Moidun was listening. "If you are certain the thing cannot be done, then remain here and fight against the Laria's minions. I want no companion who is not willing to do this venture with all his heart."

"Then you will have to excuse me," said Moidun. "I applaud your intention, but I am doubtful about its accomplishment." He looked to his fellow knights. "What do you think?"

"Do not decide now," Wladex said before they could reply. "I did not come to this decision in an instant. I will be in this place at this time tomorrow. If you conclude that you are willing to risk all in order to be rid of the Laria, then join me here. If you do not convince yourselves that we might prevail, then do not meet me." He bowed, almost as if expecting applause. "I hope that some of you will, upon reflection, see that the end results are worth every effort we might expend."

Photin's old face shone with excitement. "I could ask no finer end to my life than to go on such a campaign," he said. "But though they can bring me back to life through magic, I am still an old man, and no spell of youth is strong enough to make a young man of me for any length of time. Still, it might be worth it—one more fight for a glorious purpose."

Seizing his opportunity, Wladex said, "If you are willing to throw in your lot with me, Photin, I will welcome your experienced counsel, and your strength of character." It would make his proposal seem all the more genuine if the old paladin would consent to accompany him. And his blood was as rich as any man's.

"This is most exciting," said Hornos. "I would be glad to fight at Photin's side." He looked pointedly at his companions.

"Do not rush them," Wladex cautioned. "Reflect on what I offer and what you know of the past attempts. I will not deceive you with promises of secret weapons and easy victories. Anyone who did that would deserve your contempt." He stepped back. "I will be here at this time tomorrow." With that he turned away from the dais of honor and made his way through the crowd.

He sought out an inn offering sleeping rooms, paid for six hours' rest with a genuine coin, and shut out the bustle of Fuego in the darkness of the guest-chamber. He once again resumed his proper form and gave himself free rein to scheme. He had great hopes of his plan: to have the help of knights and paladins to assist him in bringing the Laria to ruin so that he—Wladex—could take its place was so deliciously mordant that it was difficult not to chuckle in his half-sleep. As he reviewed the boldness of his plan, he lapsed into the stupor that, in a vampire lord, passed for sleep.

By the time Wladex rose and once again assumed his spell-generated fire mage persona, the blue sun was past the zenith and was dropping into the west. The streets, always busy, were filled with those still debating the outcome of the fight staged by Cladius and Capulet. A few whose wagers had paid off handsomely were celebrating their good fortune, and others were trying to cheer themselves up after their losses. Wladex managed to ingratiate himself into one band of young men reviewing the contest in the yard of a merchants' inn, who seemed bent on reenacting the fights, by offering to act as referee in their games.

"Why should a fire mage do that for us?" the apparent leader challenged him.

"Well, I was close to the front and saw most of what happened," said Wladex. "Unless you were closer than I—?" He let the question hang, knowing he had the advantage.

The leader shrugged. "You could be useful," he conceded, and jumped onto the inn yard table to demonstrate how he recalled Hornos had made his first mistake.

Soon the rest of the group resumed their participation, a few of them taking time to confer with Wladex before they gave their interpretation of the events they had seen. Wladex made a few obvious corrections but generally let the young men act out the fight in their own terms while he decided which of these fellows would slake his thirst.

Finally the debate wound down, and the young men began to boast of their own experiences. One of the company insisted he had been in a fight with a greater swegle and lived to tell about it. Most of the others laughed derisively, but Wladex did not.

"Greater swegles are formidable creatures, with their scaled hides and their massive bodies," Wladex remarked. "Well-armed knights hesitate to confront them, but you say you were able to fend one off with a pair of torches."

"Well, yes," the young man said, adding self-consciously, "and I had purchased an invulnerability spell that was very useful, particularly when the swegle charged me directly. It almost bounced when it got within an arm's length of me."

"An invulnerability spell!" One of the others made a gesture to shame his companion. "You had nothing to fear. I wouldn't mind facing a lich or even a cloud giant if I had an invulnerability spell to guard me. Where did you get it?"

"I bought it in Terris, from an earth mage. It took almost all my money, but knowing I had to make my way here in a train of merchants with only reavers for guards, I thought it was money well-spent. And so it turned out to be," he added with defensive emphasis.

Wladex applauded his approval. "A good precaution. Many of those crossing the badlands take needless risks when they elect to depend on their guards to keep them safe from all the denizens of the Laria that haunt Delos." He saw the leader regarding him narrowly. "You think that as a mage myself I must say this. In a way, you are right, for as a mage I am often called upon to supply spells for travelers, and every time I think it a provident decision."

"Of course," said the leader. "The money you receive has nothing to do with it."

"It has less to do with it than you seem to think," Wladex countered. He rose. "It is time I left you. I have enjoyed the time I have spent with you. And before I go, here." He produced a small cluster of spells and handed them to the company. "As a gift." He did not tell them that the spells would serve as a lure to other vampires, who would make hearty meals of the young men.

A few of the young men were startled by this generosity, and one tried to give his back.

"No, no," Wladex said. "Consider it my contribution to the occasion. The spells make you attractive to seductive young women. Enjoy them."

This promise made the most hesitant of the young men accept the spells readily. Wladex did not remind them that many vampires were lovely, tempting young women; the young men would discover that for themselves. "I am off to find a proper meal," he said. "If one of you would like to bear me company, I would be glad of it."

The young man who had boasted of facing a greater swegle started to volunteer, then, sheepishly backed out.

"I'll go with you," said the leader with the suggestion of a swagger. "I'd like to know more about the young women." He winked at his companions and hooked his thumbs in his Ynglinghide belt.

"So you shall," said Wladex with a hint of an anticipatory chuckle as he led the way out of the inn yard and down the winding street into the orange shadows of the blue sun.

Chapter 5

STARIAT THE QUESTOR WAS WAITING FOR Wladex, along with Hornos, Dusho, and Brior. The knights were fully armed—Stariat was in his strange, padded apparel, carrying his long sword, two throwing axes, and a crossbow with a good supply of quarrels. All four fighters greeted Wladex purposefully.

"Fire mage Ossato," said Brior. "We have come to serve you." He made the ritual salutation with his dirk. The others touched their weapons to show their agreement.

"You have decided to fight?" Wladex asked in a gentle voice, as if their undertaking were a social diversion. "Good."

"Yes," said Dusho for all of them. "We are ready to put ourselves in your hands." If he had any doubts about the wisdom of this, it was not apparent in either his speech or his demeanor. "How do we begin?"

Wladex let himself smile. "We must go to the Lost Ruby Mine of Puerta," he said blandly, as if this could be easily done.

Hornos was the most shocked at the mention of the wizard who founded Fuego so long ago. "It is lost," he pointed out as if speaking to a simpleton.

"Not for everyone. Those who are high in the fire mages' guild have access to records others cannot see. We therefore have ways to find many things that have been lost." Wladex had had to use one of his strongest seeking spells to find the place, and the knowledge had cost him dearly—it had ended his last life.

The four fighters exchanged looks, and Dusho said, "Why must we do this?"

"Why, to obtain the most potent spells. We are going to need them to fight the Laria. The rubies of that mine are said to be the most puissant of all rubies on Delos." This was the most candid admission Wladex had made yet. "Why do you think the mine was lost?"

"If the location is known to the fire mages' guild," Stariat began, his eyes narrowed in thought, "why have they not made use of it, mined it for themselves?"

Wladex had another honest answer for them. "There is the matter of kobolds and hammets and stone giants." He paused as he let the four consider this. "Few fire mages want to confront such monsters alone."

"Hammets," said Brior. "I hate hammets. Anything with eight legs." He managed not to shudder, but that was clearly an effort.

"Then I will provide you with a spell against

them," Wladex offered. "I regret that I haven't enough power to keep all of you protected."

"Will you have that once you have the rubies?" asked Hornos.

"Oh, yes," said Wladex, knowing it was true.

"Then the trick is getting in to find the rubies, not getting out," said Dusho, doing his best to sum up their situation.

"Simply put," said Wladex, certain that once such powerful stones were in his possession, other forces would be alerted. He did not want to discourage these four volunteers, and so he kept his reservations to himself.

"I think it is good that we begin this way," said Brior staunchly, making up his mind. "I believe we must accustom ourselves to facing all the dangers and monsters that the Laria can throw at us." He made a sign to show his dedication to the work they were about to undertake. "I am willing to go to this mine, I am willing to go through the badlands and the wastes of the Old Cities, if that is what I must do to end the Laria's power."

Dusho was less enthusiastic. "We will doubtless have to face many fearsome beings, and creatures whose aspect is terrifying. If we can save our strength along the way, I would think that would be wisest."

Wladex was clearly expected to say something. "I do not want to be profligate with your talents or your courage. It defeats the purpose of our mission. But I know what we must have to bring the Laria down, and it would be irresponsible in the extreme to proceed against it without all the power we can muster. So while I do not want to fight monsters, I am certain that I must."

"Ossato is a good leader," said Stariat unexpectedly. "He does not underestimate the enemy." He made his way toward Wladex. "Had you answered less sensibly, I might have refused to go. As it is, you have my allegiance until the Laria is vanquished or we are dead beyond magic's power to restore us."

This was the very thing Wladex wanted to hear but he dared not appear too satisfied. "I would do neither you nor our cause any service by telling you the dangers are less than I expect them to be. That way lies our slaughter." He stood very straight. "The northeastern gate is open."

"If that is the way we must go, then I am with you," Stariat declared, and glared at the knights to be sure they, too, vowed commitment.

They set off toward the northeastern gate, pausing along the way to purchase food and water and heavy cloaks that would provide sufficient darkness to allow them to sleep in the full glare of one or two suns. Wladex paid for these things with genuine coins, for he did not want the integrity of Ossato the fire mage brought into question.

At the gate, bored reavers asked their names and destination, writing down *Terris*, for, as Wladex said, it was where they would have to go after they secured the rubies.

There was a track leading up into the hills; it

was narrow and tricky, more suited to scevan or Lizcanth than men. As the way grew more steep, Dusho complained.

"Why don't you use your magic to transport us to the mine? This climbing is exhausting." He was panting.

From his place in the lead, Wladex said over his shoulder, "I am afraid to deplete my magical reserves now. When we reach the mine, I fear we will have greater need of it. And," he added, "I don't want to alert the Laria to our destination by leaving magical trails for it to find."

This sobering observation silenced Dusho as well as the others, and as they continued upward, they all kept anxious watch for any hint of a follower.

By the time the green sun was setting and the red sun rising, they had arrived at a ledge high above Fuego. They paused there to rest and consume some of the food they had purchased.

"Look at that place," said Hornos. "If the emperor could see it from here, he would realize how small his domain is." He nudged Brior in the arm. "The city is nothing more than a speck on the badlands. And I can't see Astra or Terris from here. Or Dismas, for that matter," he added darkly. "How can the emperor think himself a ruler of anything?"

"Amid such devastation the emperor is all the more important," said Brior. "Without him, it would take little for the city to go to ruin."

"Do the emperors of other cities think so?" asked Hornos as he pointed to a pair of whirling storms out in the badlands near the horizon. "There's something I wouldn't want to tangle with."

"Monsters of the air," said Brior with grim satisfaction. "Only magic prevails against them, and even then, it sometimes fails."

"You know that for a fact, do you?" said Hornos with a wry smile.

"By the ancients, no, and I am thankful for it," said Brior.

"Come," said Stariat. "We have a ways to go."

They resumed their climb and reached a deep cleft in the rocks some time later, when the red sun had dropped below the horizon and the green sun stood high above them. At first the cleft looked to be nothing remarkable—a wide place where two massive boulders leaned together. On second inspection the cleft looked to be deep, perhaps concealing a cavern.

"The mine!" exclaimed Dusho as he peered into the shadows.

"That it is," said Wladex. "This is the highest level. The best rubies are said to come from the sixth level, deep in the mountain." That was truthful, and he felt pleased that he had not lied this time. "I have a small illumination spell, one that can only be extinguished by magic. Each of you will carry the stone I give you, and you will be able to make your way through the levels." He took diamond fragments from his wallet and gave one to each of the four men, saving the largest for himself. He murmured the words to put the spell in motion, and each of them had a hand that glowed like a torch. "If you are ready, come." Without waiting to see if the four were following him, he stepped through the cleft and into a cavern of formidable size.

"Amazing," whispered Dusho, who was immediately behind Wladex.

"This is the first level," said Wladex, doing his best to sound unimpressed himself. His words were echoed as if by a hundred voices.

"How vast are the other chambers?" Brior wondered aloud, and heard his question repeated endlessly.

"I don't know. I have not seen this place before," said Wladex, his voice deliberately soft and low, to diminish the echoes. "Legend says all nine chambers are huge, but the ninth is the most dangerous." He had tended to discount these tales as the exaggeration that came with repetition. Now he saw that repetition had, if anything, tended to diminish the vastness of the mine.

"Is there anything stirring in the dark?" Hornos asked, lifting his hand high in order to shed more light on the place.

"Not that I can see," said Stariat. "Though we may be watched."

This was hardly comforting to the small company as they made their way down ancient steps cut into the rock, and leading back and down. They kept their talking to a minimum, for the echoes of their footsteps created a cacophony that made it difficult to distinguish words.

The second chamber was larger than the first.

It still had a faint, red glow from the rubies high in the vault of the chamber. They made their way to the third chamber, which was a bit redder still, and showed more evidence of having been mined. They stopped briefly to get their bearings and to assign scouting duties to each.

"You, Dusho," said Wladex, trying to speak clearly enough to keep his words from being drowned out by their echoes. "You will watch ahead; go five paces ahead of me, but no more. You, Hornos, will watch the sides. Brior will watch above us, and Stariat will guard our rear. None of you are to venture off on your own, or lag behind. If you notice anything, give a warning. I will watch beneath us. There could be kobolds to deal with in a cave like this."

"Kobolds are not so bad," said Hornos, more to sound brave than to show he was unafraid.

"In the open, perhaps. Here, coming in swarms, they are very dangerous," said Wladex. "Let us go on. We do not want to linger."

"I don't want to see any hammets," Brior said with a shudder.

They had just entered the fourth chamber when they all heard a skittering noise in the dark around them. The five came to a halt, their light-hands held high to penetrate the darkness. The skittering stopped, then resumed, much more softly.

"Do kobolds skitter?" asked Brior, sounding nervous.

"No," said Stariat, and added what all of them had been thinking. "Hammets do."

Brior made a sound between a shout and a moan as he pulled his battle-axe from its holster and took a stance to swing it. The rest of the men did the same, and after a little hesitation, Wladex drew his poignard—he liked the slim, sneaky dagger—holding it carefully, since it was as likely to seek the blood of men as the blood of hammets.

The hammets were coming nearer, their many legs occasionally catching the light. They moved stealthily, unwilling to rush their prey, and reluctant to leap into the cavern.

"Get ready," said Starlat as he readied himself to strike.

The hammets came at them in abrupt, disorganized hops, their many legs scrabbling to take hold of the men. The fighters began to hack at their attackers, trying to hold them at bay while they kept their position.

"Don't let them separate us," Wladex warned as his poignard sank greedily into the body of a hammet. "They will win if they get us apart." He peered into the cavern, his vampire eyes able to see more than the men could. There were forty or fifty of the creatures around them, all of them striving to reach the men who had come into their cave. None of the hammets seemed to be evil hammets, the breed that could cast spells as well as bite and immobilize their prey with webs. That was encouraging. His poignard skewered another hammet, gaining power for itself as the hammet died.

There was a flurry of feints and thrusts on the

right—four hammets were attacking Hornos, trying to force him to move away from the rest. Stariat came to his aid, striking with deadly efficiency as the hammets tried to close in.

"There!" shouted Dusho, pointing upward where a dozen of the eight-legged monsters were gathering on the ceiling of the cave directly overhead.

"Use a spell to drive them off!" Hormos demanded as he struggled to keep three of the hammets at arm's length. He sounded dangerously frightened.

"There isn't time," Wladex told him mendaciously. He had no intention of wasting a perfectly charged spell when force of arms would do. The power of his spells was hard to maintain, and he had better things to do than fight off mindless monsters like these. "Keep fighting and they will retreat."

"At least do something about those things overhead," Stariat cried, raising his illuminated hand to reveal hammets sliding down on their silken ropes.

"Oh, very well," said Wladex, and conjured a ball of fire to rise.

The hammets shrieked and crisped as the fire hit them. Their charred and smoking corpses fell with a sound like rotten fruit falling from trees. A pale, stinking fluid sprayed as they struck, and the fighters moved back from the bodies.

This was an advantage for the attacking hammets, and they made the most of it. One of them was able to cast a length of silk around Hornos and drag him away from the others.

Hornos screamed, begging for Wladex to send more fire.

"That would kill you, too, and I cannot bring you back to life yet," Wladex warned him.

"I don't care!" Hornos screamed. "I can't stand this!"

The two other knights were upset to see Hornos in the clutches of the hammets. They continued to fight with renewed purpose as more silk was wrapped around Hornos, shiny, sticky, and deadly.

"They'll drain me!" Hornos cried out. "Don't let them!"

"Mage," said Stariat. "Spare him." He and Wladex exchanged comprehending glances, and Stariat stepped aside to give Wladex better aim.

This fire ball was not as large as the first, and it moved more quickly, burning Hornos and four hammets where they stood.

For a long moment, neither man nor hammet moved in the ruby mine cavern. Smoke rose, and the burning bodies sizzled as the fire ball burned itself out. Then the fighting resumed more frantically than before.

Stariat mowed down a group of hammets that had ventured too close. At last a few of the monsters withdrew. They made a clicking sound that might have been talking. The two knights, the paladin, and Wladex watched them, still ready to strike as soon as the attack was renewed.

The hammets paused and then fled.

"At least they've gone," said Brior, unwilling to put his weapon away yet.

"I wonder why they left," said Dusho, glancing uneasily at the charred remains of Hornos lying amid the bodies of the hammets.

"We drove them off," said Brior because he wanted to believe it.

"I don't think so," said Stariat.

As he spoke, the stones beneath their feet groaned, shook, and opened in a gaping fissure. The men and Wladex stumbled, then fell through to the cavern beneath.

Chapter 6

THEY LANDED NOT ON STONES BUT ON A vast heap of red sand. They were in an enormous cave that glowed from clusters of rubies that lined the walls and ceiling of the place. The three men and Wladex got slowly to their feet, checking for damage, their hands still lit enough to show them the place they had accidentally discovered.

"Rubies," said Brior in an awed tone. "Everywhere."

"The tenth level," said a deep, sonorous voice from the darkness.

Wladex stood as still as the fighters with him, trying to make out the location and identity of the speaker. "Who are you?" he asked, doing his best to sound unafraid.

"The guardian of the rubies," the voice replied as if this were obvious.

"Show yourself," Wladex ordered.

From high above them a long-snouted, scaled head came down. The eyes were as red as the scales and flashed in the light.

The men all stared, their emotions apparent in their faces. Wladex remained inscrutable, studying the dragon as the huge creature began to lower his ponderous head again.

"The noise you made woke me. I stretched myself, and you came through the ceiling. That's my pillow you're standing on," he said, and waited while the men and Wladex moved off the pile of ruby sand. As he went, Waldex scooped up four large handfuls and slid them into the various hidden pockets in his mage's robes.

"How old are you?" Brior asked, his attention fully on the dragon.

"I don't remember," said the dragon. "I came here in the Second Age, I think, or the First. But it may have been earlier." The dragon yawned hugely. "Old dragons sleep a lot." He lowered his head to his pillow of sand.

"Do you mind if we take a ruby or two?" Wladex asked politely. "I am the fire mage Ossato, and I need rubies for my spells."

The dragon blinked. "A fire mage, is it?" he asked as if this surprised him. "Well, if you must. No more than five, though." He closed his eyes again.

Wladex was elated. "Choose the largest you can carry," he said to the remaining three men. "Use the hilts of your swords to get them free." He stopped at a cluster where the rubies ranged from the size of cabbages to kegs. He began to pound at the base of the largest ruby.

"Do you mind?" the dragon muttered. "I am

trying to sleep. Use the right spell and it will pull out like a nail. It's quieter."

With a sigh, Wladex took out a small separation spell and used it on the ruby; the massive jewel slid into his hands so readily that it nearly knocked him over. Wladex could feel the power thrumming within it and smiled. He quickly got two smaller rubies for Stariat, and one each for Brior and Dusho.

"This is amazing," said Brior as he stared down at the ruby he held, which was larger than his head.

"No wonder Puerta put his city here," said Stariat, each of his arms around a gem the size of giant melon. "If all the caverns had jewels like this, it would have made him as wealthy as he was magically powerful."

"True," said Wladex, looking toward the dragon. "We had better not linger. The hammets could discover this place at any moment."

At the reminder that there were hammets about, Brior clung all the more tightly to his ruby. "No more hammets," he said with feeling.

"Tell me," said Dusho. "How do we leave?"

Wladex looked around the cavern and grinned. "There is magic enough here to carry us halfway to Terris without using one jot of the power in our rubies." He motioned to the men. "Here. Stand close to me." He began the spell to transport them, electing to create an air-wagon to hold them, so that they would not have to hold onto their rubies all the way. "Remember, the rubies are needed to end the Laria. Preserve them even if you are killed—the ruby will restore you to life well enough." He made the necessary gestures and recited the magical words.

There was a pop loud enough to make the dragon raise his head in annoyance, and then the mountain became like fog. The three men and Wladex were suddenly sitting in a wagon like the ones the merchants used, but one that flew through the air. Behind them the flank of the mountain rose up, massive as ever.

"We are going to Terris?" Brior asked. "You did say Terris."

"Yes," said Wladex. "We need an emerald at least as large as this ruby." He patted the huge jewel he held.

"And a diamond and a pearl, I suppose?" Dusho added.

"Yes," said Wladex. "A black pearl. At least three of each."

"I've never heard of black pearls," said Brior, not quite scoffing, but unconvinced.

"Oh, they are real," said Wladex. Everything he had learned about gaining sufficient force to destroy the Laria required a black pearl in order to harness the dark power the Laria commanded.

"Very well," said Dusho. "A black pearl it will be." Overhead the blue sun was halfway up the eastern sky, while in the west the green sun was hanging just above the horizon.

"Ossato, how are we—we have some power, but nothing approaching yours—to control such potent gems as these?" Stariat looked worried.

"I will control them with your help," said Wladex. "I will use their power, and you will stop any monster that the Laria may send to stop us."

"Is that all?" Brior asked. "A pity you haven't a legion to fight."

"The Laria could pervert a legion," said Wladex sharply. "A few dedicated fighters have a better chance against it."

To the south, clouds were gathering in the sky, towering upward like giants. Dusho pointed them out. "I am glad they are far away," he said.

"So am I," Brior admitted.

"But they are growing closer," said Stariat, who was shading his eyes to look at them. "And they are coming fast."

"With the wind, or against it?" Wladex asked, beginning to worry.

"How could clouds come against the wind?" asked Dusho. "This air-wagon generates its own wind." As he said this a sudden gust sent the air-wagon skidding sideways.

"There are things that live in the air, as well as on the ground and in it," said Stariat, taking a firm hold of the jewels he had been given.

"It could be a cloud lord, or a cloud king," said Wladex, thinking aloud as he watched the towering forms in the sky. "Or a forcelord. That would mean real trouble."

"Ossato," said Stariat with amazing calm, "what can we do?"

"We could land," said Dusho before Wladex responded.

"The most important thing is to save the rubies," said Wladex. "If we land, we will have to carry them across the wastes ourselves. If we remain aloft, we could be thrown out of the air-wagon." He looked at the men.

"Can the rubies work against a forcelord? Or a cloud king?" asked Brior. "Is there anything we can do with the jewels?"

Wladex considered the question. "I don't know. They are very powerful, but here in the air, we might have—" He went silent as a huge cloud, shaped something like a man—if a man were as wide as a city gate, four times as high, and had glowing red eyes—rose up in the sky ahead.

"What is it?" Dusho asked, shouting over the sudden roar of the wind.

"Red eyes is a cloud king," said Stariat. "We will have to use the rubies or we will crash." He shoved Wladex in the shoulder. "Use the rubies, Ossato. Use them."

Little as he liked the idea, Wladex sighed and began the ritual passes to summon the power of the rubies. Around them the clouds were growing denser and in the middle of them was a whirlwind throwing off silver sparks from a purple funnel—a forcelord in full display. The air-wagon was bucking as if being pulled over rocky terrain by an hysterical Lizcanth. Inside, the men struggled to keep hold of the open wagon and the jewels they had to guard. Stariat's crossbow slipped away from his grasp and fell out of the air-wagon, spirited off by the rambunctious wind.

"I think I can hold them at bay long enough

to get us on the ground," Wladex said as one of the rubies began to glow. He continued the magical recitation, all the while watching the weather. More cloud lords were arriving, their yellow eyes shining amid their shifting mass.

In the air-wagon the fighters were silent with determination and fear. The single radiating gem lit them all with a red light more intense than that of the red sun. As Wladex continued his spell, the air-wagon vibrated with the power of the ruby.

Then a huge gust of wind hit them. The air-wagon slid and jounced along the sky, trailed by a host of malignant clouds. The ruby shone as luridly as spilled blood as the air-wagon began a precarious descent through the clouds. Wladex kept a wary eye out for the forcelord—one good strike from it would toss them all overboard and stop the spell he was concentrating on.

As they landed, Wladex shouted, "No matter what happens, find all the jewels and stop the Laria. If I fall, you will have other help!" He leaped out of the wagon and drew his poignard to face the forcelord, shouting to the blade to drink of the might of the whirlwind.

The men were bruised and shaken, and less convinced that their weapons could prevail against such enemies as these. Stariat yelled, "I have some spells to protect us. Come back, Ossato. This will pass if we are shielded."

"My weapon hungers," Wladex replied, for once telling the truth. He turned to face the forcelord, shouting the beginning of another spell as the great whirlwind reached him, picked him up and flung him a long distance away from where the men waited within the circle of protection afforded by Stariat's spell.

"The fire mage—" Brior shouted.

All three watched in horror as Wladex was carried away, and, when no more than a speck, dropped out of the sky.

Suddenly the air was still. Wind and clouds vanished as quickly as they had materialized. The blue sun beat relentlessly down on them, showing the desolation where they had landed in uncompromising severity.

"What can we do now?" Dusho asked after a long silence.

"We can't stay here," Brior said. "Look around you. There is nothing, not even shade to keep us out of the suns' rays. We will have to leave the jewels and try to find shelter."

"Why should we leave the jewels?" Dusho demanded. "They are worth a dozen fortunes. Any mage would trade half his spells for one of these stones. I say we gather them up and start back for Fuego."

"Ossato said we were to go on. He said we would have other help," Stariat reminded them. "He was willing to die to bring down the Laria."

"Do you think we should search for him?" Brior asked a little guiltily. "He might be able to be resurrected if we found him soon enough. There should be enough magic in these rubies to restore him."

"Do you know the spells?" asked Dusho.

"How can we restore him without the words or the potions that bring the dead back to life? Where is a mage or a mentor with the power to restore him?" He waved his hand at the badlands. "Shall we see if we can summon one up?"

"Stop, both of you," said Stariat calmly. "We have undertaken a mission, one that could save all Delos if we succeed. Ossato must have known he would fall by the way and that is why he charged us to go on. We must try." He pointed to what was left of the wagon. "We can put the rubies on that and set out for Terris. We know it is to the south-by-east, and we must assume we are more than halfway there." He patted his long sword. "We can fight if we must."

"The rubies are very heavy," said Brior.

"All the more reason to make a drag. Gather them up and rig a harness. We can use our belts and scabbards." Stariat coughed. "There is dust everywhere. The sooner we move, the sooner we are gone from it."

Dusho and Brior seemed less certain, but they had no other suggestions to offer. They followed Stariat's instructions and rigged up a drag to hold the rubies, then began their long trek toward the earth city of Terris.

For Wladex, far away on an outcropping of rock, he could feel the men begin to move, for the ruby dust in his robes was still linked to the jewels the men were carrying. He smiled with satisfaction, only slightly annoyed that he had died so soon. His spine was broken, and a dozen other bones as well. A part of his left femur poked through his skin, and his right arm lay at an impossible angle. All this would have to be healed before he could resume his work. This was one other misfortune he could hold against the Laria. It had confounded Wladex at every turn, but Wladex was not turned from his purpose. Indeed, this setback made him all the more determined to succeed. The ruby sand would speed his resurrection and he would be back with the men before many red sun days passed. He began to think about his next identity. The men would be suspicious of another fire mage, so he would have to come up with something else.

All through the passage of the blue sun and the red sun, he lay dead, his vampire heart was still, no breath stirred in his lungs. and no blood moved in his cold veins. Only the ruby dust in his robe kept his undead vitality intact. He could not speak the restoration spells, but he thought them as carefully as his slow-acting brain could manage. One by one the magical words formed themselves in his mind like gathering mists taking shape. The green sun set and the blue sun rose, and then the red sun rose again, and the ruby dust drew power from the red sun.

Wladex longed for shade and darkness for that would quicken his return to life, but out here on this rocky spur there was no chance of shade, and his renewal would take time. He put all his attention in coming back to life, and gradually the power of the rubies and the words of the spells began their work. First his bones slipped into place and began to knit, then his skin healed, making long, puckered scars that would fade once he assumed a new identity. He could not yet move. That would come later, when he finally summoned life to return.

As the wind came up, the ruby dust began to blow away, and for the first time, Wladex was frightened. He might not have power enough to complete the restoration, and that would leave him a half-living wreck in the middle of a wasteland where no one came but monsters controlled by the Laria.

This realization spurred him to greater effort and he forced himself to recite the spells as quickly as he could recall them, driving himself to completion with a will that he knew was strong enough to prevail over the Laria.

"I will be back again. I will be back again. I will be back again," he muttered as the final stages of reanimation came to fruition and his first new breath began.

Chapter 7

BY THE TIME THEY COULD SEE THE WALLS
of Terris in the distance, Dusho, Brior, and Stariat
were exhausted. They had covered the distance
under a protective spell that kept them and their
jewels safe but forced them to walk the whole
way. It had taken nearly eight full green sun
days and had pushed them to the limits of their
endurance. The difficulties of their traveling had
been made worse by the occasional swarms of
animated clouds they had had to pass through,
for such opponents could only be defeated by
spells—no warriors' weapons could prevail
against them. Dusho and Brior had done their
best to master the magic they needed, and Stariat
had to use more of his strength than he would
have liked to keep those formidable enemies
away. The men had stopped at two oases and
had to fight off nits at one of them. Now that
the first leg of their mission was in sight, they
let themselves halt for a moment in the shade of
a stand of tall, shaggy trees.

"After I have a bath I want to sleep from one blue sun rising to the next," said Brior. "And then I want to eat the largest meal we can find in the city." He shifted his position and felt the grit in his clothing.

Dusho nodded his agreement. "And with these rubies, we can secure the finest that Terris has to offer."

"We cannot sell the rubies," said Stariat. "You heard Ossato before the storm carried him away. We must do this as he charged us to do."

"Ossato did not say we should beg in the streets," said Brior. "We need rest and a few minor comforts. It would be irresponsible to do less. For lack of sleep will make us careless, and failing to bathe could bring on skin-wrangles. We would not be much use against the Laria."

"We can take turns guarding the jewels," said Dusho. "And you'd best put some kind of spell on them to disguise them."

"True enough," said Stariat. "I'd best attend to that before someone from Terris notices us and comes out to see what we are doing." He straightened up, his padded clothing stiff with dust. Approaching the drag they had made, he began to chant his incantation. Gradually the rubies came to resemble large chunks of rock of no particular value. When he was satisfied with the result, Stariat fell silent.

"Do you think we will find someone to help us, as Ossato said?" Brior asked as he got to his feet and tried to summon up the strength to cover the last short distance to the gates of Terris.

"Ossato said we would," said Dusho but without conviction. It was his turn to pull the drag and he slipped the makeshift harness onto his shoulders. "I hope he was right."

"If he said so, it will be," said Stariat with the conviction all paladins shared.

They commenced walking. Now that rest was ahead of them, their efforts seemed more arduous. But they continued on, Stariat for his paladin's honor, Dusho and Brior for the promise of sleep and good food.

As they came to the gate, a stunning woman in mentor's garments stepped out from the shadows. She was tall and angular in a way that made her more handsome than pretty. She was not young, but age gave her a depth of character she would not have had in youth, and that made her attractive. She came up to the three men before they reached the knights manning the gates and made a deep reverence to them. "May the ancient ones favor your dangerous enterprise, Stariat the Questor, Dusho the Fist, and Brior the Scarred. I am Casilta, mentor from the Old Mountains." Within his illusion spell, Wladex was enjoying himself. He was still getting used to his new life, and this illusion was making it more difficult than usual, but rewarding in its way.

"Ossato sent you?" Stariat asked.

"How else would I know you?" Wladex asked, doing his best to sound mystical.

"But . . . but Ossato died," said Dusho, trying to make sense of this new arrival.

"He had potent spells prepared against the hour of his death," said Wladex, still being truthful.

"Do you know what he sought?" Stariat asked. His curiosity about this impressive female mentor was increasing with every word they exchanged.

"The end of the Laria," said Wladex. "It was his most sincere dream." He sighed. "If he had died somewhere nearer this city, or on a powerful magical site, he might have recovered. As it is, he is lost in the badlands."

"He was very brave," said Dusho. "He was as brave as a knight, and as determined as a paladin."

It was all Wladex could do to keep from smiling. He lowered his eyes, saying, "I wish I had known him. It was only when our spells touched that he and I communicated." He did his best to sound womanly. "Mages of high purpose are rare."

"That may be so," said Brior, looking at Wladex with an intensity that Wladex had not expected to encounter. "I have never encountered a female mentor before."

"There are not many of us," said Wladex. "That does not diminish what we can accomplish." He waited while Brior thought this over, then went on. "I have secured sleeping rooms for you, and a place to dine when you are rested. You must be hungry."

"Yes. Very hungry," admitted Dusho.

"I know what it is to be famished," said Wladex, who had only the day before had enough blood to satisfy him. Soon he would have to feed again, but he would tend to that while these men rested. "Follow me. The knights at the gate were told of your coming and your gate tax is already paid." He gestured to them to follow him.

The two knights did as they were bade, but Stariat lagged behind, studying Wladex. "Casilta," he called after Wladex.

Wladex hesitated. "Yes? What troubles you, Stariat the Questor?"

"I am wondering how it was that Ossato could send so much information to you when he was dying." His keen eyes narrowed. "Or did you conjure this information from his ghost?"

Wladex laughed, the illusion spell keeping the sound high and light, "You are a very worthy paladin, Stariat. I can say that with conviction. You do well to question me, for I might be in the thrall of the Laria and sent to bring your mission to an end before it has hardly begun. Your caution is commendable, for if I were one of the servants of the Laria I would be powerful and malign. But this is not so." He stopped in the street and regarded the three men with all the openness his illusion spell could create. "I was summoned here by a spell that Ossato powered with his last breaths; he'd had the spell readied for that desperate time. Mages often make such preparations. He chose me because I share his dream of destroying the Laria, and he has known of my support for some time. Fortunately I was already bound for Terris when his spell reached me."

"Yes, yes," said Stariat impatiently. "But why should we believe you?"

"Well, I could cast a spell of persuasion over you, and convince you to believe me. But that would be deceptive, and it is not my wish to lie to you." Wladex made his illusion a bit stronger. "You should not trust me for any other reason than that you share a desire to complete the work Ossato began."

They had reached the gates of the city and the guards, seeing Casilta, waved them through with nothing more than a sign of respect. They found themselves in a bustling crowd milling about the plaza that faced the gate, where the people of Terris came to see new arrivals and greet returning friends. No one paid any attention to the men or Wladex.

"But a woman mentor," said Brior. "You said yourself your numbers are few. Could that be a problem in itself?"

"Only if you think the Laria is male or female, I suppose," said Wladex. "The Laria is neither and both. It uses whatever form is useful for its purpose. Since that is the case, it may be wise to have both male and female hunters."

"She has a point," said Dusho. "She could be a powerful ally."

Stariat was still skeptical, but he nodded and said, "For the time being, I will accept that you are what you say you are, and that you will guide us as Ossato said we would be guided."

He pointed to the drag. "We have to keep these stones safe. Do you know where we can do that?"

Relieved at the turn in Stariat's attitude, Wladex said, "Of course. I am not going to expose you to the Laria's agents when you have risked so much. The place I have arranged for you to sleep has a strong room, and I will guard the entrance to it while you rest." He would also have a chance to feed, but that was not for these men to know. He was so famished that the very sound of the men's heartbeats distracted him from his purpose, but he did his best to ignore his hunger a little longer.

"But a woman?" said Dusho. "How wise is it to leave you to guard us?"

"I have magic enough for protecting you," Wladex said, somewhat testily. "Or, if you are so troubled, I can cast an illusion spell to make it seem I am a heavily armed man. Would that relieve you?"

Stariat interceded before their dispute could worsen. "I am sure Casilta will know how best to help us since she shares our goals." He smiled once, more a quick widening of his mouth than a smile. "Take us to this place, Casilta. We will go with you, and gladly."

Wladex managed to do a sweeping reverence without looking clumsy, then indicated the street they should enter. "If you will but follow me, it is done."

They went down the street to a heavy gate. Wladex made a sign and the gate opened revealing a courtyard filled with lush plants and the music of fountains. The men, following their mentor, stopped in astonishment at what they saw.

"Is this a spell, or is it genuine?" asked Stariat, his eyes huge as he looked around.

"It is real enough," said Wladex. "The place is owned by a great lord of the city. His family has for generations cultivated plants. They hope to bring Delos back to life with new strains of plants that will grow in the badlands, but so far they have not been able to." He pointed to the center of the garden. "Those who strive to defeat the Laria are welcome here."

"It would be a great thing, wouldn't it?" Brior asked. "To defeat the Laria. What kind of place would this be with it gone?"

"That is a great mystery," said Wladex, adding to himself that he intended to solve it as soon as he could. "There will be a meal laid for you, and sleeping rooms prepared for your use." He made a gesture and two liveried servants appeared. "These are the heroes I spoke of. See they are honored according to their deserts."

"And the . . . stones they carry?" One of the servants indicated the rubies which just then looked like nothing more than river rocks, thanks to Stariat's spell.

"I will tend to them," said Wladex, almost too quickly. "Go along with the servants," he advised the three men. "I have to provide safety for these stones." He chuckled, but not loudly enough to be overheard.

"Very well," said Stariat. "We're hungry and tired, and you appear to be the woman mentor you claim to be. For Ossato's sake, we will do as you command." He bowed formally and snapped his fingers. "Dusho. Brior. Come."

They had not gone more than three steps when a green mage came out of the plants and stood before them, blocking their way. "Who are you, and why are you here?" he demanded, his full attention on Wladex. "You are not what you appear to be."

Wladex laughed, high, tinkling, feminine laughter that made the men with him look slightly shocked. "We are on a mission, green mage. It would be good of you to aid us."

"To what end?" The green mage pointed a finger at Wladex. "You are putting these men at terrible risk and you do not care?"

"I care," said Wladex before the men could speak—if they had decided to speak at all. "No one values their lives as I do."

The green mage took hold of an amulet hung on a chain around his neck and began to recite a spell. There was something dangerous in the tone of his voice; Wladex did not trust him.

"What are you doing?" Stariat asked bluntly as the ancient words of power went on. "We are not your enemies, good mage, we are your allies in purpose." He took two strides toward the mage and was suddenly frozen in place.

Aghast at this, Dusho and Brior drew their weapons—Dusho a throwing axe and Brior a short lance—and launched both at the green mage. The axe struck a glancing blow on the mage's shoulder, but the lance fell an arm's length short of its target as if it had struck an impenetrable wall. The knights reached for new weapons, now determined to stop the chanting, for they were convinced it would do them no good.

"Hold!" Wladex ordered the knights, and flung himself on the green mage, giving the appearance of trying to wrest the amulet from the mage's hands, but actually feeding on the mage's blood. The power of the mage flowed into him even as the man gave a cry of despair. Wladex took the amulet and rose from the drained body; he was strengthened, his thoughts sharp and clear now that they were no longer driven by hunger. He held the amulet as the treasure he suspected it was.

Stariat came out of his immobility so suddenly that he almost tripped over the dead mage. He blinked in surprise, turning to Wladex. "Casilta. What happened?"

"You should have seen her," Brior exclaimed before Wladex could answer. "She was splendid. Fought as well as any knight could have done, or paladin, either."

"Hardly that," said Wladex with more honesty than humility. "The green mage was casting a spell that would have brought you to harm. There was not enough time for a counterspell, particularly if the green mage has minions to do his bidding. I did the only thing I could." He did not add that it was what he most enjoyed doing.

"Very good of you," said Stariat. "And what have you there?"

"I have his amulet. I did not want him summoning knights or reavers, or something worse. And it may have spells I can use to help us find what we seek." He twitched his skirts away from the mage. "He must have been using a most formidable spell. Breaking it has killed him."

"You could reanimate him," said Dusho with a slight chuckle.

"So I could," said Wladex, who had no intention of such an action. "But he would not be grateful. In fact, he might make himself obnoxious." He began to walk again. "I will tell the master of this place that there is a dead green mage in the garden, and that the mages' guild should be sent for. They can reanimate him if that is what they want." It would be a difficult task, Wladex knew, for a vampiric death was more comprehensive than most others. "Do not let this stop us from doing our duty."

The knights retrieved their weapons before going on. Brior bent over the green mage to be certain he was dead. Wladex did not like that, and motioned to him to follow. "The man looks sucked dry," said the knight as he rose.

"Perhaps he was under an illusion spell," Stariat suggested. "That could account for it." He was already following Wladex. "Casilta, did you notice anything that made you think he was not a green mage?"

Again Wladex used the opportunity to his advantage. "It is possible. For if he were trying to maintain two powerful spells at the same time, he might well be unable to survive both of them." He held up the amulet. "Perhaps this will tell us more."

"Do you think so?" Dusho asked.

"Most certainly. Come, gentlemen. You have to bathe and rest, and I must spend an hour or so trying to discover what is in this amulet." For the sheer, malignant fun of it, he added, "Who knows? That mage might have been one of the Laria's creatures."

The two knights exchanged uneasy glances. Stariat looked grave. "Then be careful of us as we sleep," said the paladin as he went into the big house at the center of the garden, the others close behind him.

Chapter 8

THE AMULET WAS COVERED IN MINUS-
cule, archaic writing that Wladex had to squint
at in order to read. It took him most of the transit
of the blue sun to realize the importance of what
he had found, and when he did, he had to stop
himself from waking Stariat, Dusho, and Brior in
order to tell them. His excitement had to remain
unobvious for now, or the men might wonder
about the green mage, which would not suit his
purposes at all.

To test the amulet, Wladex generated a pur-
loining spell, bringing the disguise of rubies
under his control. He decided he would tell Stariat that it was better to have protection of the
jewels in Casilta's hands than in the hands of
fighters, who might be too occupied with combat
to give the rubies the enegetic shielding they required. As he ran the explanation through his
mind he decided it had a nice, mentorish logic
to it. Besides, the spell was cast, and the matter
settled already.

By the time Dusho came to the dining room, Wladex had hit upon a strategy that suited him. As the knight greeted him with a respectful reverence, Wladex said, "I begin to hope that we may have found something most useful in this amulet. I am reluctant to say for certain that this is so, but I am encouraged."

"How is that, Casilta?" Dusho asked, regarding Wladex with curiosity mixed with satisfaction. "It would be a good thing to have a worthwhile spell or two from that." He pointed to the amulet. "What do you think you have found?"

"I am not quite certain," said Wladex, shading the truth. "It may be that this amulet provides instruction on how to find the Emerald Treasure House. I am not absolutely certain that it does, but it appears to be possible."

Dusho grinned. "That would be wonderful, wouldn't it?" He looked up as Stariat came into the dining room. "What do you think, paladin? Casilta here thinks she may have found the way to the Terris emeralds."

Stariat looked startled. "How?" he asked.

"Here," said Wladex, holding up the amulet. "The inscription is very, very old, and difficult to read. It may be that I have not read it right, and it may be that over time the location of the treasure house has changed. But given the power of this amulet, I believe we may be able to find what we are seeking."

Stariat was less enthusiastic than Dusho, but

still his eyes gleamed in anticipation of adventure. "Do you think you can find this place?"

"I hope so," said Wladex, disguising his certainty. "I believe the location we seek is directly beneath the Great Square of Terris." He paused, letting the two men think about the magnitude of the problem this created.

"Why so glum?" asked Brior as he came into the dining room. He stifled a yawn as he stretched, throwing off the last of his sleep.

"Not glum—thoughtful," said Stariat. "Casilta has stumbled upon something that may well serve our purpose, if we are able to put it to use."

"Why not just take us to the vault with a spell?" Dusho suggested.

"Because so great a treasure, and one with such power, will be protected by many spells," said Wladex. "We must go there on our own. That is the only way to avoid the guardian spells."

"There will be guardians for such a treasure," warned Stariat. "Monsters as well as spells."

"Of course," said Wladex. "Which is why Ossato sought out fighting men like you. Any monsters we face you can defeat."

The three men considered this, and Brior spoke up again. "How do we defend ourselves if the spells keep us from being able to fight?"

"That is my concern," said Wladex. "I do not fear fighting," he went on. "Not all women are afraid to do battle."

"But not all women are trained for it," said

Brior, and shrugged to show he did not mean to insult Casilta.

"I am a mentor," Wladex reminded them all. "I am prepared to do whatever I must to bring about the end of the Laria. I will even fight the most dreadful monsters that can be spawned. If my spells are not strong enough, I will find other ways to fight."

Stariat was impressed by this dedication, and said, "I don't think we can question her devotion. She was willing to attack the green mage, and that may have saved us already." He saw the servants appear in the doorway, two of them bearing trays of food.

"I took the opportunity to order your breakfast for you. And to pay for it," Wladex added with a quick glance at Dusho. "Have all you want and enjoy it."

"That I will," said Dusho, sitting down and pulling up one of the platters laden with succulent viands. "Never miss an opportunity to eat."

Brior sat down across from him and took another of the platters. He grinned as he began his meal. Only Stariat hesitated. "Are these meals magical?"

"Only in the sense that the chef is an artist," said Wladex. "I have conjured nothing. You will want real meat and bread for the strength they provide, and you do not need anything that may lessen the power of spells you may cast." That was all fairly true. It was also true that eating magical foods could thin the blood, which Wladex did not want. "While you eat, I am going to scout the Great Square. I need to see how much of it has changed since the amulet was inscribed." He also needed to find some hapless mortal to feed on, for he knew he would need to assuage his hunger before they went in search of the Terris emeralds.

"Very good," said Brior through a mouthful of bread. "Go on."

Wladex curtsied to the men. "Be ready within the hour. I will return for you then." He left the men to their meal and went out into the streets. His head was filled with greedy thoughts, and he had to remind himself to be careful, that he could not risk any exposure now, in this place. So he contented himself with looking for enthusiastic young mages in students' robes who would take a mentor's attention at face value.

The youngster who approached him was almost too easy a target. He saluted Wladex with a reverence worthy of a master and said, "If you are new to this city, I would consider it an honor to show you what it offers a mentor of skill." His over-eager smile made Wladex satisfied.

"You are gracious, young mage. Do you happen to know if in the Great Square there is a monolith with the words 'On this site in the era before the millennia were counted stood the monastery of the Land'?" The inscription on the amulet identified this as the marker for the emerald treasury.

"The seventh monolith. Yes," said the young mage enthusiastically. "I can show you just where it is, if you will accompany me." He started off, hardly bothering to see if Wladex was behind him.

The Great Square had a section of ancient wall standing near it, and Wladex realized that it played a part in the treasure he sought, for it held a magical presence as persistent as the hum of insects. He asked his escort, "What is that, and why is it still standing?"

"That is to remind us of the sacrifice of Tremayne Baric, the great bard," said the apprentice mage with an expression bordering on adoration. "This is where dead heroes can be returned from the dead, if they are worthy."

"I have heard of this place," said Wladex slowly. "It was part of an ancient monastery, wasn't it? The same monastery the seventh monolith marks?" He was convinced that he had found what he sought. "This is a most remarkable place, apprentice. You are to be commended for bringing me here."

The young mage blushed. "If you are gratified, then so am I."

"Not quite yet," said Wladex. "But I will be, shortly. If you will do one more thing for me?" He knew his illusion spell made his smile feminine and seductive. "I am a stranger here, and I rely on your help to end my loneliness." It was so blatant that he feared the apprentice mage would laugh aloud. Instead the young man fairly panted in anticipation. "Is there someplace where we could be private for a while?"

"Yes," said the mage eagerly. "If you will come with me, no one will disturb us."

"Good," Wladex said, and set out to the quarters the mage kept for himself some little distance from the Great Square in the heart of the city. As he went up the stairs behind the young mage, Wladex had trouble keeping himself from acting immediately.

"Here," said the apprentice, opening the door to a small suite of rooms. "If you will come inside, I will be honored to accommodate you in any way I can."

"How very good of you," said Wladex, waiting only for the door to be closed before he overpowered the young man and drank deeply of his life-blood. He left the body lying on the antique carpet in the room where the mage had studied, his head pillowed on a book; Wladex thought that was a nice touch. He then made his way back to the ancient wall and summoned the disguised rubies, placing them amid the rubble of the wall. He thought they might need to have them close at hand when they left the emerald treasury, and could think of no better place than this. Satisfied with his efforts he made his way back to where his companions were. He found the streets crowded and the people active, but thought nothing more about it but that it was inconvenient.

"Have you made any progress? We will need to act quickly if we are not to be stopped in our efforts, won't we?" Brior asked when Wladex returned to the grand old house with the elaborate garden. The men had finished their breakfast and had been talking about the things they had to do to preserve themselves from the Laria and its agents; the arrival of Wladex made their concerns all the more keen.

"Yes," said Wladex, almost drowsy now that he was replete. He forced himself to put his languor aside; rest was for later, when the emeralds were safely in their hands. "I have been to the Great Square, and I have discovered an inscription matching the one on this amulet. That is the place we must search first."

"And how do you propose to do that?" asked Dusho, still a bit testy. "There are many people who might watch us. If you use an illusion spell, another mentor could notice and that would bring us trouble. I have been thinking about our situation."

"Ah, but that would mean the cloaking spell was not powerful enough," said Wladex, his manner gently chiding. "I have just such a strong spell that, if it were detected, would only reveal another spell beneath it." He saw that the men were doubtful. "I am certain that this magic is strong enough to do what we need. But it will mean I will have little power left to protect you against anything we may find in the treasury itself." This last warning brought a smile to Brior's face.

"Just as well. It isn't a real victory unless we do the fighting for ourselves." He saw Dusho nod.

Stariat was not convinced. "I have a spell or

two at my command. Do you think they will suffice?" He glanced at Wladex. "You already have our rubies disguised to look like ordinary rocks. Now you propose to undertake a double-layered spell? Is this too much for you?"

"I hope it will not be," said Wladex, who did not mention his own spell that made him appear to be a female mentor. He would be spreading himself quite thin, but not so much that any of his spells would fail. "I will do my utmost to be sure our activities are not discovered." This pledge seemed convincing enough, for it won a gesture of respect from Stariat. "As soon as you have your weapons, good knights, worthy paladin, we should go from this place."

"Very good," said Stariat. "We will make ready." He paused. "Our other stones . . . what of them?"

"They are safe enough. I have them where no one will notice them," said Wladex. "They are stacked with many other rocks." It seemed prudent to tell them that much.

"Will you have any trouble finding them again?" asked Dusho nervously as he prepared to arm himself.

"No. They are disguised by a spell I control; they cannot be hidden from me. I would know them scattered across the badlands." Wladex was confident of that, and for this once, he let his certainty show.

"Very good strategy," said Brior. "For it means that we must preserve you if we are to have access to the rubies." He smiled. "That is nothing to your discredit, mentor. In fact, I have a good opinion of one who is clever enough to protect herself as you have done."

"You are very gracious," said Wladex, curtsying. "But we have much to do." Then he turned away. "Be ready."

It did not take the three men long to prepare themselves to depart. In a short while they stood before Wladex again. "Lead on," said Stariat, and followed Wladex through the garden to the edge of the street, which was now so filled with people that it was like a river in flood. The population of Terris was all bound for the Great Square, moving with such inexorable force that not even spells could stop it.

"What is this?" Dusho asked as the men paused with Wladex at the edge of the surging mass.

"I don't know," said Wladex resentfully. "Should we wait until it is over?"

"It depends on what has caused this—this disruption," said Stariat. "I think we would draw too much attention to ourselves if we did not go along."

"Oh, do you?" said Brior, looking at the mob uneasily.

"Yes," Stariat said firmly, and without waiting for any of his comrades to follow him, he plunged into the street and began to move away from the knights and Wladex at a good speed.

"Should we follow?" asked Brior, clearly bewildered by what had just happened.

"We had better," said Wladex, concealing his

annoyance. "If we do not, who is to say where we shall meet again." Saying that, he, too, stepped into the roiling mass.

With a shrug, Dusho and Brior followed, striving to keep Wladex and Stariat in sight among the many bobbing, churning heads. Moving with the flow of the people, they all reached the Great Square in a short time, where the confusion was magnified a hundred-fold, for all the streets had carried the same turmoil, dumping them in the Great Square in ever-increasing numbers.

Wladex came to the foot of the fourth monolith, which held the inscription: *This marks the spot where the paladin Demarest slew the last of the Dragons of Wrath during the Night of Fire.* He grabbed hold of it and hung on tenaciously. He wanted to shout for his companions, but the noise was so great that he knew beyond all question that he would not be heard. He raised one hand high in the air and waved it, hoping that one of the knights would see him. All the while, he did his best to try to determine the cause of this sudden unrest. The citizens of Terris were not given to riots; something had to be causing this upheaval. For Wladex, the only force powerful enough to disrupt a whole city was the Laria.

Dusho appeared at Wladex's side. "At last," he panted. "The people will start fighting soon, if only to try to reduce the crowding."

"That is what I think," said Wladex. "And when they do, there will be more pandemonium than we see now." He pointed across the Great Square to another monolith where Stariat had found a haven from the tumult. "Look. All we need now is Brior. Look for him."

Dusho shaded his eyes and peered into the commotion, hoping to find his fellow knight. Finally he pointed. "There he is. At the edge of the square."

Wladex nodded. "Very good. That is the direction we wish to go. If he will only remain where he is—" He decided to cast a minor spell of immobility on Brior. That would simplify finding him. "You and I and Stariat need to go to him."

"Through this?" Dusho asked, appalled.

"Certainly," said Wladex. "In fact, this may benefit us. In this ruction, who will notice us when we go in search of the emeralds?" He smiled without a trace of humor. "Think, Dusho. Who can tell in all this what the four of us may do? No one will notice, and if anyone should, there will be no way for anyone to determine the truth of any accusations that may be made. For everyone who sees us will be discounted by all those who will not." Heartened by his own encouragement, Wladex plunged into the crowd and began to make his way toward the place where his spell held Brior immobile. He had the satisfaction of seeing Stariat come down from his perch to go in the same direction.

"Slow down!" Dusho shouted from behind him.

"You hurry!" Wladex countered, continuing on with all the determination he could muster.

Chapter 9

THERE WAS A DARK CLEFT IN THE BACK of the wall, small enough to be ignored. Out of the path of the milling crowd the four stood together facing the cleft. "This is the entry," said Wladex. He clasped the amulet in one hand and pointed with the other. "That is a portion of ancient script meaning 'emerald.'" There was more to it than that, but he did not wish to reveal the whole of his understanding.

"If that is the case, how come no one has gone into this cleft before us? Or have they?" Dusho was very suspicious. "Anyone who found that amulet could have gotten into the treasury and taken the emeralds. We may find nothing when we go to look."

"Possibly," said Wladex. "But we will not know for sure until we have inspected the place ourselves."

"That is correct," said Stariat. "I would have to agree that we must go in." He was briefly distracted as a basket full of half-rotten fruit came flying overhead.

"Whatever the situation may be under the Great Square, we had better go through the cleft before the fighting gets worse up here," said Dusho.

The howls and shouts from the mob were now a continual din. The four had to shout to be heard over them. Brior made a belligerent gesture in the direction of the Great Square, muttering, "Louts!" as another mass of spoiled fruit came sailing overhead. "They'll be all over us soon."

"Go through the cleft," said Stariat. "We must act while we can."

"No doubt," said Brior with feeling. "Either that or we must start throwing rocks."

"No," said Wladex hastily, aware that the rubies were among the rocks they might throw. "I must fit the amulet into the old script. Then the inner door will open."

"Are you certain of that?" Dusho eyed the old inscription with narrowed eyes and stared at Wladex. "Is that on the amulet, too?"

"Yes," said Wladex, leaning forward, trying to find the right way to put the amulet into the ornate, archaic word carved in stone. His first two tries failed, and he was becoming exasperated. To make matters worse, the riot was growing closer and the people of Terris were determined to make the most of this occasion to be as rambunctious as possible. More bits of garbage flew threw the air in all directions, and now and again, stones were added to the rotten fruits and vegetables.

"Is that going to work, or not?" Stariat asked. He wasn't angry, but he was growing uneasy. "Is there another entry we might find?"

"This is the one specified on the amulet," said Wladex, concentrating on what he was doing. "It is supposed to fit in here." As he spoke, the amulet slipped into an ornamental swash on the first letter of the inscription, and in the next moment there was a rumbling that was more impressive than the clamor of the riot. Before his eyes, the stones drew back, revealing stairs leading down into darkness. "There!" he exclaimed, unable to conceal his excitement.

"Good hopping hoards!" Dusho burst out, peering into the darkness. "What a sight that is."

"Better to view it from inside," Stariat recommended as a scrabbling group of citizens barreled their way by.

The men did not need another invitation. They bustled through the narrow opening and waited while Wladex contrived to retrieve the amulet and the opening narrowed once again.

"Do you think you will be able to get us out of here?" Brior asked as the stones rumbled closed.

"I have no doubt," said Wladex. "That's why I took the amulet." He did not add that there had been whispered stories in Terris for generations that hinted at foolish men who had stumbled into this vault and were unable to get out because they left their amulets outside, fixed in the inscription. He looked ahead into the dark, holding up the amulet and saying a few ancient words that turned it into a torch. "Now we can go on. But tread warily. This vault is sure to have guardians."

The knights took the lead this time, and Stariat brought up the rear as they made their way down the long, rough-hewn stairs into the vaults beneath the Great Square of Terris. As they reached a section that was more corridor than stairs, they paused to look about.

"No hammets at least," said Wladex, and could have bit his own tongue for the slip.

"We fought hammets when we found the rubies," said Dusho heavily. "The Laria probably won't repeat itself."

"Probably not," agreed Brior. Ahead were three doors, each firmly shut. "What do we do now?"

"We choose a door," said Wladex, trying to recall if he had seen anything on the amulet that would advise them on which door would lead to the treasure they sought.

"How do you propose to go about it?" Dusho asked. He fingered his sword as if anticipating monsters to fight.

"Well," said Wladex, "the center is the most obvious, which may mean it is the door we want, because it was supposed by the ancients who built this place that we would not select the door that seemed most obvious. If they made it the right door, they assumed we would not take it." He scowled at the left door. "This might be the most likely choice, because it is the door we would probably not choose."

"I say we go through the middle," said Brior. "It is the most direct."

"All the more reason to avoid it," said Dusho. "And the left door is least likely because it is the one that they would think we would decide is unlikely and therefore would take." He made a sign with his hand indicating how futile the matter was.

"The right door could be the safest choice," said Wladex distantly. "It is the one that we might decide upon when it is apparent that the center is too obvious." He licked his lips. "Still, I say it is best to try the center door after all."

"You are the mentor," said Brior, doubt coloring his encouragement.

"This is a difficult problem," said Wladex, and impulsively reached out for the massive latch on the middle door. Behind him, the warriors held their weapons at the ready. The door swung open, revealing a large room stacked with chests of treasure—gold and silver coins, most so old that all images upon them had been worn away, caskets of moonstones and opals, bags of tourmalines and sapphires, ropes of amethysts, peridots, and beryl. Riches beyond measure lay strewn about as if they were nothing more than dust.

"Where are the emeralds?" asked Stariat as he pawed through the myriad jewels.

"Not that these are shabby," remarked Brior, taking a particularly fine ring inlaid with tiger's eye and turquoise. "Do you think it would be all right to keep this?"

Wladex didn't answer. He held the amulet high, letting its glow suffuse the room. Finally he pointed down at the stones paving the treasury. "There. Look."

The floor was a rich, effulgent green; emeralds as large as stepping-stones were fitted together underfoot. Their luminous shine was enthralling; the three men and Wladex stared in stupefaction at this splendid discovery.

"How do we get them out?" asked Dusho after their silence had grown long.

"I don't know," Wladex admitted. "No doubt they have a spell holding them here." But as he said it, he doubted it. The door had turned out to be the obvious one, and the emeralds were hidden in the gaudy treasury by the presence of other gems. Perhaps it would be possible to remove the paving stones by nothing more arduous than prying up a portion of the floor.

"Well?" Dusho was getting nervous. "I don't think we should linger in this place, do you? I think we should take what we need and leave."

"Take what we need," said Stariat as if he had been overwhelmed by the riches around him. "The old monks who built this place might have let us take what we needed."

"Then I'll use my axe blade to lever out the emeralds," said Brior, and began to suit his actions to his words. He worked the blade of his axe deep into the very narrow joint between the emeralds and leaned on it, doing his best to pry the jewels out of the floor. The blade of his axe bent.

"You must be careful," Wladex warned as he saw what was happening. "You may still need that as a weapon." He picked up some discarded jewels for himself.

"If I have an emerald the size of a brick, I can buy more axes," said Brior, continuing to labor. He grunted with effort and had the satisfaction of seeing the green stone shift the tiniest bit.

Inspired by Brior's success, Dusho set to work on the next stone, concentrating his efforts on lifting the emerald up. "This thing is . . . is good-sized. It must be a hand's breadth deep."

"At least," Stariat agreed, and joined the other two at this work. He pushed a mass of coins aside and felt the floor for any irregularities that would give him purchase on the emeralds. He bent over and went to work.

Wladex almost itched to work along-side them, hesitating only because his illusion of being female might be compromised if he did. He contented himself with standing guard, his dagger at the ready, his sword hidden in the vast folds of his mentor's clothing. For a short while all he could hear was the sound of the three men, straining to get the emeralds loose. They occasionally made sounds of progress, and at last Dusho was the first to pull up one of the green jewels. It was half again as large as a paving brick and it shone with a verdant luminescence that hinted at its powers. "Wonderful," Wladex exclaimed as he touched the gem.

"I'll try to get another up," Dusho said, his excitement making him giddy. He handed the emerald to Wladex and redoubled his efforts to pull up another stone.

Holding the emerald in his hand, Wladex began to hit on a notion that was as audacious as it was practical: he would disguise the emeralds in an illusion spell that made them look like bricks! That would be the easiest way to get them out of the city, for what guard would bother with a cart of such ordinary objects. He grinned with delight. Small boulders and bricks. After a riot, who would notice such things? He slipped the emerald into one of the concealed pockets in his mentor's robes and waited while the men pried up another four bricks. As he slipped these into other pockets, he heard something in the hall beyond them, a strange, shuffling sound as if large bags of wet clay were being dragged along the corridor. He held up his hand for silence.

"What is it?" Brior asked, pausing in his selection of a string of opals. He thrust this into his wallet and looked about anxiously.

Dusho drew his sword even as he scooped up loose gems. "Trouble?"

"I hear it, too," said Stariat. He, too, drew his sword.

"Kobolds," said Wladex. "They must have been summoned when the emeralds were taken up."

These powerful monsters were determined, if mindless, fighters. The men sighed, knowing the kobolds were hard to beat. "What do you think?" Stariat asked Wladex. "Do we make a stand here, or go out into the corridor to face them?" He made a sign to the two knights. "Make ready," he said.

"I think it would be best to fight in the corridor. This is a box," he said, indicating the room, "and hard to get out of once we are in it." He wished for an instant that the emeralds were not so heavy, but he quickly dismissed such an unworthy sentiment, for he was keenly aware that their weight came as much from their magical power as their actual mineral density.

"I agree," said Stariat, and flung the door open before any of the others could speak.

Kobolds filled the corridor, shambling along so close to one another that it was difficult to find a position in which to fight them. They had one purpose—to destroy their enemies, and right now, that meant Wladex and the three men in the treasury.

"Can we defeat them?" asked Brior, unafraid but troubled.

"If we can get them to move apart, I think so," said Stariat. "If we had more room to maneuver."

"What about the other two doors?" Brior suggested. "If they are thrown open, they might give us some chance."

The kobolds were almost upon them now, their enormous cudgels and sledgehammers raised.

"Well, do something," said Dusho, preparing to rush their lumbering attackers.

Wladex squared his shoulders and began a spell to confuse the kobolds, one that made them unable to recognize friend from foe. If this could get them to fight one another, then he and his three companions might be able to escape. As he finished the spell, nothing much happened, and he was distressed to see it might have been blocked. "Get ready!" he shouted.

The three men prepared to land the first blow, their weapons seeming puny against the immense clubs and hammers of the kobolds. Brior said, "Too bad we won't be able to defeat the Laria," and began to rush toward the monsters.

"But we will!" Wladex roared, his hands rising to release the spell. He was not about to be stopped now, and by something so lumpish as a kobold! He was going to defeat the Laria, and nothing—*nothing*—would keep that from happening, not even the Laria itself.

The air of the corridor crackled with the energy of the spell, and an odor of a cross between soap and boiling vegetables filled the air. The three heroes hung back, not knowing what was coming next, until Dusho let out a whoop.

"Look!" He pointed to the kobolds. "It's working."

The great, squat-bodied creatures were beginning to mill, the purpose of their attack gone. They were still ready to fight, and they chose the nearest targets they could find—their fellow kobolds. The drubbing began slowly at first, and gradually grew in fury as the monsters warmed to the battle. It was a confusion of huge weapons in massive hands as the kobolds continued their assault.

"How do we get past them?" Brior asked as they watched the continuing slaughter among the kobolds. "They will fight anything getting near them."

"So they will," Wladex agreed. "We will have to put ourselves in a protective bubble and go quickly, for we cannot have them stumbling upon us."

"That was a very good spell," said Dusho, watching the kobolds fight. "I am very impressed. You have done something most remarkable, mentor, even though you are a woman."

"Perhaps it is because I am a woman," said Wladex, doing his best not to laugh. He ducked as a huge severed kobold arm came flying out of the close-fought battle. "If we wait a little longer, they may make themselves useless."

"Better to go now," said Stariat. "I do not like the look of them. They could kill us just falling from a blow."

"True enough," said Wladex, and once again began to recite the spell that would keep them all safe. "We will have to move quickly as soon as the spell is in place," he added as he took hold of the small wedge of Fuego ruby he had concealed under his robes. He put this atop one of the emerald bricks; the power of these two potent stones together gave added strength to his spell. "Be ready."

A glowing, crackling orb settled over Wladex and his companions, like a clear bowl turned upside down. Wladex urged the men to move at once, for he knew the spell would protect them utterly, but it would also shut out their air, and in so closed a place as this, they would grow weak quickly.

The men needed no more encouragement than that. They hurried ahead, shoving and climbing through the pile of kobold casualties, and then into the precarious heart of the fighting. There were clubs and fists moving all around them, and the sounds of blows thudded like landslides. At one point three kobolds locked together in a confusion of arms and legs, and proved too much to get by. Stariat stepped beyond the spell and plunged his sword into the shoulder of the nearest kobold, then led the way through the enormous, squirming bodies to emerge at the rising steps.

"Go up," said Wladex, dismantling the spell. "I am coming after you." He had one more spell to do.

As the three men rushed past him up the stairs, he made one more spell, and brought the walls crashing in on the kobolds and the treasure.

Chapter 10

THE MERCHANT LEADING THE CARAVAN was a leather-faced old fellow with a sly look and a knowing laugh. "Astra, is it?" He studied Wladex and the three men with him. "I don't usually hold with taking women along on journeys. It's hard going. But seeing you're a mentor and you have your own guards with you . . ." He made a gesture showing he was willing to accept the four of them. "It'll cost you."

"No doubt," said Wladex. "How much?"

"Oh, two jewels apiece. Real jewels, mind, not something you conjure up with a spell." He held out his hand. "Make them worth my while. I don't want bits of this and that."

Wladex pulled out a string of opals he had purloined from the treasury. "Will this do? The stones are not magic, except for the magic they rightly contain." He dangled it in front of the merchant's eyes. "You will find it is good quality."

The merchant took it and squinted at the opals.

"Very good quality, by the look of them." He stared at Wladex. "They had better not be false, is all I can say."

"They are not," said Wladex as if offended. "Take them now, and when the journey is done you will see that they are not ensorcelled."

Stariat spoke up. "We are fighters. Your reavers can surely use our help if we have to fight. A paladin and two knights are a good addition to your escort."

"True enough," said the merchant. "But you are coming along to protect the mentor."

"In a fight, we will protect all," said Stariat.

"So you say now," said the merchant. "But when you must do it, will that still be so?" He looked at the sleds piled with rocks and bricks. "Strange cargo."

It was an observation Wladex was ready for. "It is for a mentor stronghold we seek to build, a place that can be proof against the Laria."

"And there are no bricks or rocks where you are going to build?" The merchant laughed. "I won't meddle in magical things, but you have made yourselves the butt of jokes for crossing the badlands with such goods as those." He fingered the opals. "Still. This will silence jibes, won't it?"

"I don't like that man," said Brior when the merchant had ambled off to speak to the captain of the reavers who was in charge of the armed escort that would see them across the badlands to Astra.

"He is typical of his calling," said Wladex. "He probably thinks we are smuggling."

"Which we are," said Stariat.

"Yes. But not what he would be inclined to suspect." He smiled at his three companions. "He also thinks that you are my lovers."

Dusho spat, Brior laughed, and Stariat looked baffled. "Why should he think that?"

"A woman alone with an armed escort with a load of bricks and rocks? Why else would two knights and a paladin accompany her?" Wladex asked, enjoying himself. "It is probably wise to let him continue to think this, for he will not bother any of us if he has such notions."

The two knights nodded, but Stariat looked worried. "Won't that lead to trouble?" He fingered the hilt of his axe. "If the reavers decide that they are entitled to the same privileges we appear to have, what will you do?"

"Oh," said Wladex with elaborate nonchalance, "I will use a disguise spell to make them think I am something dreadful—a vampire lord, perhaps—and that will serve to keep them at a distance." He nodded in the direction of the walls of Terris behind them. "When we return, let us hope there is order in the city once again."

"Do you know why the people rioted?" asked Stariat.

"No," said Wladex. "Why should I?"

"Well, you are a mentor, and you have access to special information that the rest of us do not. I thought you might have discerned the cause of the riot for your own curiosity." He watched Wladex closely.

This scrutiny made Wladex uneasy. "I had other things on my mind—more pressing to our purpose." He tossed his head in what he hoped was a feminine gesture of exasperation.

"So you did," said Stariat, and let it go at that.

The merchant was coming back down the line of his company, announcing their imminent departure. As he reached Wladex and the three men, he said, "I thought you might like to know, the reavers have an elf to help guide us. Very reliable, elves are."

"That they are," Wladex agreed, doing his best to look satisfied with this information. He knew he would do well to avoid the elf, for occasionally elves could penetrate cloaking and disguising spells, which would not please him or his comrades. "You are wise to have so perspicacious a scout with you."

"I think so," said the merchant. "We will be moving as soon as the red sun sets behind the walls of Terris. Be ready. We will not tolerate stragglers."

"An excellent precaution," Wladex approved, and adjusted the harness he wore that attached to the smallest sled; it held stout bags filled with their clothes and food and bedding. The three men pulled the sleds with their bricks and stones.

"How long until we reach Astra?" asked Brior.

"We haven't left Terris yet," Dusho reminded him.

"I know. But still, how long?" He rocked back on his heels. "I want to know."

"Four, five green sun days," said Wladex, repeating what he had overheard the merchant say to one of the others in the line.

"And must we bring up the rear?" Brior persisted.

"We joined the caravan last," said Wladex. "We must be at the end." He didn't like it much, either, but knew there was no point in complaining.

"We will eat dust all the way to Astra," said Brior, disgusted by the prospect.

"There are worse fates," said Dusho. "We could have had to make the crossing on our own." He gave Brior a hard look.

Brior said nothing, but his expression revealed his dismay at such a prospect.

"It is better to bring up the rear, I think," said Stariat, and added, "We can be alert without drawing too much attention to ourselves."

Brior sighed. "I'll try to remember that when my mouth is full of grit."

Then the shadows changed. There was a shout from the head of the line, and one of the reavers made his way back along the line, ordering the caravan to start moving. As he reached the end of the line, he glared at the two knights. "You will keep a watch behind us. There can be trouble from there as well as from the front."

"Or the sides, or beneath us, or above us," said Dusho with a kind of world-weary aplomb.

"Yes!" barked the reaver, then trotted forward as the line began to move.

"How many in this caravan?" asked Brior as he took his first step.

"The merchant said forty-one, counting us," said Wladex. The weight of the sled was minor now, but he knew that it would become heavier as they traveled. He did his best to look optimistic and to move easily.

"Well, on to Astra," said Dusho, and began to move with the rest.

They kept on for several hours. The walls of Terris disappeared behind them and they were left in the great wild expanse of wastes that claimed most of Delos. Here wind blew constantly and the very rocks hummed as the planet basked in the changing light of its three suns. The caravan kept on, pausing occasionally for food and water. Finally, as everyone was getting tired and the red sun shining overhead, the reavers came back along the line of travelers announcing that there was an oasis ahead. They had sent half a dozen of their men ahead to secure it from any creatures that might make staying there unpleasant. "We will rest there. You may all sleep for one sun." This meant until the next rising sun was in the same place the red sun was now.

"Good of them to offer so much," said Dusho sarcastically.

"Be glad of it," said Stariat. "We will all need to sleep, and to drink, in an hour or so." He bent forward as he pulled his sled.

"I am tired," Brior said without apology. "I am longing for a good sleep. An oasis is a better place than the side of the road." He chuckled. "No doubt the others in the caravan think the same thing."

Wladex said nothing. He was too hungry to think clearly, and knew that he would have to be very, very careful if he wanted to go undiscovered. He licked his lips. "I could do with something to drink," he said, and heard his companions agree.

They trudged on for a while, and then saw a patch of green ahead of them, emerging from the dust like a mirage. As they drew nearer they saw trees and bushes and heard the unmistakable sound of running water. The others in the caravan were moving more quickly, eager to reach the oasis.

"Be careful!" the captain of the reavers warned. "There is sucking sand all around the oasis. Follow us, and do not deviate from our path, or you will be lost."

"Sucking sand," said Brior. "That is all we need."

"You could get us out of it with a spell, couldn't you?" Dusho asked Wladex. "You've got magic enough for that, don't you?"

"If it is necessary, yes, I do," said Wladex impatiently. "It would be better if you did not step into it. While it would not be difficult to retrieve you with a spell, it would be much more difficult to get our stones out again and keep them disguised."

The significance of this warning struck Stariat at once. "You mean we could lose some of our . . . stones to the sucking sand?"

"If any of us are unlucky enough to fall into it, yes," said Wladex. "Take that as fair warning, and pay attention to where the reavers guide us."

The three men were quite subdued, and paid strict attention to the instruction of the reavers. They were making their way along a narrow track when, half a dozen paces ahead of them, someone did not watch where he was going. At once he was sinking in a vortex of sand. He screamed and those near him froze for fear of being sucked down with him. The elf came along from the front of the line and began to make spells, but the merchant sank deeper.

Wladex sighed. "I suppose I must do this," he said, and began a spell to release the merchant. The other travelers would regard him and his three comrades with resentment if he stood by and let the sand swallow the man up. His magic was strong enough to pull the man from the sandy maw, though most of what the merchant carried was lost—all but a pack of what had looked like cloth and was now revealed to be gold and silver leaf. Those standing near the terrified merchant looked on him with contempt.

"How many of the merchants' cargos are disguised, do you think?" asked Dusho.

"Certainly more than half," said Wladex. "Most do not wish to be a greater target for marauders than they already are. They would be foolish to show the world what they carry. I suppose some of their fellow merchants would not be above stealing."

The man who had been in the sucking sand looked toward Wladex and bowed deeply to show his gratitude. A few of the merchants stared at Wladex with respect, although one or two of them looked edgy, as if they feared that their cargos would be revealed by Wladex's magic.

"We are going to have to be careful," said Dusho, watching the merchants. "They could change their tune about us very quickly."

"So long as Casilta helps them, why should they mind our presence?" Brior looked mildly defensive.

"They will mind it if they decide that we are not as cautious for them as we are for ourselves," said Stariat.

They had reached the oasis, and the reavers were assigning places to pitch tents. "We will be keeping watch. You may all rest," they said, and the captain of the reavers added, "We will have a cooking fire built for you when you all waken."

"You," said a reaver to Wladex while pointing to a spot near a low-growing bush, "you and your lot will put your tents there."

"Of course," said Wladex, who would have preferred another site for them; this was very near the sucking sand.

"Set the tent posts carefully," the reaver advised. "If one gets into the sucking sand, it'll take everything."

"We'll be cautious," said Stariat, looking at the reaver with ill-disguised annoyance. "The fellow is insolent. He would not mind if we had all our goods lost. He might enjoy it."

"So he might," agreed Wladex, vowing he would feed on that reaver before they reached Astra. He turned his attention to setting up their tents. "Remember to keep your sleds inside with you. We do not want anyone inspecting our cargo while we are asleep."

"Are you really going to disguise yourself as a vampire lord?" asked Brior.

"Why not?" said Wladex, thinking it was risky, but the kind of risk he thoroughly enjoyed. "I could present a very good appearance of one, I think."

The men with him chuckled as they began to put up their tents. "That would be something worth seeing," said Dusho as he put the stakes into place and stretched the thin, opaque fabric over the supports. "Shall I set up yours?"

"No. I'll do it myself in a bit," said Wladex. He looked around the oasis, watching the merchants and the reavers set up their own tents. Some were large, with two and three chambers; others were small, like Dusho's, with room for a man and a sled. It was as if a flock of strange, dark creatures had settled down on the oasis, making the place seem oddly sinister.

"Have a little dried meat and water before you sleep," Stariat recommended. "Otherwise you will be groggy when you wake."

"We're not completely without experience,

you know," said Brior, stung that Stariat should be instructing him as if he were a green recruit.

"Do not squabble," said Wladex. "It does nothing useful." He pointed to the fountain in the center of the oasis. "I am going to refill our water casks, if you will hand me yours?" He waited while the three men gathered up their casks. "I will be back directly." He put the casks on his sled atop his cargo and went off toward the fountain. He was hoping to encounter the elf, for he had to assess how much of a danger the elf posed. At the fountain, while he held the casks under the spouts, he glanced about with what seemed to be mild curiosity. Then he saw the elf deep in conversation with the merchant who had been in the sucking sand, and he gritted his teeth. Pretending disinterest, he continued his general observation of the camp, hoping to determine how the guards would be posted. When he was satisfied, he corked the casks and took them back to his men, saying, "I am going to stay up a short while, just in case. Will one of you take my sled into his tent?" It was a reasonable request, and one none of the men would refuse.

"I have the biggest tent," said Brior. "I might as well take it."

"Good enough," said Wladex, and shrugged out of his harness. "Thank you."

Brior smiled. "I'll take care of it, Casilta. Don't worry. And I'll pitch your tent for you, too."

"I won't worry, and I thank you," said Wladex, and left the men. He walked around the edge of the oasis, taking careful note of where the sand had that rippled look that meant danger. He made his purpose clear, so that anyone watching him would not question what he was doing. Finally he sat down on an outcropping of ancient masonry and stared off into the badlands.

"Looks like we'll have a storm soon," said the elf as he came up beside Wladex a short time later.

"The wind is building up," Wladex agreed.

"Are you doing it?" the elf asked politely.

"Of course not," said Wladex.

"I couldn't help but wonder," said the elf. "After what you did for the merchant. Mentors are powerful magicians."

"Some of them are," Wladex agreed again, and moved near enough to strike. The elf struggled once, then went limp in Wladex's grasp as his blood flowed out. Wladex drank greedily, and with intense satisfaction. It was good to be rid of a potential enemy and be nourished at once. When he was done, he tossed the body into the sucking sand, then made his way back to where Brior had pitched his tent, knowing he would now sleep soundly.

Chapter 11

BY THE TIME THE MERCHANT CARAVAN reached Astra at the edge of the sea, their numbers had been depleted by a dozen. From the loss of the elf, the travelers had been plagued by a number of strange mishaps. Once a day, someone disappeared, or was found dead in the wastes beyond the trail they followed. The reavers stepped up their guard, but to no avail; an unseen force was stalking the travelers, and all they could do was hope that the evil would not strike them.

Wladex arrived at the diamond city greatly restored. He had made the most of his opportunities while traveling and was now ready for the next phase of their mission. He could not help but be cheerful as they entered the gates of Astra and stopped to explain to the guards at the bridgehead gate how it was that they were carrying a cargo of rocks and bricks. Wladex's glib explanation about a safe retreat for mentors was grudgingly accepted, and they were allowed in with minimal tax. "Where might we find an inn, my companions and I?" Wladex asked the guard as he paid his entry tax in gold coins.

"In the Street of the Old Gods, there is a good hostelry," said the guard, who was a functionary of the city, not a warrior or other fighting man such as had guarded Fuego and Terris. His expression was affable and he made careful records of all those he admitted to Astra. "You take that bridge and continue along the bank of the canal to the second square. The Street of the Old Gods is across the square."

"We will look there," said Wladex, and signaled his companions to come with him.

"Probably his brother-in-law is innkeeper," said Brior.

"Does it matter if we have a good meal and a dark room to sleep in?" countered Dusho. "His whole family can profit, for all I care."

"Well enough," admitted Brior, relenting. "So long as there is food and a bath, I don't care if every guard in Astra profits." He sagged against his harness. "Let's go on. I'm worn out."

"We all are," said Wladex, looking spruce and glossy. "A good sun's sleep and we'll all be ready to try to find the diamonds we need." He smiled ferociously. "Astra may have more to offer us than diamonds."

"It may," said Stariat as he began to pull his sled again.

The streets were not wide, but the canals were, carrying boats and barges of all descriptions. The city was lively, as if the wind off the ocean had somehow invigorated the people. Following the guard's instructions, they soon reached the inn on the Street of the Old Gods, which was a pleasant place with an open yard and a large taproom.

Wladex paid for three red sun days for all of them, reinforced the illusion spell that made their rubies and emeralds appear to be stones and bricks, and then set out to find the hall of the mentors' guild where he hoped he might learn more about the diamonds of Astra. As he arrived at the hall, he found a group of mentors gathered in serious discussion of the latest word from the more remote islands of the city—islands that continued to fall to the Laria's monsters, displacing their human occupants.

"This is most distressing; I had hoped to hear better news upon my arrival in your great city," said Wladex when he had listened to the disturbing reports. "Liches and skeletons, you say?" He had not bothered with all the ceremonial greetings that would usually take two hours, for it was apparent that the mentors of Astra had more immediate concerns on their minds.

"They have overrun Lidan," said one of the mentors heavily. "That was the latest."

"How close is Lidan?" asked Wladex. "I am just arrived in Astra and I confess many of the islands are unknown to me. Tell me all that you can, and perhaps I can be of help."

"It is the Laria," sighed the oldest mentor. "It sends its monsters nearer and nearer the city, and we can do nothing to stop it. Our spells are not strong enough."

Wladex managed a grim smile. "Then perhaps you can aid me," he said in a strong voice. "I have sworn a mission to bring down the Laria."

Three of the mentors held up their hands in dismay. "Say nothing. The Laria has agents everywhere."

"But I need your help," Wladex declared. "Without it, I can do nothing."

"That may be," said the nearest mentor. "But do not speak of it, or you may have to pay a high price for your temerity."

"I may indeed. But if I do not make the attempt, by the sound of it, the Laria will eventually have this place all to itself, for the delight of its creatures. Surely you cannot want that to happen." He was shocked at how frightened these powerful magicians were, and he decided he could use that fear to his advantage. "You need not say you will help me, if that will spare you trouble, but you may want to consider how things could be if you all could band together in resistance to the Laria. There are other mentors, and many mages, who would rush to assist you."

"For the diamonds, woman, be quiet," ordered the tallest of the mentors. "You have no idea what you are proposing."

"But I do. I am gathering jewels to restore Delos to order and to bring down the Laria and the monsters it controls." He put his hands on his hips. "I have rubies and emeralds already. I need diamonds and pearls to do the task."

"You are not of Astra. It is an easy thing for you to condemn our circumspection," said the tallest of the mentors. "You will not have to see the results of your recklessness."

"But I can—"

"Say nothing," the oldest insisted. "The Laria will hear of it."

"I must suppose the Laria already knows," said Wladex. "My companions and I have done much to acquire the jewels, and we are prepared to do more. If we could find the diamonds of Astra, we would have power enough to hold off most of the Laria's monsters until we gain the pearls."

The tallest mentor shook his head. "You are a dangerous fool."

"Perhaps," Wladex allowed. "But at least I am doing something. I am not wringing my hands while the Laria's creatures claim my islands and take the lives of my people."

This condemnation struck home. Two of the mentors stared at him, and one nodded slightly. "You are willing to fight whatever the Laria puts in your path? That could be a reckless course."

"Yes, I am willing, and so are my companions. I travel with a paladin and two knights. They have fought all manner of beings to bring us this far." He smiled. "We will take on your fight if it will secure us the jewels we seek."

"You ask a deal too much," said the oldest

mentor. "You do not know how dangerous that can be."

"If you were of Astra, you would understand," said the shortest mentor. "As it is, you have nothing to lose if you fail, and we have everything."

"I can see that," said Wladex, trying to sound more conciliating. "I have no wish to bring misfortune to Astra. I wish to preserve the cities of Delos and see them flourish again. As it is, that cannot happen, for the Laria makes it impossible. Once the Laria has no more power, Delos will thrive." *And I will be the one to master it*, he added to himself.

"You say you have rubies and emeralds already?" asked the oldest mentor, as if he had finally become curious.

"Yes. We obtained them at great risk, and the loss of . . ." He almost said "one" but caught himself in time. "Two of our company, a mage and a knight."

"And you go on," said the tallest mentor.

"Yes. We will go on with or without your help." He did his best to look pleasant as he said this. "I would prefer to do it with, of course."

"I can't say I blame you," said the oldest mentor. He frowned. "Well, I can give you an old map that shows where the diamonds were kept in the past. Some of them are still there, according to our records." He ignored the shocked expressions on his fellow mentors' faces. "I will send my apprentice to fetch it for you. I had better warn you that this is not the most current record, for that is with Lord Tennebrea, and he will not readily relinquish it to anyone."

A few of the mentors raised their voices in protest, but the tallest mentor stopped them. "It is fitting that we follow the will of our senior," he said, nodding in Wladex's direction. "We have not been willing to undertake such a venture as this woman has, and it is fitting that we do what we can to help her on her way."

Wladex had the disturbing sensation that the mentors were hiding something in their sudden acquiescence. Still, he did not want to appear suspicious. He bowed his head. "Your generosity is most touching. I thank you from the depths of my heart."

"My apprentice will bring the map. I should warn you that the coastline is not as it was when the map was drawn, and you may have some difficulty locating the precise site indicated on the map. The old lighthouse on Delondos may help you to determine where you must go." The oldest mentor made a quick gesture with his hand and a youngster in apprentice's robes hurried off. "It is the most we can do, I am afraid."

"It is more than many would do," Wladex said, wondering how much the mentors' guild would expect from him for his efforts.

"If you could bring a single diamond to us, we would be amply rewarded," said the oldest mentor.

So that was it, Wladex thought. "I would be honored," he said.

"Then it is our intention to do all we can to

assist you," said the tallest mentor, smiling a bit too widely.

"As soon as my apprentice returns, you may be on your way," the oldest mentor said, and added, "We look forward to welcoming you back from your excursion. I hope the paladin you have with you is a superior fighter."

"He has certainly been thus far," said Wladex, still not satisfied that he was not being led along for purposes he could not fathom. He tried to look pleased. "Your assistance is very much appreciated. Is it too much to ask for a spell to support what we do?" He wanted to sound innocent, and very nearly succeeded.

"I do not think that would be wise," said the oldest mentor. "But we will not do anything to hinder you, or allow anyone in the guild to interfere with your quest." His expression was so bland that it was hard to think ill of him. He looked up. "Ah. Here is my apprentice." He took the scroll the young mentor was carrying, opened it, then rolled it up again. "Take it. Be very careful. The parchment is quite old and fragile, and we have no copy of it. If you do not handle it cautiously, it could crumble, and then you would be entirely on your own."

Wladex accepted the scroll with a curtsy. "Thank you. I know I will have much to report to you as soon as I return."

"Excellent," approved the oldest mentor. "May fortune favor your enterprise."

"Thank you," said Wladex, and left the hall of the mentors' guild. He made his way down the narrow streets along the canals back to the inn, where he took the time to lure a young boatman from his work with the promise of a drink and a useful spell. The young man's blood was rich and fed Wladex well. As soon as he had disposed of the body, he sent word to his companions to waken and join him.

"Look," he said as he rolled the scroll open on the tabletop. He handled the ancient map with meticulous care. "This is supposed to be the caves in which the diamonds were hidden before the storms were calmed." He cocked his head as he studied the map. "There are not many bridges; we will have to investigate."

Stariat was engrossed with the details recorded on the parchment. "If the shoreline is still like this, we should have little trouble finding the cave."

"Um," said Dusho. "Which leads me to wonder why no one has bothered to look there before now." He turned to Wladex. "Do you think this is a trap?"

"I think it may well be—that, or a riddle. But if we do nothing, we will rouse the suspicions of the mentors' guild, and that could be as dangerous as facing whatever is in those caves." He pointed to the map again. "I think we should keep in mind that the mentors' guild will be watching us."

"Will they help us?" Brior asked.

"They said they would not," Wladex admitted. "But they said they would not hinder us, either, and under the circumstances, we must be thankful for what we have been offered." He looked out the window. "When the blue sun rises, we should depart for the caves. Otherwise we may appear unwilling to act, which is not to our purpose."

"That gives us time for a meal," said Stariat. "We should make the most of this opportunity. No wine, though, until after."

"Very prudent," Wladex said, and summoned the barmaid to take their orders.

When their meal was finished, Wladex paid the bill while Stariat, Brior, and Dusho went to get their weapons. He rolled the parchment and slipped it into one of his interior pockets, in case they should need to consult it again. Then he added his own weapons, including a small ruby and a sliver of emerald as added protection, then went to join the three men.

The canals and streams and inlets all led to a rocky, eroded shore, with high bluffs torn and clawed by the sea. The six changes of tide during the full day were not very dramatic—hardly more than the height of an elf—but sufficient to cause the men to be wary as they made their way over the slippery, salty rocks.

"There's the wreckage of the lighthouse," said Stariat, pointing to a small island some little distance offshore. It sat on the end of what had once been part of the cliff and was now a hollowed arch of stone.

"It won't last much longer," said Brior, shading his eyes to study the old, worn tower. "That arch will collapse some day, and the lighthouse will go with it."

"So long as it is not today, I do not mind," said Dusho bluntly.

Wladex would not be distracted. "There should be a cave entrance over that way," he said, pointing toward the place the map indicated the diamonds were hidden.

"If you have the right part of the bluffs. They've changed since that map was made," Dusho remarked.

"Yes, but the lighthouse hasn't moved, and since the old seaward tower is still over there"—he pointed to a place on the city walls where all merchants had once had to report when Astra had still been a port to sailing men—"it means that this section of the beach should be where the cavern is."

"It might have been looted," said Dusho. "The cliff could have fallen in."

"Yes, all those things are possible," Wladex allowed. "But this is the best lead we have, and if we do not use the information here to search for the diamonds, who knows where they might be, or how long we would need to find them."

"Casilta's right," said Brior. "We have to start somewhere."

"Well, I don't like the feel of it," said Dusho, clutching the hilt of his sword.

"If it comes to that, neither do I," said Wladex, who was growing more certain by the moment that they were walking into a trap.

Stariat drew his battle-axe, holding it up

against his shoulder. "There is a spell working in this place. It bothers me."

"Where is it the strongest?" asked Brior, looking along the beach. "Is the tide turning?"

"Coming in," Wladex confirmed. "And the spell is strongest over in that direction, by those high shelves of rock."

"Then let's look there," said Dusho, getting down to business. He had taken three strides when there was a loud sound like a gong being struck, and a moment later Left-Handed Ninnian walked out from behind the ridge of stones, accompanied by a hideous crew of liches and skeletons.

Ninnian bowed sarcastically. "Well, Stariat, how good to see you again."

"You've made a strange alliance since we fought in Fuego," said Stariat, his tone level. "Or are these your masters?"

Wladex took stock of the situation, and knew they had to fight. If these creatures, and one disavowed paladin were servants of Astra, it would be risky to do battle, but if they failed to fight, their fate was already sealed. He pulled two short swords from within the folds of his robes and shouted, "Now, men! For your oath!" Then he rushed toward Ninnian, prepared to strike.

Chapter 12

NINNIAN BLOCKED WLADEX'S ATTACK without difficulty as he signaled his liches and skeletons to fight. The liches, which from their decayed appearance should have been slow and disjointed, were fast and relentless warriors, incapable of fear. There were more than a dozen of them and they swept silently toward Stariat, Brior, and Dusho. Ninnian yelled to his skeletons to attack Wladex.

Now that the first fury of his assault had gone, Wladex was aware of how desperate their situation was. He whispered a strengthening spell to the pieces of ruby and emerald he carried, and felt his swords become more powerful, hungrier for the blood of enemies. This excited Wladex, and he renewed his charge on Ninnian.

"I do not waste steel on women," said Ninnian contemptuously. "I have knights and a paladin to destroy." He swung his sword as if expecting an easy victory.

But Wladex caught Ninnian's sword on his

scissored blades and had the satisfaction of seeing Ninnian's sword shatter. He began to smile. "I may be a woman, but I am also a mentor."

"Mentors are not fighters," said Ninnian, his voice uncertain as he took a star-headed mace from his belt and hefted it.

"Many are not," said Wladex as he struck at his opponent. He could hear his men fighting behind him, but dared not look around for fear of giving Ninnian an advantage.

"Mentor and woman, you are a fool to fight," Ninnian blustered as he brought his mace around in a vicious side swipe.

Wladex ducked and heard the mace swoosh just above his head. He thrust out and up with his short swords and had the satisfaction of hearing Ninnian grunt in pain as the sword grazed his hip. Taking advantage of the moment, Wladex rose up while Ninnian was preparing to make another swing with his mace. That left Ninnian's side exposed for an instant, and Wladex struck true and deep. Then he flung himself on Ninnian to drain the life from him before the wound did that. As he got to his feet, he was struck from behind by a lich wielding a short pike. Wladex pulled his short sword out of Ninnian and turned to feint at the lich. Seven skeletons were bearing down on him as well, and he steadied himself for a long, exhausting fight.

The three men were not doing well. There were four liches and two skeletons bearing down on Brior, who was bleeding from half a dozen wounds. He fought with the dogged determination of the truly wretched. Some ten paces from him, Stariat held off six skeletons and two liches. Dusho was backed up against a tremendous boulder covered with trailing seaweed where he battled against five skeletons and four liches.

The skeletons were hard to defeat unless a straight sword-thrust could break their necks, or separate legs or arms from the ribs and pelvis. This was more difficult than it appeared, for if the weapon did not strike true, it did nothing to the skeleton and left the living opponent open to a short, deadly strike. Stariat was holding his own, but gaining no ground, and Wladex could not fight his way through the skeletons around him to reach his comrades to help them. He began a spell, only to find that it had no power against the skeletons.

"The Laria," Wladex exclaimed as he realized what was giving his opponents their unnatural might. He swung his swords with greater determination. He would not be bested by the Laria, not now, when he was getting so close. With a shout, he lunged at the two nearest skeletons and felt his magic-strengthened swords hit their targets.

The skeleton directly in front of him broke apart and fell to the ground, a jumble of bones. The second skeleton did not fall, but it flailed an arm that ended at the elbow. Wladex kicked out sharply, hitting the skeleton on the side of the knee, and it went down, one whole arm still waving a fleshless fist at him. Wladex had already turned to face another skeleton and a lich. He managed to cut the skeleton in half, but the lich proved more formidable, shambling with remarkable swiftness in an attempt to get behind Wladex.

Brior howled and crumbled with skeletons piling on top of him. Dusho saw this and fought more aggressively than before. He smashed one skeleton, then a second, then a third, and had to face a lich which was bearing down on him. He met it with a combination of sword and pike, using the two weapons with terrible efficiency, so that in a short while, the lich was dismembered and useless. He fought on, making his way to Brior's side, and there he battled all that came against him.

Seeing this, Stariat began to make his way through his foes toward the two men. "We can stand together!" he shouted.

"Brior's dead," Dusho answered, his voice filled with emotion.

"No." Wladex was not willing to accept this. He crushed his way through three skeletons and sliced a lich to pieces, all the while making his way toward his companions. "Hold on!" he shouted. "I'll deal with Brior."

The men were too busy fighting to respond. They hacked and bashed at the remaining skeletons and liches with all the strength they had. Wladex tried to extend his force spell to the blades of his companions' weapons, but did not have the uninterrupted time he needed to complete the magic. He used his sword to stop a charging lich, then put all his attention to breaking up skeletons as the two standing warriors did the same. Wladex had never fought so long and unrelentingly. By the time this was over, he would need another meal of blood, or he would have to sleep for one full sun before he regained all his strength. This was going to be difficult, he knew, and he did his best to pace himself. He could not dine on skeletons and liches, and he would not take the blood of his companions—at least not yet.

The fighting went on, and the men were showing signs of exhaustion. More than half of their opponents had been killed or disabled, but they were still outnumbered. As horrible as it seemed, Wladex was afraid they might not be able to win their fight. If they did not win, he would never have the four jewels, he would never defeat the Laria and would never be able to make himself absolute ruler of Delos. This alone kept him fighting as he saw Dusho drop to his knees, still swinging his sword, but too worn out to stand.

Three lucky blows shattered three skeletons, and the next one cut through a lich from shoulder to hip. Wladex whooped in triumph, then slapped aside the sword of another lich, and drove his other sword straight through the creature. At the same time Stariat felled a skeleton and bashed a lich in the head so powerfully that the monster's skull hung on by only a few tendons—its fighting became aimless. Wladex dispatched it with a stab through the side that separated the upper and lower torso.

Abruptly the few remaining skeletons fled, and the liches were right behind them.

Stariat sat down beside Dusho and panted. Dusho fell forward and sighed.

Wladex went up to Brior. The knight had over a dozen wounds on his body, and his face had gone pale. Wladex bent down and laid out the limbs properly, then began the revitalizing spell that would restore Brior to life. The other two men watched from where they lay.

As the magic played over and through Brior's body, his eyes opened, looking like pebbles in his face, and his movements were clumsy. Then there was a crackling sound and Brior rose, his expression alert. "What happened?" he asked, befuddled. "Did they kill me?" His eyes were wide and his demeanor was impossible to read.

"Yes, they did," said Dusho.

"Luckily Casilta knows the spells to revivify, or you would be as lost as—" He could not say Hornos or Ossato.

The other two men nodded somberly. Dusho clapped Brior on the shoulder. "Well, no lasting harm done, though?"

"I doubt it," said Brior. "But I'd rather not do it again." He looked toward Wladex. "Thanks, Casilta. I am very grateful."

"You should have seen her fight," said Dusho, trying to bring a note of enthusiasm to his voice. "You wouldn't think a mentor could fight like she did. I always supposed mentors stayed out of battle and cast spells, but nothing of the sort with Casilta. She took on Ninnian and beat him."

"And he will not be reviving," said Stariat, his expression grave. "A pity that he should turn away from all he valued, to be a servant of the Laria."

"Probably thought he would be more powerful," said Wladex, remembering how potent Ninnian's blood had been.

"Power of that sort is not the goal of a paladin," said Stariat, his voice haughty. "A paladin seeks the inner strength that fortifies against all evil."

"Yes, well," said Dusho, "the first duty of any warrior is to survive. Ninnian was trying to do that, and he chose the wrong side." He shrugged to show indifference. "You have done much for us, Casilta. We're grateful."

"As I am grateful to you," said Wladex, smiling in what he hoped was a humble way.
Then he changed his demeanor. "Enough of this. Who knows when the monsters might be back. We still have a cave to find, and we had better do it quickly."

"Do you think we will find the diamonds?" asked Brior, who was still a bit dazed.

"I didn't until we were attacked. Now I have reason to believe that the diamonds are somewhere inside these caves." He was more encouraged than he could admit.

"Where shall we begin?" asked Brior, staring at the cliffs. "The caves could be anywhere."

"That they could," said Wladex, "but according to the map we were given, we have a limited area in which to look. The lighthouse shows us that we are not far from the cave on the map."

"Then where do we go from here?" asked Dusho, picking up his weapons and getting to his feet.

Wladex studied the face of the cliffs, trying to imagine how they looked two millennia ago. They would have been nearer to the lighthouse, which was on a point of land when it was built. The map showed a deep series of caves immediately to the north of the lighthouse, and in the cave farthest back from the ocean the diamonds were hidden, at least that was what the map indicated. He cleared his throat. "I think if we go up the beach a couple hundred steps, around that outcropping, we might find what we are looking for."

Stariat sheathed his weapons and prepared to follow Wladex. "Why would the leaders of Astra hide their diamonds here? Isn't there a safer place in the city?"

"No," said Wladex, who suddenly realized what the reasoning had been. "They put the diamonds in water, in a pool inside the cave where they could not be seen. They were very clever." His praise was genuine, particularly because he was certain he was right. His stride lengthened as he continued. "The old lords of Astra knew the diamonds would be sought by many. So they put them where they could not be found by accident. No one will find the diamonds unless they know to look in water."

"But how are we going to do that?" asked Brior.

"We will have to feel in the pools in the cave. We must use our hands to see, for our eyes will not be useful." The more he spoke, the more convinced he was that he was right. Wladex led the way with the vigor of confidence. This would be precisely what he wanted, and he would find the diamonds in spite of everything.

Four hours later, he was beginning to get discouraged; his search of the foot of the cliffs had revealed nothing, and that annoyed him more than he could say. He did not want to admit defeat, but he knew his companions were tired and needed rest. They could not search much longer without hurting themselves, as well as endangering their search. The tide had risen and was now falling again. Wladex promised himself one last scrutiny, and then he would retire for a full blue sun day and resume his search the next time the blue sun rose.

"Casilta," said Stariat. "We are hungry and thirsty, and if we do not rest, we will become a liability to you. Must we continue here?"

"Not much longer," said Wladex, letting his discouragement color his words. "I know you are haggard, and I am depleted myself." This was not quite true, but it came near enough to accuracy to satisfy him. "Just a little while longer."

The two knights sighed, and Brior said, "I am in need of sleep. I don't complain, but I must warn you that I can't go on much longer." His face was wan and his voice was thready.

"I do understand," said Wladex, drooping a little. "There is that one little cavern, just over there. I want to look at it before we leave this place."

Stariat came to his side. "Very well," he said. "I will come with you. These two can remain on the beach."

"No," said Brior. "We will come with you."

"Yes," said Dusho. "You must have someone to help you, or you could be in there for hours." He was plainly annoyed, but he did not turn away from his duty.

"Good," Wladex approved as he made his way toward the entrance to the cavern. "This should not take long."

The entrance was low enough that all of them had to bend down to get inside. The sea rushed in with every wave, running up to three deep tide pools at the back of the cavern. The place echoed with the sounds of the waves and it smelled of seaweed and damp earth. What little light there was came from the reflections carried by the water, making a fretwork pattern on the walls and ceiling of the cave, but it was not enough for the comrades to make their way without difficulty. Wladex drew out a small amulet and recited the words to make enough light for them to see their way.

"Look at this pool," said Stariat, as he paused at the edge of the largest of the three. Sea creatures moved along the bottom of the pool, and a variety of fishes and shrimps moved about in it. "This is amazing."

"Stare all you want," said Wladex. "Just feel along the sides and the bottom for the diamonds. There may be sand on them, or there may not."

"Isn't this an odd place to put such valuable jewels?" asked Brior, who had apparently forgotten Wladex's explanation for putting the diamonds there. Such lapses in memory were not uncommon in those brought back to life, and so Wladex did not become impatient with Brior.

"Water hides diamonds very well," he said as he climbed into the most remote of the three pools. The water made him uncomfortable, but he began to feel his way along the sides, deliberately not looking at where his hands touched.

"Do you really think we'll find anything?" Dusho asked as he got into the third pool and began the same kind of search Wladex was conducting.

"Why not use magic to find them?" Brior was getting crabby, and made no excuse for it. "You have magic enough to do that, don't you?"

"If these diamonds do not have a cloaking spell on them, I suppose I could locate them magically," said Wladex as he continued his search. "But if there is a cloaking spell, such an attempt on my part would ensure we do not find them. No, keep on as you are."

Brior grumbled under his breath, but did as he was told, and a short while later he let out a little yelp. "I cut my hand," he complained.

"On what?" Dusho inquired with minor interest.

But Brior began to laugh as he pulled something from deep in the tide pool. "On this," he said, holding his hand up to the light and grinning with delight, for there in his palm was a diamond the size of a melon.

Chapter 13

THE OLDEST MENTOR STARED IN AMAZEMENT at the diamond Wladex held out to him. "So you found them?"

"We found some," said Wladex cautiously. He did not add that he and his companions had kept the largest for themselves, hidden in their water-casks for their trek to Dismas.

"Do you think there are more?" the tallest mentor asked as he took the scroll Wladex offered.

"There may be. We did not find many, and they were securely hidden." That, Wladex thought, was no more than the truth, but he did not elaborate on it.

"Did you have any . . . trouble?" the stoutest of the mentors asked.

"Nothing that my companions and I could not handle." Wladex made himself chuckle to imply that the foes they faced were few and trivial.

"Tell me," said the oldest mentor.

"There were some skeletons and some liches

guarding the place. It may be that the Laria is eager to keep us away from the diamonds." He rubbed his upper arm as if it were stiff. "They were persistent fighters, but not particularly tough. There are worse opponents."

"That there are," said the youngest mentor, grinning as if he thought he might try to fight some skeletons and liches himself.

"So you have your scroll back, and a diamond," said Wladex. "As agreed."

"Very good," said the oldest mentor, smiling a trifle too widely.

"Tell me, how soon do you think you and your companions will leave Astra?" asked the tallest mentor, so casually that Wladex was immediately on the alert.

"Soon," Wladex replied, deliberately vague. "We have plans to make, and we will need to find a caravan bound for Dismas." He had already decided they would have to travel alone for this leg of the journey—there was too much at risk to be in the company of others.

"Perhaps we can assist you there," offered the oldest mentor. "There are merchants who are more reliable than others, and it would be prudent to travel with such men."

"You are most gracious," said Wladex with a slight bow. "If we have questions, I will bring them to you before we leave."

"Mentor Casilta," said the tallest of the mentors. "Dismas is a dangerous place. If you go there, you must remain alert to all manner of trouble."

"I am aware of that," said Wladex politely, beginning to feel an urge to escape this place. "You cannot think that I know nothing of Dismas, surely?"

"We do not want your successes to blind you to danger," said the oldest mentor, and made a gesture of dismissal.

Wladex left the hall of the mentors' guild with growing apprehension. He was almost prepared to bolt from Astra, but he knew that the mentors' guild would expect that and would have men on the alert for it. So there would have to be another way to go. He stopped at a market square, ostensibly to purchase supplies, in actuality, to try to find someone he could pull aside and drain. He settled on a young merchant selling footgear. The merchant looked bored and readily accepted Wladex's offer of a drink.

"It's been slow today," he said to Wladex as they went down an alley that boasted a tavern at the far end.

They never arrived. Wladex tugged the young merchant into an archway and savaged his throat before the young man could cry out. The blood restored him, and he hid the body behind a stack of barrels.

At the inn, Wladex told the three men of his plan. "So you will each leave the city at different times and by different gates. You will carry nothing—not even your weapons. We will meet at the edge of the bluffs where the old mariners' chapel stood. You'll know the ruins when you see them. I will leave in disguise with our jewels and your weapons. No one will realize that we have all gone until we are well away from the city."

"So you do expect trouble," said Dusho.

"I fear we may have some." Wladex did his best to smile. "I will find a cart, and when I leave, no one will think I am anything more than a villager from out in the wastes, bringing a few necessities back from Astra." He saw that these men had doubts, and so he added, "We all share the same goal. Do you think I would jeopardize our mission when we are so close? Once we have the black pearls we will have power enough to defeat the Laria. I cannot abandon this great enterprise. I trust you cannot, either."

Stariat looked slightly embarrassed. "Do you intend we should pull the cart ourselves?"

"Why not?" Wladex asked. "Merchants do it."

Brior looked slightly ill at ease. "Fighting men do not pull carts."

"Then consider it a useful disguise," snapped Wladex. "You do not want to let every monster on Delos know that we are still determined to do our work, do you?" He folded his arms. "This isn't a contest in a city square, as you should know."

"No," said Brior quietly. "It isn't. And you are probably right—we would do well to disguise our purpose when we go to Dismas."

"That is a most dangerous place," said Stariat. "More dangerous than anywhere we have been thus far. The Laria is very strong in Dismas, and we must plan to stand against it where it has the most allies."

"True enough," said Wladex, who thought Stariat was being a little pompous with his pronouncements. "But we will have to face it sooner or later, and now would be a very good time. We have three of the four jewels we need to give us the power we must have to overthrow it." He grinned wolfishly. "By saving Dismas for last, we are better prepared to deal with the power it wields."

Brior looked mildly confused. "You say this, but you cannot be certain that even with all four jewels that we will be strong enough to accomplish our mission."

"Are you losing heart, Brior?" asked Wladex. "No doubt caution is wise, but we have known from the first that we must one day face the Laria. Or did you think it was impossible?"

"If a mentor woman is willing to take this on, you should be, too," said Dusho, his expression unexpectedly stern. "You are behaving as if you have no will of your own, and no ability to resist the evil the Laria commands."

"You should remain with us only if you can keep your determination to face this thing and risk all to end its power." Stariat was warming to his theme. "You may not think we have any chance to end the Laria's hold on Delos, but that serves only to give strength to the Laria. You are half-defeated already."

This stern rebuke pleased Wladex, who nodded several times. "Yes. Listen to him. You have to decide if you are willing to do what we must do. If you are not, then leave us to our mission." He saw Brior wince, and added, "Perhaps your death troubles you more than you know."

Brior, shamefaced, shook his head. "That's not it."

"Then what is?" The question was a challenge, and Wladex waited for his answer with a composure that startled him.

Brior shrugged. "The Laria is so . . . so overwhelming. I dreamed about it, and I began to understand how impossible our mission is."

"Dreamed about it," Wladex repeated. "So it has started to work on us. It is aware of our purpose and it is trying to stop us. I have been expecting this, but not quite so soon." He sighed. "We must all be vigilant, the more so when we are asleep. I will provide you with spells to stop its intrusion into your dreams."

"Can you do that?" asked Brior.

"Of course I can," said Wladex. "The Laria may be powerful, but our spells still work." He chuckled. "If that is satisfactory to you, Brior, then let us prepare to leave the city. You know how it is to be done. I will meet you at the mariners' chapel. Be waiting for me there."

"I'll leave first," Dusho volunteered. "I'll tell the guards that I want to look at the ocean, that I have never seen it before."

"Clever," Wladex approved. "You other two will have to come up with other explanations for leaving the protection of Astra's walls, but whatever you choose, do not let it be too complicated. You don't want the guards asking questions, or remembering you." He stood up and curtsied. "Do not be alarmed when I find you. My disguise must be complete and convincing."

"All right," said Dusho for all of them, and left the inn, bound for the city gate.

"I will leave in an hour or so," said Stariat.

"And I will go an hour after the paladin," said Brior. "I want to go to the market, to find a waterskin."

"Good," Wladex approved, for he wanted Brior to be restored to confidence. "I'll ready my disguise spell and I'll make sure we have our cargo cloaked." Saying this, he left to purchase a cart.

The markets were busy, with many people thronging the various small squares, arriving on foot and by boat to purchase the goods spread out in merchants' stalls. Wladex disguised himself as an old merchant—this would account for his interest in a cart—and strolled the market squares as if he had something specific in mind. At last he found a man selling carts with runners as well as wheels, and this caught his attention. "A very clever design," he commented.

"You do not want to have your wheels bog down in sand," said the man selling the carts. "This way, if you lower and lock these two levers, you can use the runners over deep sand, and the wheels when the earth underfoot is hard." He smiled with the certainty of making a sale. "You will find it a most useful design."

"No doubt," said Wladex, and began to haggle

the price. When they finally agreed, he paid in genuine coins and took the cart in hand, pleased it was well-balanced so that it would be easily pulled. He resumed his disguise of female mentor and went back to the inn to reclaim the jewels and weapons of his companions which he disguised as boards and sticks. He made a point of lashing them in place with a section of tough cloth over them, as any prudent merchant would, then left the inn and turned back into the old merchant for his departure from the city.

The guards at the gate laughed at his cargo. One of the men made a slighting remark about old age stealing the wits of good men, but Wladex only laughed.

"You may not see the worth in this cargo," he remarked in a quavering voice, "but I know its value."

"Probably good enough to build an oasis hut from," one guard suggested.

"No doubt," another said as he waved Wladex on with only the smallest tax demanded.

The road along the bluffs was in fairly good condition, and Wladex made good time, walking briskly, knowing he was being watched by the guards. As he approached the ruins of the mariners' chapel, he slowed his pace, so that his pausing there would not look suspicious. As he drew up beside the collapsed wall, he heard Dusho call out a greeting.

"Good to see you," said the knight. "Though you do look a fright."

"I did not want them associating me with Casilta," said Wladex with a trace of pride.

"No chance of that," said Stariat with as much humor as he ever displayed.

"Then we must make ready," said Brior energetically as if to make up for his earlier vacillation. "I don't think they're paying any attention," he added, with a nod in the direction of the gates.

"Probably not," said Wladex, and transformed himself to Casilta again. "Come. Your weapons are under the tarpaulin. Arm yourselves and we will set off. Dismas is at least six days away."

"Why don't we just go there by magic?" asked Brior.

"Because that would be noticed," said Wladex. "And it would use magical power we had best save for when we really need it." He took his own sword and strapped it on over his shoulder. "As soon as you are ready?"

Dusho spoke for them all. "Let's be off."

They followed the shore for some distance, but finally the road turned inland, toward a spine of low mountains that lay on the horizon like a gigantic sleeping swegle. "I hope that isn't an omen," said Brior with an uneasy laugh when the shape was pointed out to him.

"Impossible," said Dusho, laughing to prove his point.

"That may be, but it will be wise to be cautious," said Stariat. He was scowling at the mountains ahead, too. "They look bad because of the time of day."

"They could also hide things we would not like to fight," said Brior. "Perhaps we should take a moment to study the lay of the land."

"Or perhaps our mentor should turn herself into a bird and fly over to have a look," said Dusho.

"If they are lying in wait, they are also disguised," said Stariat. "A mentor could see no more than you or I, and if we fly over, we might alert anyone watching that we are ready to face them."

Wladex held up his hands. "This is enough," he declared. "I think we must assume that something is hiding in those mountains because they are a good place to hide and by now we have enemies to deal with." This sensible pronouncement held the attention of the men. "If we are circumspect and if we hold ourselves ready, then we can face them well enough."

"At least, that is what we hope," said Dusho. "I suppose it would be foolish to stop here and sleep before we go into the mountains?"

"Not at all," Wladex said with an emotion very like enthusiasm. "You may do this and I will applaud your efforts. I will add a protective spell to shield us, and then we will be restored when we go into the mountains. Very good, Dusho."

This unexpected praise and agreement made Dusho blush. "It just seemed sensible," he muttered.

"And you were right," said Wladex. He pointed to a hollow not far away where an ancient and half-dead tree rose out of a nest of rocks. "That would be the best place for the protective spell. But we will have to be careful upon waking, for such a place as that hollow could make us vulnerable if our foes come down to meet us."

"Would we be any less vulnerable on a mountain trail?" asked Stariat with a trace of sarcasm in his voice. "At least this way we will be rested."

"True, very true," said Wladex, who could not admit he was longing for a fight so he would be able to refresh himself with blood. "Well, let us drag the cart into the hollow and put up your sleep-tents."

The men were eager to comply, and Wladex could not blame them for it. He followed after, already beginning the recitation of the spell that would protect them while they all had some much-needed rest.

Chapter 14

THERE WAS A RUSTLING AROUND THE PRO-
tective bubble, a sound of branches waving in
the wind. At first Wladex thought it was the old
tree, but then he stuck his head outside of his
sleep-tent and saw that just beyond their shield
of protection, a host of ball-shape plants, about
half as tall as a man, had rolled up to their bar-
rier and were now hovering, waiting.

"By the jewels," Brior swore as he emerged
from his sleep-tent. "Where did all the brognabs
come from?"

"I would guess they came down from the
mountains," said Wladex, and glanced up as a
double shadow crossed him. "And floaters, too.
We're going to have to be very careful." He
scowled as he looked at the creatures confronting
them. "I'd be glad of a swegle," he admitted,
trying to make a joke.

Dusho was awake now, and as he caught sight
of the silent hoard around them, he muttered a
few ferocious words to himself. Then he shoved

himself out of his tent and raised his fist. "I've fought brognabs before. They're dangerous for all they look like nothing. They whip you until you are too badly cut to fight, then they wrap their tendrils around you, sting you to immobility, and devour you at their leisure."

"I've fought them once or twice," said Brior. "We set fires."

"We're in the middle of rocks," said Dusho in case Brior was unaware of it.

"But there is that old tree," said Wladex, pointing to the spindly-limbed trunk rising over them. "It could burn. That would slow down the floaters, as well."

"You mean we have floaters to contend with, too?" Dusho asked, peering up in time to see one of the sinister shapes drift overhead, accented by two shadows, one green, one red, and black where they overlapped.

Stariat had emerged from his tent, too, and was arming himself while doing his best to count the number of brognabs. "I make it thirty-eight," he said at last.

"And at least a dozen floaters," added Dusho. "The fire is probably necessary."

"We must be careful not to burn the cart," said Dusho, glancing toward Wladex. "Can you protect that, at least?"

"Yes. And if two of you will pull it, going at a run, once I start the fire there should be enough confusion to let us get away." He also planned to send an incendiary spell to wipe out the brognabs once he and his comrades were out of the hollow.

"We'll still have to fight them," said Brior, sliding his sword into its scabbard but without securing it.

"That we will," said Wladex, annoyed that he would have to waste his time and energy on bloodless plants.

The men packed up their tents, and put them on the cart with their precious cargo. Brior and Dusho took their places on the shafts, and Stariat went to the rear of the cart to keep the brognabs from attacking from behind. As soon as they were all in place, Wladex began his spell to set the tree on fire.

This was tricky, for as soon as the tree started to burn the protective shield that kept them safe would collapse and they would have to act quickly. Outside the shield the brognabs were crowding in, anticipating their assault, and overhead the floaters gathered, already letting down their long, stinging tendrils to snare the men.

The tree roots began to smoke and then smolder. Then the first wriggling flame appeared. In the next instant the protective shield fell, and the brognabs struck out with their deadly flails, writhing as if driven by a powerful wind. Then, as the fire took hold of the tree, Dusho and Brior rushed headlong through the brognabs, scattering them with kicks and blows from the flats of their swords. Trotting backward behind the cart, Stariat managed to keep the brognabs from swarming over the cart. A few steps behind him,

Wladex increased the fire in the tree, and made it as smoky as he could.

The floaters rose up, trying to get away from the tree that was now beginning to burn in earnest. One of them managed to leave a horrible welt on Wladex's face before it drifted some distance away from the smoke, while on the ground a few of the more aggressive brognabs began to burn.

As they came to a stop some distance away, the men fought the rest of the brognabs as best they could. Wladex, irate from his injury, summoned fireballs and launched them at the brognabs. The third fireball grazed the cart, charring the protective cloth over their cargo. Stariat turned and slapped the sparks out, leaving himself open to brognab attack. One of the sly creatures had rolled near enough to strike a crippling blow with its flail, but Wladex saw what was happening and stopped the attack with another fireball.

The brognabs were now in disarray, some rolling around aimlessly, some lashing their own branches with their flails, trying to put out the fires that were spreading. The smoke from their smoldering branches filled the air, making it impossible for the floaters to return.

"Hurry!" shouted Brior. "We have to get out of here. If there are more of these monsters, they will know something has gone wrong and will flock here at once."

"Brior's right," said Stariat, motioning to Wladex to get into the cart. "That welt looks nasty."

"It is," said Wladex, glaring from pain.

"You better rest until you can heal it," Dusho recommended. "We'll carry you on the cart so you can work your spells."

"And watch the sky," Wladex added. He could not keep from squinting upward, wondering if the Laria—for he was certain that the attack had been masterminded by the Laria—would send anything more to fight them.

"If you see anything, let us know," said Brior as he leaned into his task of pulling the cart off toward the road winding into the mountain.

They found a spring about halfway up the first line of mountains where they stopped to refill their water casks. Since the casks all contained diamonds as well as water, it meant their supply had to be replenished often. It was good to stop pulling the cart, and for Wladex to have a short time to restore his face. When this was done, he smiled as if testing the new skin. "That was just the beginning," he announced. "There will be more to fight before too long. The Laria wants to exhaust us, to frighten us into surrendering even more than it wants us dead." He said this with great certainty, for it was what he would do if their circumstances were reversed.

"Do you think it will succeed?" asked Brior, who was bathing his face in the spring.

"We must make sure it does not," said Wladex with such conviction that his companions were inspired by his resolve.

"If a female mentor can do this without fear, then so can we," said Stariat.

"We must," said Brior.

Dusho put his hand on his sword. "Until the death that cannot be broken."

Wladex nodded as if humbled, but actually was delighted. When he finally came up against the Laria, he would not have to fear that his men would fail him. "You are heroes, all of you."

"Let us hope that we are," said Stariat.

"And if we are to survive," said Dusho with great practicality, "then let's get ready to move on. The longer we remain here the greater the chance that something will find us." He got to his feet and stretched. "I will be glad when we get to Dismas."

"Let us hope you do not change your mind once we arrive," said Stariat as he put the stopper in his water cask.

"Why should I do that?" Dusho said as he refilled both his cask and water skin.

"Dismas isn't like Terris or Fuego or Astra," said Brior. "I've been there once. It is a most . . . amazing place." He looked about as if he were afraid of being overheard. "All kinds go to Dismas. All kinds."

Wladex had a fondness for Dismas that he had for no other place on Delos. "It has made itself free," he said.

"Free from what?" asked Dusho.

"Anything," said Wladex, making no apology for his enthusiasm. "We will have to be careful there. The people live by their own rules."

"It is disorderly," said Stariat. "There anyone may aspire to anything."

"But that's good, isn't it?" Dusho stopped in the middle of loading his water cask on the cart. "Too much restriction leads to trouble. We saw that in Terris."

"And too much liberty can lead to trouble, too," said Stariat. "All I can say is, hold onto your wallet and believe nothing when you are there."

"I think," said Wladex, interrupting the discussion, "that Stariat and I should pull the cart until our next stop."

Neither Dusho nor Brior objected to this plan. They took up positions in the van and the rear of the cart and made their way up into the crags, following the merchants' road that was occasionally no wider than a stride and so steep that sometimes the cart had to be lifted up on ropes since its wheels could not hold the face of the slope.

"This is taking forever," Brior complained as they paused on a rocky escarpment high over two desolate valleys. "How much longer until we're out of these crags?"

"Another full red sun day," said Wladex, not at all sure they would reach the other side of the range so quickly. "Perhaps two." He paused in his healing spell on Dusho's blistered hands. "If there is no more trouble, one full red sun day. If we pause to sleep, then more than that."

"Sleep would be welcome," Dusho admitted. "But I'd rather be out of the mountains. I say we keep going."

The other two men agreed, but neither one

was very enthusiastic. Stariat rubbed his chin and said, "I say we keep moving. Because I think we're being followed."

"So do I," said Wladex as calmly as he could. "Unless my senses have failed me, there is a pack of scevan behind us. They've been there since we crossed that narrow stream on the rope bridge."

The men exchanged uneasy looks. "Do you think they're hunting us, or just hunting?" asked Brior.

"I think we have to suppose they're hunting us. Scevan can be very particular about their prey." Wladex smiled as the blisters on Dusho's palms disappeared. "There. You shouldn't have any more trouble with your hands now."

"Thanks," said Dusho, giving his hands an experimental flex. "Yes. They feel fine."

"And a good thing, too," said Brior. "We've got to be ready to deal with those scevan." He looked back the way they had come as if expecting to see those scruffy, lupine creatures peering at them from behind the rocks.

"That we do," said Wladex. "I think they will try to cut us off when we reach the next pass." He saw his companions' startled expressions. "Well, they are not stupid, and the Laria can control them."

"Have you fought them before?" asked Brior. "I haven't."

"I have," said Dusho before Wladex could answer. "They have cunning and speed and they are very strong, but a sword or a pike can end them at once." He paused. "Pity we don't have a crossbow—that would be the best weapon against them."

"Tell me how you plan to stop them," Stariat said directly to Wladex.

"I thought we would find a place where we had the higher ground, and we would take a stand against them." Wladex looked at the others. "What else can we do?"

"We should engineer a rock-fall," said Stariat bluntly. "There are four of us and who knows how many of them. If you put a strengthening spell on our weapons, that will help, and a rock-fall will slow them down."

"What about a spell that could halt them altogether?" suggested Brior as he readied himself to fight.

"I could cause a fissure to open beneath them, but that would mean that there would be tremors through the whole of this ridge, and we might suffer because of it." If it were not for that risk, he was willing to undertake such a spell. "And if the fissure does not appear in just the right place, it will do nothing to slow the scevan. I would rather we make a stand here and now than set these mountains to trembling."

"And that would alert the Laria," added Dusho. "Who knows what it might send against us once we betrayed our position and situation to it."

"We cannot be sure it does not already know," said Brior, looking up at the sky. "It has such great power that we are little more than blue nits to it."

"Then why bother with us at all?" asked Dusho sarcastically. "We must have alarmed it sufficiently that it is taking steps to stop us." He went to the edge of the trail and looked back. "Dust is rising, down there." He pointed.

"Scevan," said Stariat, hoisting his pike in one hand and sword in the other.

"They're coming fast," said Brior, doing his best to keep the concern out of his voice. "Look."

"That they are," said Stariat. "Well, we won't have time to arrange a rock-fall."

"No, we won't," said Wladex, who took his sword, anticipating the thrill of absorbing all the lives of the scevan through his sword. He recited the spell to strengthen their weapons as he stood with his companions.

"Not much longer," said Dusho laconically. He looked ready to face anything that might come up the narrow road.

As he finished speaking, the first of the rugged creatures came around the bend, letting out an eerie wail that set the men's teeth on edge. Behind the two leaders came a pack of more than thirty.

"This isn't good," said Brior without a trace of nervousness.

"No, it isn't," said Stariat, preparing to strike at the first of the scevan as it rushed toward them.

Wladex changed his spell, and his weapon was no longer a sword, but a long lance with a double blade on the end. He slashed with it and the first two scevan fell, baying defiance and fatality.

"Hold your weapons up," he ordered his comrades, then hurriedly extended the spell to their weapons. "Now, kill as many as you can. Don't let them get behind you."

Brior actually grinned. "I will take the rear if they get around."

"Very good," Wladex approved before slashing at another three of the voracious scevan. He felt his weapon bite deeply into their attackers, and the force of their lives traveled up the shaft of his lance into him. It was glorious! He began to revive as the excitement of the kill filled him.

"Look out!" Dusho shouted as four scevan together charged them, mouths agape.

Wladex swung his lance in an arc, mowing down all but one of the scevan. A few of the pack had drawn back, whining nervously—those that had been injured but could still walk joined their pack, whimpering, not entirely from pain. Wladex was tempted to take a few steps toward them to see what they would do, but he held back, for it seemed to him that the scevan were apprehensive about more than Wladex and the three men with him.

His reservation was prudent for an instant later the scevan fled, howling in terror as a troop of gargoyles came rushing down from above them, leathery wings flapping, their weapons at the ready, their beaks open, their talons extended.

Chapter 15

WITH A SHOUT OF TERROR AND RAGE, WLA-dex turned to face the gargoyles. There were fourteen of them, great ugly brutes with the violence of storms built into them. They stank of carrion. When a sword or lance was driven into them, the ichor that came from their wounds reeked and burned like acid, stripping flesh to bone. The three men reeled back from the fight, trying to avoid getting any of the horrible blood on them.

"Get a shield!" Wladex roared, feeling a gout of gargoyle blood burn down his raised arm from his elbow to his shoulder. This, he knew, was going to be bad. Even with healing spells he could not continue to maintain his mentor disguise while he restored himself. He would have to die and trust Stariat, Brior, and Dusho to carry on until he could catch up with them once again in another persona. He continued to strike at the hovering monsters, then shouted, "Get shields! Wrap your sleep-tents around you! I will hold them!"

"Their blood is burning you!" Brior cried aloud in distress as he reached for his sleep-tent while transfixing a gargoyle with his lance. The point of the metal blacked and curled like a blighted leaf, and in spite of his best intentions, he let out a cry of dismay. "How can we fight on against this?"

"Get under your tents!" Wladex repeated. He could feel the skin stripping away on his hands, and the tendons beneath grow spongy. If he were not a vampire lord, he could not have continued to fight. But vampires were notoriously hard to kill, and Wladex was one of the most powerful of his breed.

He held his sword in a skeletal claw and brought down four of the repulsive brutes before too much of his flesh was gone. By this time he had lost one eye and could no longer see what was attacking. He was glad of the few small rubies, emeralds, and diamonds hidden in his now tattered robes, for it would speed his recovery.

As he pronged one more gargoyle out of the sky, he called out, "Leave me! Stay true to the mission! Another will come to take my place. Follow him and you will prevail!" Then he stopped wasting time with words and threw himself into the fighting. It was disconcerting to see exposed bone in his upper arm and to hear the rattle of his fleshless feet, but he did not allow himself to be distracted. His face—the disguise and the real one beneath it—slid off his skull, and he finally collapsed in a pool of ichor from the dead and dying gargoyles. Only two of them still flapped overhead, and one of them was injured.

As Wladex closed his remaining eye, he made one last shout. "Go on!" It sounded dreadful, but the three men were clearly moved by it. He let himself die, hoping that the three companions would not be so foolish as to try to bury him, for that would only slow his restoration process.

"She's almost a skeleton," said Dusho quietly as he came up to the body.

"She fought like the finest paladin," said Stariat.

"What should we do?" asked Brior.

"She said to go on," Dusho pointed out.

"But . . . we can't just . . . leave her here," said Brior.

"She told us to," Stariat pointed out. "She—"

"I heard her!" Brior interrupted. "But we can't just leave her, not out here like this."

"She said to." Dusho stared down at the remains. "And I don't want to touch that gargoyle ichor. Leave her where she is. It's not as if anything can do much worse to her." He wiped his sword on his sleep-tent, then stuck it back in its scabbard. "We should get out of here. We don't know what else may be coming our way."

Stariat gave a single, austere nod. "You're right." He, too, put his weapons away. "The mission is more important than any of us. We must go on, and go on now." He folded his hands. "She was as valiant as any fighter I have ever encountered."

"And clever," said Brior. He looked a bit

shame-faced as he turned away from the body. "I still think we should do something."

"What we can do is get out of harm's way. There is a long walk to the crest, and we will be exposed on the trail for every step of the way." Stariat motioned to the cart. "Let us go. Now."

Reluctantly Dusho and Brior moved into position to pull the cart, keeping their weapons ready at hand. They moved out of the small grove around the spring, and went back onto the narrow road that twisted up the face of the mountain to the crest.

Wladex could sense their going, and felt relief and sadness at once. He put his last efforts into a cloaking spell so that no monsters would be able to see them or smell them as they made their way through the mountains. It would hold until the blue sun set again, but that should be time enough for the three heroes to get over the crest and begin their descent through the long foothills that led almost to the gates of Dismas. That done, he once again began his process of revivification, withdrawing inward so that only the merest spark of him remained, burning with the full heat of his will.

By the time the three men were over the crest, they were numb with fatigue and another emotion they did not want to name—grief. Stariat had said almost nothing since they left Casilta's body near the spring. He had occupied himself during the first part of their journey away from the courageous mentor with watching for monsters of all sorts. He was very diligent, for he knew they were very exposed on the face of the mountains. But as they continued to climb and nothing came near them, he began to be less watchful and put his mind on making good time.

"Can we rest when we're over the crest?" Brior asked, his voice sounding strained.

"It would help us," said Dusho. "I can't keep up much longer without food and drink and a little sleep."

"Let us see what the other side of the crest reveals before we make too many plans," said Stariat, squinting toward the blue sun which was now edging west from mid-heaven. "We have this one light for a while longer. Let us wait until the green sun rises, and then we can decide. That isn't so very long from now."

The other two reluctantly agreed. "Very well," said Brior for them both.

"You have done well," said Stariat. "Be proud of that." He pointed a short distance above them where the road cut a notch in the rock. "That is the crest. We are almost there."

The two knights gave a sigh of relief, and Dusho swore to indicate his approval. With increased vigor, they made their way toward the notch. They got through it without incident, which surprised them all.

"You don't think Casilta's ghost is guarding us, do you?" asked Brior, looking about uneasily.

"I don't know," said Dusho. "I'm just glad we

had respite from fighting." He looked down, seeing the long, twisting trail that wound its way among scattered boulders. Then something much nearer caught his eyes. "Look at that," he said, pointing to the deep incision in the rock looming over the road.

DISMAS it read, with an arrow pointing down the slope. Over that single name was scrawled *crush* in a rusty-brown substance.

The three comrades studied this for a short while, and then Dusho shrugged. "At least we can find the way without getting lost."

"Unless this is intended to confuse us," said Brior, looking about nervously.

"Since the only direction we can go is down the mountain, unless we make a new road, the point is moot," said Stariat, with a half-smile.

They went on silently, still alert to possible attack, and burdened with the loss of Casilta. As they found a good site to camp in the shelter of a huge boulder, Dusho said, "I wonder who will take her place?"

"We do not know," said Stariat in a stuffy manner. "But we must hope that whoever it is knows how and where to find us."

"Casilta did," Brior said. "After Ossato died, she came right to us." He began to set up his sleep-tent.

"Let us hope it will go as well now," said Stariat, also beginning to set up his sleep-tent while Dusho brought out their food.

"We'll need to reach Dismas, or somewhere, in a week, or we will have almost nothing left," he said to the other two as he busied himself with the minor preparations that would make their evening meal.

"We should have a sentry for our sleeping," said Brior, looking down the slope. "We don't know what's down there."

"That's a good idea," said Stariat. "Each of us can stand a two-and-a-half-hour watch. I have a small timing spell that will time the watches. We'll all be the better for sleep, but we won't be left vulnerable."

"Good," Dusho approved as he handed the sliced thread cake and dried meat that was the basic part of their meal. "I have red thorn ale as well. If we don't drink more than a cup of it once a day, it should last until we reach Dismas."

Brior went still, then said, "That sign, the one at the crest? What do you think it meant?"

"I think it meant that Dismas lies in this direction," said Dusho. "Have some ale. You'll feel better."

"Should we believe it?" Brior took the cup and drank a generous sip.

"We discussed this before. We have to get down the mountain and this is the only road. If it is meant to deceive us, we will know in a while. In the meantime we might as well get all the way to the flats. The foothills are not too rugged, but they are barren, and we do not want to linger in them." Stariat accepted his food and drink without a complaint, although the fare was terribly simple. He sighed.

"Do you think Casilta was able to summon

her replacement?" Brior was chewing on the tough dried meat. "If she didn't, what can we do?"

"We must assume she did—she ordered us on and promised another would join us." Dusho began to eat. He looked very tired, as if sitting down had enabled him to accept the exhaustion he had been fighting for so many hours. "We have three of the four stones. It would be foolish to abandon our mission now."

"But—" Brior shrugged. "You're probably right. But I can't help but think that there is more we need to do if we're to get what we seek."

"And we will need a powerful magician to use the four stones when we have the black pearls," said Stariat. He finished eating in silence.

"Who is to take the first watch?" Dusho asked as he put away their few pieces of eating materials, then took his sleep-tent from the cart to set it up.

"I thought," said Stariat, "that you would take the first, I the second, and Brior the third." He waited for an argument, but none came. "Very good. Since each must do his share, there is little point in disputing it."

"Good," said Dusho, and stowed their food and eating supplies on the cart once again, then went into his sleeping tent. He emerged a moment later with a walking staff with a chip of ruby embedded in its head. "This will help me stay alert. I will walk the camp while you sleep."

"Excellent," said Stariat. "My spell will sound a chime when we are to change places. Brior, you make yourself comfortable. I will call you in five hours."

"I'll be ready," said Brior, and ducked into his sleep-tent, securing the flap behind him.

"Remember to watch the skies," Stariat recommended before he left Dusho to guard duty.

"I will," said Dusho, beginning to walk around their small encampment, occasionally looking up the mountains, then down, then into the skies, then over their sleep-tents and carts. He soon had made a rhythm of it, making it almost too automatic, for he almost didn't see the movement of a small, squamous head on the far side of the trail. He raised his stick, prepared to give the alarm.

The scaly creature disappeared, and despite Dusho's renewed vigilance, did not reappear again. Dusho went back to walking his rounds, doing his best not to be tired. When his watch was finished, he was glad to leave the duty to Stariat to go into his sleep-tent and rest.

But the very rest he sought eluded him; he found himself visited by troubling dreams, visions of destruction and ruination that left him sweating and miserable. By the time Brior summoned him to wake, his temper was short and he had much less energy than he had before. He snapped at Brior and had trouble packing up his sleep-tent.

"You look ill," said Stariat.

"I slept badly, if you must know," said Dusho, glaring at the paladin.

"Are you hurt?" Stariat persisted.

"I said I slept badly," Dusho responded testily. "Surely you can understand that, can't you? Our mentor died yesterday and we've been traveling hard."

"Did you have bad dreams?" asked Brior, and would not let Dusho answer. "Because I had bad dreams, too."

Some of the irrational anger that had been building in Dusho was calmed. He looked at Brior. "What kind of bad dreams?"

"It was like everything was ruined. The cities were gone. The oases were gone. We were gone. There were monsters everywhere, things worse than any we have seen." His face paled as he said it. "I told myself they were only dreams, but I could not banish the fear." He looked embarrassed, unable to meet Stariat's steady gaze.

"I dreamed much the same thing," said the paladin. "I didn't know why I could not banish the images, but I think I know now." He went to the cart and took out some of the smallest jewels. "Keep these with you at all times. They should help hold off the Laria."

"Was that the cause of the dreams? Again?" Brior sighed, looking defeated. "How can it do that?"

"It knows we are striving against it," said Dusho, with a nod of comprehension. "My dream was everything I seek to end."

"Keep these small jewels with you and you will hold off all but its direct attacks," said Stariat, then glanced up at the huge boulder above them, stared, and pointed.

There on the face of the rock was the incised word DISMAS with an arrow pointing to the road and another scrawl across the incision: *cut*.

The three men stared up, a grue sliding its gelid fingers up their backs.

"Did you see that carved when you were on watch, either of you?" Stariat asked after a long moment.

"No." Dusho shook his head firmly. "I didn't hear anything. Carving like that would make a racket."

"Unless it was done magically," said Brior, looking over his shoulder.

"And we must suppose it was," said Stariat.

"But who?" Brior marveled.

"And why?" Dusho was less impressed than Brior. "Is this a warning, or are we meant to be frightened?" He kicked at the sandy earth. "If it's a warning, what is the nature of the warning?"

Stariat studied the word for some time. "If Casilta were here, she would be able to tell us."

"Perhaps this is because she isn't here," said Dusho. "This may be some guiding spell she left to guide us when she couldn't."

"Possibly," said Stariat. He slung his packed sleep-tent onto the cart. "You take scouting, Dusho. I'll help pull the cart." He took hold of the vehicle. "And be on the lookout for more signs."

"Do you think there will be more?" Brior asked, looking about apprehensively.

"How should I know?" asked Stariat. "We will have to wait and see."

Chapter 16

"I WILL BE BACK AGAIN. I WILL BE BACK again. I will be back again," Wladex repeated to himself as he gathered his consciousness and began to put body to spirit once again. It had been a near thing, he thought as he sat up in his proper vampire lord form. He looked toward the setting sun, wondering how long he had lain on the mountain. At least a full green sun day, perhaps two. This had been more of an ordeal than he had thought. The poison in the gargoyles' veins had made his restoration difficult. He had used more magic than he had thought he would need, a realization that made him angry. How dare the Laria try to enervate him? He got unsteadily to his feet, hating the weakness that made his bones feel like jelly. As he made his way to the fountain again, he searched the tatters of his clothes for his weapons and the jewels he had hidden there. All were intact, which reassured him. The Laria was powerful, but not against any of the four jewels.

"That's what saved me," Wladex muttered as he drank water, wishing it were blood. He dared not go on from there until he had blood to restore him, and that could mean a long delay, for he had purposefully chosen a trade road many merchants avoided because of its ruggedness. He might have to wait for days for the chance to drink down the blood of merchants or reaver escorts. He found himself a bit of shade under an outcropping of rock, and sat back to husband his strength. He did not bother with any disguises, for that was a needless consumption of magic, and tiring as well.

By the rising of the red sun, his hunger was getting the better of him. He was ravenous. All he could think about was blood. Right now, had the Laria presented him with either blood or the Laria's power, he would have chosen the blood. Hunkered down, his head covered by a scrap of cloth, he might have been a smuggler come to grief or a traveler who had taken the wrong path—or so he told himself. He thought of using a summoning spell, but was worried that it might be felt in the wrong places and bring creatures to him that would be more dangerous than nurturing.

Most of the gargoyle bodies had rotted away to a scattering of bones, the monsters' corpses eaten away by the acid of what passed for their blood. This reminded Wladex that he might have to be ready to fight before he ate, which worried him, for his hunger was making him weak.

He was dozing, doing his best to forget his

privation, when a small band of men who might have been rogue reavers came up the slope. All were armed, and two of them carried trophies of human heads hanging from the ends of their pikes. Wladex sat up, his full attention on the approaching men.

The leader was a reaver, but clearly one no longer working for the cities or for merchants or high-born families. The man had a long scar on his scalp that indicated he had not been given any healing spells in some time. He motioned to his followers—there were five of them—pointing to the spring.

"We need water," he reminded them as if he were the only one who could be thirsty. "This is where we can be sure it is good to drink."

"You might be thirsty," grumbled his nearest follower. "Some of us are not."

"It is a long way to the next spring. Over the crest and down the slope," said a man missing his right hand.

Yes, thought Wladex, *they are clearly men who have turned rogue.* They would do for him, and no one would miss them, or lament their passing. He sank back into the shadows, hoping they would pause to sleep.

For once, fortune favored Wladex. "We might as well rest here," said the leader. "There's nothing behind us and we don't know what's ahead. Put up your shelters and make the most of the time. We'll eat when you waken."

"You're going to stand guard?" one of the men called out.

"You need the rest, and I do not," said the leader, as if to show his power. "Sleep. When it is time to move on, I will waken you."

This was better than anything Wladex had anticipated. It was all he could do not to leap out and savage the nearest man. Only the conviction that the others would rush to his victim's defense kept him where he was.

"Remember, you're to sleep. No fighting, no gaming, and no stealing," said the leader as he went to the spring to fill his water skin first. He was only three strides away from Wladex, but did not see him for he was keeping watch over his men.

"All right," said another of the rogues. "We'll put up double shelters; two of us in each." He pointed to the place where Stariat, Brior, and Dusho had rested. "It's enough off the road to give us an advantage against other travelers."

"So it is," said the man who was apparently the leader's lieutenant. "And that is a good thing. For us." He chuckled.

"Set up the shelters a little apart from one another," said the leader. "I don't want any crawling back and forth, and I don't want us to be caught in a tight bunch. That would only help our foes."

Wladex grinned in anticipation. The precaution the leader was taking would be prudent against Lizcanth and scevan, but it was very much to Wladex's advantage. While the shelters were set up and the rogues went into them, the leader sat down with his back to the spring, looking back down the trail. It was hard for Wladex to wait, but he made himself do it. Finally, as he saw the leader nod and then catch himself, he moved quickly and silently.

The rogue leader could make no sound as Wladex's hand closed inexorably over his mouth and dragged him back into the long shadows. The leader squirmed and fought, but he could not break free of Wladex's hold, and could not make enough noise to waken his followers.

It was tempting to howl in victory, but Wladex made himself be quiet as he straddled the rogue leader's body, making escape impossible. As he took his first, long, sweet bite, he felt the strength returning to his body, and the narrow focus of his thoughts began to broaden. He finished the rogue leader as quickly as possible. Then he carried the body to the edge of the spring hollow and slipped it down a small defile, taking care to make as little noise as possible. Then he went back to the shelters.

Slipping into the nearest, he attacked the nearer man, drinking greedily as the man sank into unconsciousness. The other man fought a little, but by now Wladex's full might had returned and the rogue was no match for him. He debated finishing off the lot, but reminded himself that if he were sated he would not be able to travel swiftly and that his mind would be torpid. Better, he insisted to himself, to have the three and get away, than have all and be weighted down by their blood.

Reluctantly he slipped out of the small encampment, making his way up toward the crest before beginning a transportation spell that would take him down to the foot of the mountains where he would meet his companions again.

He had to decide what he would be this time. He did not want to give any of the men reason to doubt him, but he did not want to repeat himself, either. At last he settled on an elf. That pleased him more, the more he considered the possibilities. He would be an elf. Heroes trusted elves, he was fairly sure of that, and these three men would be expecting someone to come after their mentor. An elf would not be a difficult disguise spell to maintain, either—far less demanding than a female mentor. He chuckled as he reached the notch and looked down the slope.

His powers were sufficiently restored to allow him to see down the mountains to trace the progress of the three. He could see that they had one narrow bridge over a rocky gorge to cross before they were beyond the most demanding part of the road, and would have an easy descent through the foothills. He studied the bridge, and realized how tempting a place it could be for an attack. He leaned back, contemplating the approaches to the bridge, looking for potential hiding places for enemies. It did not take him long to find them. Worried now, he assumed his elf disguise and carried himself down to the far end of the bridge by a transportation spell. He made sure his weapons were ready at hand and his bits of jewels were tucked into the many pockets of his elvish clothing, as well as his large leather wallet that hung from his thick belt. Emboldened by all the blood he had drunk, he took up a stance in plain view, his attention on the road behind him and the bridge and the mountains in front of him. The pediment stone caught his attention for there was a newly cut upside-down word on it: DISMAS with an arrow pointing to the road behind him. Across it was printed *confuse* in a clumsy hand.

"Well, it does confuse," Wladex said aloud, his elvish voice rough and a bit higher than he would have liked. He knew his companions would arrive shortly, so he kept himself alert by measuring the depth of the chasm by dropping stones into it and listening to them land.

Then he saw a darting shadow on the rocks across the ravine, and he looked about in dismay. "Lizcanth," he muttered, knowing how pesky and nasty they could be. As a vampire lord he admired their tireless, relentless hunting, but just the same he wanted no part of them. He loosened his sword in its scabbard, ready to fight the creatures if they began to swarm.

More of the Lizcanth were gathering on the other side of the gorge. They bounded lightly from rock to rock, their scaly tails flailing about, their heads bobbing in anticipation. It was clear they were preparing to hunt, and Wladex had a good notion who their prey was. He glowered at the reptilian bodies as they skittered up rocks and lay almost motionless on the tops of boulders.

Far up the slope Wladex could just make out Dusho and Stariat handling the cart with Brior helping them, guiding the awkward vehicle down the treacherous incline. The men were concentrating on their labors and paid little attention to what was happening below them. Their progress was slow—it took more than two hours to reach the approach to the bridge. By then, ten Lizcanth were lying in wait for them, and Wladex knew he would have to fight with the men to save the jewels.

Dusho was the first to spot the Lizcanth. He gave a loud shout and pointed, doing his best to hold onto the cart while he drew his sword, readying himself to fight.

From his position on the opposite side of the bridge, Wladex watched and at last drew his sword from its scabbard, knowing that the Lizcanth did not want the three men to get across with their cargo. Wladex stepped onto the bridge and felt it sway. He took hold of one of the woven cables and steadied himself.

Stariat now drew his sword and brandished it in a warning gesture as the Lizcanth bounded toward the three, taunting the men with rapid feints toward them and then quick backward bounds that gave the men nothing to strike at.

"Paladin!" Wladex shouted in his gruff elf's voice. "Come ahead! I will help you and your knights!" The sound echoed down the gorge as if he were falling.

Two of the nearest of the Lizcanth turned as if noticing Wladex for the first time. The darker scaled of the two bounded onto the bridge, setting it bouncing and swaying. It began to advance on Wladex, mincing carefully to avoid being thrown off-balance.

The men had taken a stand at a bend in the road where there were few rocks the Lizcanth could use. They put the cart in the most protected position and made ready to fight off their attackers.

On the bridge, Wladex was trying to keep from falling at the same time he was attempting to move closer to the Lizcanth. He held his sword extended before him, and he tried to divide his attention between the Lizcanth and the motion of the bridge. As the Lizcanth became aware of this, it began to jump deliberately, so that the bridge jerked with every move he made.

Wladex found his elvish body inconvenient for this kind of fighting, and he almost concluded that the only answer was a magic spell. He let the Lizcanth come a little nearer, so that anything he did would be cloaked by the monster's body. Then he used a transportation spell to lift the Lizcanth into the air, carry it over the cables of the bridge and move it some little distance from the bridge. Then he withdrew the spell and let the Lizcanth drop.

The remaining Lizcanth were closing in on the three men as Wladex trundled up the slope, a fire spell blasting ahead of him, driving off the Lizcanth as he came. Finally, as the creatures retreated into the boulders, Wladex came up to the three and bowed. He noticed that all three men looked tired and hungry. He would have to remedy both those things before they reached Dismas—Dismas was no place to be weak.

"Good elf," said Stariat, answering Wladex's bow with one of his own. "How fine to see you here, and in so timely a manner."

Wladex grinned. "I thought you might be waiting for me. Godoh, at your service. I was visited by the ghost of a mentor named Casilta, who told me your goals and where I could find you. I came as fast as I could—used a flying spell to get here." He looked at the men. "Which of you is Brior?" he asked, although, of course, he already knew.

Brior bowed. "I am." He studied Wladex. "Why did you come? Just for a ghost?"

"Well, I have long hoped for an end to the Laria. I haven't been in much of a position to do anything about it, but the hope was there, nonetheless." He made a face that he intended to be self-effacing. "This is the opportunity I have longed for."

Stariat nodded with approval. "Yes. We, too, long for that time. The Laria has poisoned our home for ages and it is time that came to an end."

"You are very dedicated," Wladex approved. "This is not a fight to begin and abandon. Many others have done just that, and all Delos has suffered for it."

"You speak true," said Stariat. "We cannot turn back."

With a chuckle, Wladex nodded in the direction of the bridge. "Then let us go ahead," he told them, and started back down the hill. "There is an odd inscription on the far side of the bridge: the name of Dismas and an arrow—"

"With something written across it," said Dusho. "Yes. We have encountered these before."

Wladex did not say anything, but he had a shine in his eyes that he had some understanding of the meaning of such things. "Dismas is a strange place."

"So we understand," said Stariat as he readied himself to help carry the cart over the bridge. "Be careful and go slowly," he warned his companions. "We cannot afford to lose this."

"Permit me," said Wladex, and began a levitation spell, then a transportation spell that lifted the cart and all its contents as easily as if it were a bit of down on the wind. This he moved over the gorge and set it down lightly on the far side. "You had best hurry and cross. You don't want anyone to claim your cargo for himself."

Brior was the first onto the bridge. He rushed over it, setting his stride to its sway so that he had no trouble in crossing.

"Very well done," Wladex approved as Brior took hold of the cart, waiting for the others.

"You next," said Dusho to Stariat. "I will come after you." He seemed uneasy, an impression he confirmed when he looked at Wladex. "It is a failing in me. I am troubled by heights. Not high places, but a bridge like this one brings out the worst in me." He ducked his head. "I am ashamed of it, but I cannot stop my fear."

Wladex concealed his vexation. "Do you want me to go with you? Would that make it easier?"

"No," snapped Dusho as Stariat reached the far side. "I am not as craven as all that. Let me have a rope around me, and I will not embarrass myself or you." He glanced at Wladex. "Godoh, I am loathe to ask this, but I will do better if you will extend your—"

Wladex waved impatiently and conjured a rope from a handful of sticks lying beside the road. He handed one end to Dusho. "Here. Go in safety. I will not let you fall."

"You are very good to me, unworthy as I am of it," said Dusho as he secured the rope and stepped onto the bridge. He walked swiftly, his legs stiff, and was bounced about for this, but he was never in any danger of falling, Wladex realized as he followed half a dozen paces behind Dusho.

As he came off the bridge, Wladex decided to keep the rope.

Chapter 17

THERE WERE THREE STONES AT THE ENtrance to the large oasis; each one had DISMAS carved on it, with an arrow to point the way. On one the word *confound* was scribbled in a yellowish substance, the second said *collapse* in mud, and on the third, *compel* was written in blood fresh enough to be tacky to the touch.

"What do you make of that?" asked Stariat, turning to Wladex. "Six different words, and all of them suggesting a warning."

Wladex shrugged. "It is Dismas. You cannot expect anything else of Dismas."

"Doesn't it bother you?" Dusho, who had been helping to pull the cart, looked over his shoulder as if he expected something to leap out of the oasis.

"It puzzles me," said Wladex. "That alone is enough to make me cautious, but elves long ago learned to be wary. This is the Laria's world and those of us who do not bend to its will go charily." He pointed to the road. "This does not seem to be dangerous."

"But there are shrubs and trees," said Brior, catching some of Dusho's malaise.

"Better than the arid expanses of the badlands," said Wladex. "Storms can catch you in the open, and so can swegles and other large creatures, to say nothing of the weather monsters. An oasis offers a respite from the barrens as well as giving protection to us as much as it might to any other. We might as well take advantage of this opportunity, for we are not likely to have another. Let us find a sheltered place and rest." He paused, knowing these men had no reason yet to accept his orders. "Unless you would rather press on to Dismas."

"No," said Stariat. "We are all in need of rest. You're right, Godoh. We will make camp here, restock our water supplies, gather ourselves, and begin our plans for Dismas." He pointed to the stream that flowed through the oasis. "Let us be sure it is good to drink."

The others nodded in agreement and followed him to the edge of the stream. There were reeds growing in profusion along the banks, and trees with long, graceful branches drooped over the waters. Among the reeds and down the banks were strewn the bones of countless creatures. Here and there lay bodies not yet wholly decayed, although they did not stink. The men drew back, Brior cursing.

"Tush, tush," said Wladex, going to the edge of the water. "Do not fret. There is a spell that can render this water wholesome. I will drink some to prove it works, if you like."

Without waiting for permission, he bent down, scooped a handful of water, muttered the spell and drank. "There. You see?"

The men watched him suspiciously. Finally, when Wladex showed no ill effects, they came nearer to the water. Brior studied Wladex carefully. "How do you feel?"

"I am well, as you see. And refreshed." He nodded to the men. "So can you be, if you will permit me to recite the proper spells."

The men exchanged glances, and Dusho said, "Perhaps later."

"Quite right," Wladex told him. "You cannot be certain that I will not succumb later. I think you are being very strategic. I will be glad to wait here until you are satisfied that I am not harmed and that the spell lasts." He added to himself that having died so recently he was not about to do it again anytime soon.

"At least you understand," said Stariat as he looked about for an appropriate place to set up their sleep-tents. "We do not intend to offend you, good elf."

"Nor do you," said Wladex, grinning again. "I would probably do the same, were I you." He began to stride about the clearing, listening to the rustling of the leaves and the murmuring of the stream. He thought that this place was much too peaceful, and that made him nervous.

Brior came up behind him, doing his best to conceal his worry. "You are not ill, are you? The water has not poisoned you?"

"Not with the spell to take care of it," said

Wladex, a bit annoyed at being questioned. He had to keep reminding himself that the men did not know him yet and that their doubts were a good thing for all of them.

"You do not feel anything . . . wrong?" Brior persisted.

"No. Not that I am aware of," said Wladex, certain he could not be harmed by the poisoned water. "But watch me, if you are reassured."

"I will, for a little while. Then I must set up my sleep-tent, or I will not be rested when we move on." He matched his stride to Wladex's. "Have you come far to be here?"

"Far enough," said Wladex, frowning to discourage more questions.

Brior caught the reprimand in Wladex's voice at once. "I didn't mean—"

"No matter," said Wladex, and walked on while Brior turned back. He went along a bend in the stream, not thinking of anything other than the black pearls they would have to find at Dismas, when he heard a familiar noise from the bushes. He stopped still, listening as the sound came again; it was low and haunting, between a purr and a murmur. He made a gesture of impatience. "Vampires," he said aloud. "That's all I need."

The sound ceased immediately, and a moment later the bushes parted. A voluptuous young woman in seductive clothing stepped up to him, smiling enough to show her sharp teeth. "Elf. Are you alone?"

"I have companions," said Wladex, and dropped his disguise spell. "They are mine."

At the sight of this vampire lord, the female vampire drew back, half-afraid, half-angry at Wladex. "You are disguised?"

"Yes. And for a good reason that I will not tell you." He glowered at her, his eyes flashing red. "These men are mine. Mine. You are not to touch them, nor are any other vampires. If you do, I vow you will regret it bitterly."

The vampire smiled more seductively. "You say so now, but do you mean it? There are several of us and we are all famished. Those three could satisfy us very well."

"You will hunger no more if you make any attempt to drink from my companions. Nor will you rise from the grave, no matter what spells are spoken." This was more a promise than a threat. "I will not hesitate to kill you, or any other vampire who attacks these men."

"But they are men," the vampire protested, pouting. "Just men. They are filled with blood. What else are they good for?"

"They serve a purpose greater than your need. Nothing else matters," said Wladex. "I will defend them against anything that tries to keep them from fulfilling their mission."

"Oh, a mission, is it?" the vampire scoffed. "Well, that does make a difference, I suppose." She made a sarcastic click of her tongue. "Who are you, that you command me?"

"I am Wladex," he said, and saw her expression change. "You know of me, as do all our kind. And therefore you know enough not to challenge me."

She hissed, showing her teeth. "You are as much a monster as anything the Laria creates," she said, spitting at him.

"You are too generous," he said with a mocking bow. "In time I may be worthy of such comparison, but not yet."

"Very well," she said slowly. "I will do nothing against the men with you, nor will any of our kind at this oasis, but we will watch you, and if you should falter or fail, we will take the men as our prey."

Wladex laughed once. "All right. If I do not succeed, you may have them." He made this concession with the certainty that if he failed to overthrow the Laria and claim its power, anything the vampires could do to Stariat, Dusho, and Brior was minor in comparison to what the Laria would demand.

"Good. We will want them." She licked her lips.

"Perhaps," said Wladex, then hesitated. "There have been signs for Dismas. Do you know anything about them?"

She pretended to be startled. "Signs?"

"Carved signs, cut in stone, pointing the way to Dismas with cryptic words written over them," said Wladex, a bit impatiently. "Have you noticed them?"

"I might have," she said coyly. "Why do you ask?"

"The words inscribed on them. Do you know

why they are there? Do you know what they mean?" He wanted to shake her to get an answer from her, but he knew she would resist him and then refuse to answer—it was what all vampires did.

"No, I don't. Oh, I know the meaning of words, but not those words. If I know what you are talking about. Which I may not." She gave him an arch, flirtatious look.

"You must have some notion," he pursued. "You have been at this oasis some time and you must have seen how the words are written, and who writes them. You must know."

"If I do, it is no business of yours." She stared at him for a long moment, then silently slipped away into the bushes.

As soon as she was gone, Wladex resumed his disguise, and not an instant too soon, for Stariat came walking hurriedly along the stream, concern in every aspect of his demeanor. Wladex hailed him with a casual wave. "I didn't realize I had come so far," he said, nodding to Stariat.

"We were worried," said Stariat. "Since you drank the water—"

"Nothing has happened to me," said Wladex. "As you can see." But he turned back toward the direction he had come. "I will put the same spell on the water for you. You will not have to be thirsty." As he said it, his own thirst rose in him like a red tide and he had to calm himself.

"When we waken," said Stariat, and walked along with Wladex back to where the sleep-tents had been set up.

"Where do you intend to sleep?" Stariat asked, as if suddenly aware of his lack of sleep-tent.

"I don't know," said Wladex. "In a tree, perhaps." He had no intention of sleeping; he wanted to find something or someone to feed on and counted on his comrades to sleep while he did it.

"You cannot intend to—" Stariat began.

Wladex raised his hand to signify his desire for no more questions. "We will learn more of each other when we are rested and restored." He pointed to the two knights who were trying to make a meal out of the last of their food. "I will purify the water for you and that will make things easier for you. You will gain strength from the water."

"If you are still alive when we waken, we will be glad to let you do that," Stariat said as he went to the cart to fetch his sleep-tent.

"You don't look badly off," said Dusho, looking over Wladex's elfin self. "If that poison has touched you, I cannot see it."

"That is because it hasn't," said Wladex bluntly. "I will abide with your decision not to drink until you waken, but I know I am unharmed." He sighed, then admitted, "It will take time for you to come to trust me."

"We trusted Ossato and Casilta. They were worthy of our trust," said Brior. He was about ready to crawl into his sleep-tent.

"May I be so fortunate," said Wladex, bowing slightly.

"Are you mocking us?" asked Dusho, more amused than angry.

"No, I am not," said Wladex. "I am speaking truly."

"We'll see," said Brior as he closed the flap of his tent.

Dusho also climbed into his tent. He did not bother to speak before he shut himself in for sleeping. His silence troubled Wladex, who did not like to think Dusho was wary of him. He watched Stariat set up his tent, and saw the paladin check over the cart before going in to sleep.

"I will sit on the cart, if you like," said Wladex as Stariat readied his tent.

"I suppose you know what is on the cart?" Stariat looked worried. "You know that it must be protected at all costs."

"Yes. Casilta revealed much to me." He paused. "If I wanted to take your cargo, I could have done it at the bridge, and none the wiser. I might have used spells to take it away. But I haven't. I am sworn to the same task that you are. You do not have to trust me, but it would make our mission easier if you would."

"Godoh," said Stariat, his voice low and serious. "You have not endured all that we have in securing the . . . cargo. You are not yet shown to be as dedicated as your predecessors were. You will have to give us time." He thrust his weapons into his tent. "Stay with the cart, and if you have guarded the cargo well, it will make us more inclined to believe in you."

Wladex heard this out with impatience. "I will

do that, not to prove myself to you, but because I am determined to end the Laria's power, as you are."

Stariat nodded his approval. "Well enough. Let us sleep for one full sunrise to sunset and we will review your performance."

"All right," said Wladex, doing his best not to be too annoyed. "Sleep well."

"And you, watch well." He slipped into his sleep-tent and closed the flap.

Wladex climbed onto the cart and lifted a corner of the cover. This would be as good a place to sleep as any, he supposed, if he were not growing steadily hungrier. He would have to find blood soon, his need was imperative. He stood on the cart and looked up and down the oasis, looking for something that would provide him a meal.

At last he sighted a young swegle grazing at the edge of the oasis. This was not the best source of nourishment for a vampire lord, but it would do until they reached Dismas and he could find richer fare. There were no signs of other swegles, and so Wladex began to make his way toward the beast, saving his magic for the moment he would pounce on the swegle.

The tall reeds rustled as Wladex inched along; the sound was like a whispered conversation incompletely overheard. He kept alert, for he knew that he was not the only vampire stalking food. Nearing the young swegle, he was suddenly aware of other hunters ahead of him. An instant later three vampires flung themselves on the young swegle, wrestling it to the ground and worrying at its neck.

Infuriated, Wladex rushed forward, leaping upon the nearest vampire and pulling him off the prey. "I saw him first!" he shouted as he flung the vampire off, tossing him into the poison stream.

The other two vampires rounded on Wladex. "You dare, elf?" one challenged.

Wladex once again dropped his disguising spell and rose over the other two. "The swegle is mine. And the men are mine."

One of the vampires made a rush at him. Wladex met the attack squarely, catching the vampire in mid-spring and breaking his neck in a single jerk. He glared at the other vampire.

"You can't claim them all," the vampire protested.

"I can and I do," said Wladex, feeling proud of his own might. He had maintained his disguises so long that he had almost forgotten how terrifying he could be. "Leave this to me and do not approach the men."

The vampire backed away, then rose into the air and sped away.

Wladex took as much of the swegle's blood as he dared, then trudged back to the three tents, taking his place amid the disguised jewels on the cart where he dozed until it was time to wake Brior, Dusho, and Stariat for the final leg of their journey to Dismas.

Chapter 18

THE CITY WAS VISIBLE IN THE DISTANCE, shimmering in a haze that was not entirely the result of heat. Dismas was filled with deception and illusion, which spilled out of it in dense waves. By the time the blue sun rose, the three men and their elf companion would be at the gates.

"There is another sign," said Brior, sounding ill-used.

Sure enough, on a nearby outcropping of rock, DISMAS and a pointing arrow were etched in stone. The word written over it this time was *curdle*. More than the shadows cast by the two suns shining, red in the east and blue in the west, there was a darkness on the face of the rock, one that could not be accounted for by either of the suns.

"The Laria," said Wladex quietly. "It knows we have come."

"You can't be certain," said Brior with a jaunty grin. "Everyone knows Dismas is a peculiar place."

"Not this peculiar," said Dusho, looking about as if expecting to find hidden enemies. "I think the elf is right. The Laria knows we have come, and it's playing with us."

"Could be," said Stariat thoughtfully. "But if that's the case, why doesn't it attack us and be done with it?"

"We're being tested, to determine if we are worth such effort," said Wladex, all doubt gone. "If we are not able to gather all four jewels, it will not have to bother striking back with force, for we will be no real threat."

"Listen to Godoh," said Dusho, his face set in uncompromising lines. "He has the right of it."

They went on in silence for a while, until another, much darker and smaller stone was found lying directly in their path: DISMAS it read, an arrow pointing them toward the city. In a blue liquid, the word *claw* still dripped, filling the incised M and A with the fluid.

"What do you think?" Brior asked Wladex. "If this is the Laria taunting us, should we continue?"

"Why not?" Dusho answered before Wladex could speak. "What is the point of waiting? It would only provide the Laria more opportunity to harry us with monsters. We have three of the four jewels, which means we have strength enough to act." He looked at Wladex. "Do you agree, Godoh?"

"I agree," said Wladex, privately pleased that Dusho had come to be so much in favor of him.

"And what is more," Stariat said, "the Laria

might use this time to confuse us. The sooner we find the black pearls, the sooner we are going to be able to make the stand we have sworn to make." He looked directly at Wladex. "You will stand with us."

"Of course," said Wladex, kicking at the dark stone as they went on.

Shortly after the blue sun had set and the red blazed down from above, they reached the first of four guardposts set out around the city. The sign over the high, crenelated tower said DISMAS, and chalked across it, *clash* glowed. The reaver guards did not notice this addition as they looked over the small company and the cart they pulled.

"What do you have there?" the leader of the guards asked as he walked carefully around the cart.

"Stones and bricks. We are going to build with them." Wladex sounded as calm as the most innocent person on all of Delos.

"A fortress, for those who have fought honorably," said Stariat, surprising Wladex.

"And you have come to Dismas for what reason?" asked the reaver. He was lifting the edge of the cover of their cart with the point of his spear, frowning. "Stones and bricks. Sleep-tents and water casks."

"We have been told that there are powerful ensorcelled stones to be had here, stones that will make our walls proof against all but the most powerful spells," said Brior, going up to the reaver. "Have you heard of such stones? Do you know where we could look?"

The reaver laughed. "Everyone in Dismas has something they claim is strong magic and worth all the diamonds in Astra." He shrugged. "Go on in. We won't bother to tax your bricks and stones." He looked to his comrades and they all laughed together.

Wladex thought of the splendid Astra diamonds they had hidden in their water casks and forced himself to laugh, too. "Such treasure is beyond our ambitions," he said as if aspirations to the jewels was absurd. "Let those with aims at great power seek the diamonds." When he took the place of the Laria, he would be able to show these reavers what the diamonds could do, but until then, he was willing to make a joke of the very thing he sought.

"You have the right of that, elf," said the reaver. "Jewels of that kind can blast those who try to control them as well as those the stones are used against." He pointed to the rough paved road. "Go on."

As they moved along the last stretch of road toward the city gates, another shadow passed over them, as if a floater of enormous size had come between them and the sun. Caught in the intense green of the red sun's shadow, Wladex and the three men faltered, looking up to see what might be hovering over them.

"Nothing," said Stariat, and the shadow vanished.

The two knights clutched their weapons more

tightly and looked over their shoulders as if expecting to see monsters on the prowl, but aside from the bustle of the city and the merchants heading into and out of the gates, nothing more dangerous than a few small bugs could be discerned.

The gates yawned wide, and merchants clustered around them, their stalls and wares gaudy. Along with the merchants there were men— rogue reavers and rogue knights singly and in bands, offering themselves to anyone who had money enough to pay for their services. Mages and mentors of questionable character also called out their skills and wares, from spells to amulets to curses.

Beyond the magicians were lovely women, many of them in suggestive garments, all whispering seductive promises. Wladex recognized the female vampire from the oasis; she lay on silken pillows and turned an enticing smile on all who came past her. She was a reminder to Wladex that he would have to find real food soon, and a warning that he would not be the only one hunting.

"Look how beautiful they are," said Brior, pointing to five astonishingly gorgeous women who beckoned to him, their finery glowing like gems.

"You'd be a fool to touch them," said Dusho. "I've seen women like them before. Once you are alone with them, they become hags. They are ghouls, and their disguises are always lavish." He shook his head to show he was not deceived.

"Is anything in Dismas what it seems?" Brior asked.

"We are," said Wladex. "I will not vouch for the rest of this place." He chuckled and soon the men were chuckling with him.

Vivid banners hung over the streets, offering everything from meals to weapons, to treasures, to assassinations. The noise was constant, a boisterous jumble of all kinds of exchanges. The people of Dismas paid no attention to the cacophony, but went about their tasks with the kind of ease that revealed how common all this commotion was. Vendors of every kind plied their wares, a few of them working with troupes of cutpurses or pickpockets.

"Is it always like this?" Brior marveled, not completely happy about what he was seeing.

"Usually. There are special festivals when it is worse," said Wladex, thinking of those occasions with an emotion very like enthusiasm. "Those who live here are not distracted by the crowds, and are not taken in by the thieves."

"They may be thieves themselves," said Dusho, doing his best to be amused by what he saw.

"That they may," said Wladex. He pointed to a small plaza where a crowded hodgepodge of buildings faced a carved fountain. Few market stalls were set up in the plaza, and those few that were sold mainly food and drink. There were not too many loiterers about, suggesting that their wallets and purses were not in immediate danger. "We should be able to find lodging there.

The gambling houses aren't very large or very important in this quarter and the rooms are safe."

"You have been here before, Godoh?" Stariat seemed mildly perplexed. "I thought elves did not often come into Dismas."

"Oh, we do, from time to time, when it suits us," said Wladex, as nonchalantly as he could. "Everyone comes to Dismas from time to time."

Stariat shrugged. "I don't know what to make of this place," he admitted as they went down into the plaza.

"No one does," said Wladex. "Not even those who live here. They do not try to understand it, only to get used to it." He pointed to a sign over a brightly painted door: Wizard's Rest.

"Is this an inn? It doesn't look like one," said Dusho, regarding the place skeptically.

"In a manner of speaking," said Wladex. "This is a gamblers' haven, where they can come when they need to get away from gaming but do not wish to leave the city. The rooms are closely guarded and there are protective spells available to conceal and shield any winnings that the gambler may bring to this place." He looked at the men. "I think we might avail ourselves of that service."

"There is a spell on our cargo," said Stariat. "A powerful one."

"And a second would not be unwise," said Wladex. "We do not need to risk what we have with us through complacency." He went and knocked on the door.

The master of the house was a sharp-faced, stooped man with tufted eyebrows and long, gnarled fingers. He peered at Wladex. "An elf," he said at last.

"And two knights and a paladin," said Wladex, undismayed by the scrutiny to which he and his companions were subjected. "We come here seeking chambers where we may rest and keep our cargo"—he shrugged in the direction of the cart—"without fear for our fortunes or our lives."

"Then you have come to the right place," said the master of the house. "I want two fingers of real gold—none of those enchanted pebbles one finds everywhere—and some possession of value. That will be returned when you leave if you have not attempted to cheat me in any way."

Aware that no such items had ever been returned, Wladex offered the master of the house a silver-hilted dagger that he had brought along for just such a bribe. As a weapon it was fairly useless, but its elfin workmanship made it worthwhile for superior craft. "Take this, and these three fingers of gold." He held them out to the master of the house. "We will be here for three or four green sun days. If we must remain longer, we will pay more before the green sun sets three days from now."

The master of the house took what Wladex offered. "Done. Come into my house. I will give you keys and locking amulets for two chambers."

"I think the men would be best sharing one

chamber. Give them one large enough for all three. I do not need much room. I will take a small compartment," said Wladex, and noticed that this proposal was met with approval from the three men.

"That is very good of you, Godoh," said Stariat as he and the two knights pulled the cart into the house.

They found themselves in a broad entry with large closets on both sides of the door. Straight ahead there was a flight of stairs, and in back of that was a dining room of fine proportions with high windows overlooking an expansive garden. The master of the house smiled a little at the men's startled expressions.

"Nothing is as it seems in Dismas," the master said. "Take your cart up to the room with the green door." He handed a key and an amulet to Stariat. "There is a bathroom behind the yellow door. The use of it is included in the fee. We serve meals every sunrise and every midday. The meals are extra, but I must tell you we have a magical chef here and any meal he prepares is a feast to remember." His obsequious expression was modified by an avaricious gleam in his eyes.

"A bath would be welcome," said Brior, scratching his shoulders.

"And we are hungry," said Dusho. "We will come for your next meal." He did not bother to look at the others for consent.

"Very good. We will set four places," the master of the house said, bowing slightly.

Wladex held up his hand. "Set three. I have

tasks I must be about before we can do the business we have come to do." He managed a self-effacing grin. "I will fend for myself while I am out."

"As you wish," said the master of the house.

The three men began to climb the stairs, lifting the cart with them carefully. Stariat went first, holding the front of it, Dusho and Brior came up behind, holding the cartwheels on their shoulders to keep the bed—and its cargo—level. From the top of the stairs, Stariat called out, "We will keep this with us. Secure it with a guardian spell."

"That I will," said the master of the house, nodding repeatedly to show his reliability. He glanced down at Wladex. "Do you know where you have to go, or may I advise you?"

"That is all right," said Wladex. "I know where I must go. Thank you for your offer." He added to himself that no one would learn where he was going. It would have to remain a secret or it would be worthless.

"When shall you return?" The master of the house rubbed his hands together. "Is there anything you will want to have waiting for you?"

"I will order what I want when I come back, and that will be when I am finished with the task I must do." He made no apology for the bluntness of his response. "See that the men dine well," he added, not wanting Stariat, Brior, or Dusho to be given short shrift because of him.

"Certainly," said the master of the house, somewhat mollified.

Wladex left the Wizard's Rest without any more discussion, and made his way through the streets with the ease of familiarity. He finally reached an old quarter of the city, where the buildings were dark and leaning together, where more shadow than sunlight penetrated from above. He made his way carefully, aware of the many eyes upon him from the darkness. At last he found the door he sought. It was two steps down from the pavement, so low that even in his elf body he had to duck his head to enter.

The chamber was ill-lit and smoky, with braziers supplying what little illumination there was. There were almost no furnishings—only an ancient divan against the far wall on which reclined an ancient mage in rust-colored robes. His face was seamed and twisted with a lifetime of evil. His many crimes hung about him like a noxious odor as he sipped from a tall glass of opalescent liquid. As Wladex approached, the mage turned blighted eyes upon him, and after a long moment smiled.

"Ah, Wladex," he said with a profound sigh of appreciation. "Why have you sought me out this time?"

Wladex was not surprised at being recognized, for he had come before this rogue mage before. "I am here on a mission," he said.

"Of course." The old voice was silky, but left an invisible trail of slime. "What do you want me to do?"

"I seek information," said Wladex, planning

how he would kill and drain this vile old mage when he had obtained the knowledge he wanted.

The mage smiled more broadly. "All who come to Thanor seek information of one kind or another." He beamed at Wladex. "If I know what you seek, I will tell you. You have a capacity for wickedness, and the ambition to use it."

This compliment did not deter Wladex from his purpose. "I want," he said, "to know where the black pearls are hidden."

Chapter 19

"THE BLACK PEARLS?" THE OLD MAGE began to laugh, a kind of subterranean rumbling that might portend an earthquake. This continued for a short while, during which Wladex said nothing. Finally the mage wiped his eyes with the sleeve of his robe. "Oh, Wladex, Wladex," he said, gasping for air between more laughter. "You do amuse me. You do."

"You praise me too much, mage-who-must-not-be-named," said Wladex in a flat tone that belied the title of respect he gave.

Thanor coughed and laughed some more. "You are outrageously enterprising, I give you that. But the black pearls—have you any notion of what you ask?"

Wladex was tempted to say he had a very good idea, for he had already obtained rubies from Fuego, emeralds from Terris, and diamonds from Astra, but he knew that such a boast would leave him open to all manner of trouble, so he only replied, "Why don't you tell me?"

"I might. I just might," said Thanor as he drank more from his glass. "You have the madness to go after them, and that could prove entertaining." He rocked back on his divan, staring up at the dingy ceiling. "I have amassed wealth and power, and this has led to having many enemies. They toil day after day to ruin me, to bring me down and end my power." He was musing now, hardly noticing Wladex. "It would be worth much to me, to see them all scrambling to stop you."

"Does that mean you will tell me what I have to know?" Wladex demanded, disliking the way Thanor was acting.

"Yes," said Thanor slowly. "I suppose it does." He drank more and shifted himself to a more comfortable position. "Although how you are going to reach them is more than I can think."

"Are they in vaults? In treasury guarded by monsters? Hidden well beyond the sight of the world?" He was trying to contain his impatience, but with limited success.

Thanor wheezed a little more laughter. "No, no. They are more fiendishly hidden than that. They are in the open, in plain sight to anyone high above the city."

"In the towers, then?" Wladex asked, realizing the task of reaching them was going to be much more difficult than he had first anticipated. "Which tower?"

"Oh, no, nothing so easy as that. In Dismas that would only encourage rascals and adventurers to try their luck." His smile vanished. "No, Wladex. They are in caskets set atop the Great Square monoliths. There are caskets on all of them, but only three have the pearls."

The magnitude of the problem struck Wladex like the flat of a sword to his head. "Do you know which three?" he managed to ask, his mouth dry.

"Of course I do. I would not be who I am if I did not." He folded his big arms. "They are atop the second, fifth, and seventh monoliths. The Great Square is filled all the time, and no one may come near the monoliths—let alone climb them—without being attacked by the reavers from the walls of the city. Furthermore, all the mentors and mages who have come to Dismas will use all their might to stop such a theft. And," he added in a condemning tone of voice, "the death you would suffer for your temerity would be absolute. Not even a vampire lord would return from it."

"Well," said Wladex, "I am warned." He considered everything he had just been told, and wondered if it might be a lie. "It is a clever solution to the problem of hiding the black pearls— I'll say that."

"Clever and sly. The whole of the city becomes the guardians of the pearls, all unknowing." Thanor made a gesture of dismissal. "You have what you came for. Now leave me."

But Wladex did not move. "Who else knows this?" he inquired politely. "Are you the only one?"

"A few of us know. Not very many, and over time our numbers diminish. Two remain within the city, and another two beyond it." He cocked his head. "You cannot eliminate all knowledge of the black pearls. The rogue mages—those of us still living—have long maintained our protection. That way Dismas always has a place for us." He pointed to Wladex with a finger as round and firm as a sausage. "You cannot change that, no matter how much you may wish to."

"The rogue mages," said Wladex, ignoring the last, "they must be dangerous to have so much knowledge and power at their command."

"Yes, and you would do well not to forget it," said Thanor. "All of us have names that may not be spoken, so you will not find it easy to locate any but me."

"That does not mean it cannot be done," said Wladex, his thoughts whirling. How could he find the others before he made his attempt at stealing the black pearls? The Laria would be aware of what he was doing, and might send monsters to aid the other mages, or to hunt him down before he could do anything. He regarded Thanor. "You say you have four brethren?"

"That is one word for it. I would say colleagues," answered Thanor, growing bored with Wladex. He took another long drink from his glass; it was now nearly empty. "I am going to have to summon my servant. You do not want to be here when he arrives. Leave me, Wladex."

Little as he wanted to obey, he bowed. "Thank you for what you have told me."

"For all the good it will do you," said Thanor, and waved in the direction of his low door. "I like the elf disguise. It is so much more innocuous than a mage would be."

"I hear you with gratitude," said Wladex, doing his best to be courteous.

"Good-bye," said Thanor, and lifted a silver bell to summon his unspeakable servant.

Wladex hastened away from the place, entering the street with care, to be sure he was unobserved. He knew that Thanor was guarded by many devoted followers who would take his intrusion as a sign of trouble and contempt. He would have enough to do to gain the black pearls without worrying about those devotees of the mage-who-must-not-be-named. He also suspected that Thanor was in league with the Laria directly, and anything he said to the mage would be relayed at once to the Laria. Wladex considered that inevitable, so he did not attempt to cast a shield around Thanor; it would just create more suspicions and that wasn't worth the risk. Better to put his energies to securing the black pearls, and to doing that in as unnoticeable a form as possible.

He made his way to a busy market where he used the confusion to hide long enough to change identities again. He was no longer Godoh the elf, he was now an ogre lord, brawny and powerful, swaggering just a bit as he shouldered his way toward the Great Square to get a sense of the difficulty ahead of him. He whistled as he went, a jaunty, repetitive air he had heard ogres chanting before fighting. His face, as formidable as granite, had a suggestion of friendly pugnacity, a combination that got people out of his way as he strode along.

At the Great Square he saw that the place was filled with activity, including a contest of champions that the promoter boasted to have gone on for years as one challenger and then another came and tried to keep his title for as long as possible. Wladex stood at the edge of the fighting field, watching two reavers bludgeon each other with cudgels, using only a leather square shield for protection. One of the two had bruises on the side of his face that looked like masses of purple paint. He moved jerkily, showing injury and fatigue. For a moment, Wladex had to fight the urge to seize the fellow and drain him of what little life he had left. But that would defeat his purpose, exposing him to his enemies, so he kept his place and bet a handful of coins on the battered reaver, then sent him a strength spell to enable the reaver to best his opponent in a sudden surge of energy.

As he collected on his wager, Wladex looked around the Great Square, trying to see which were the monoliths he would have to raid—assuming Thanor had not led him astray, which was not unlikely. He ambled over to the second monolith: *When Dismas was much smaller, the town square of the small village of Detae occupied this spot. In one generation Lingame produced Cluth the Con-*

queror, Pottre the Maker, and Orlow the Beastmaker. Know by this marker that those of humble origins can move the pillars of the world. Wladex read the inscription twice, and decided it would be a nice irony to have some of the black pearls atop this monolith. He noticed also that the top of the monolith was visible from three of the city towers, making aim easy for the guards of the city.

With a nod, he strolled on, looking at the third and fourth monoliths before checking the fifth. *In this tragic place the guild master Lee of Shirl died in the final hour of the Night of Horrors. Surrounded by vampire lords, he fought valiantly until overwhelmed, allowing the high lord and his family to escape.* That was not quite the way Wladex remembered it. He shrugged, no longer moved by events that happened so long ago. Still, he did think it was unnecessary to make vainglorious Lee of Shirl into a hero simply because he was too stubborn to know when he was beaten. Again he noticed that the line of sight from the city towers to the top of this monolith was excellent.

"Lost?" asked a voice beside him.

Startled, Wladex looked down to discover an apprentice merchant standing slightly behind him. "No."

"It's just that you've been wandering around the monoliths. I thought you might not know the city." The boy wore an ingratiating smile and a tunic that advertised mead and ale. "If you need a guide—"

"Thank you, no," said Wladex, his tone stern enough to catch the youth's attention. "It is a long time since I was here. I am reacquainting myself with this place." He motioned the lad away.

The boy laughed, a sinister note in his mirth. "You think you know how to do it, but you don't." With that, he darted into the crowd and disappeared.

Wladex stood fixed to the spot. His head rang with the apprentice's words. He told himself he was imagining hearing what he had heard, that it was a trick of sound, nothing more. But he could not convince himself. He was being watched, beyond all doubt. The Laria had its agents following him, and no disguise, no matter how convincing, would be proof against the Laria's perception until Wladex controlled the four jewels.

Cursing, Wladex stomped away from the Great Square without bothering to look at any more of the monoliths. He would do that later, when he was stronger and in his elfin form. He was a fool not to have brought more of the first three jewels with him, but he had not wanted Thanor to be aware of them. He decided that had been a useless precaution, one that made no sense now that he had the Laria scrutinizing his every move.

Reaching a side street lined with bazaars, Wladex shifted form back to Godoh, and in that guise wandered into a weaponmaker's shop. He smiled at the two men behind the display

counter—father and son by the look of them—
and said, "I was wondering if you have any
crossbows?"

"They are very costly," said the elder.

"Yes, I know. But do you have them?" Wladex
did his best to sound genial, but he could feel
his jaw set in aggravation.

"We have a few," said the younger man,
very cautiously.

"And quarrels for them?" Wladex pursued.

"Yes. We have plenty of regular quarrels.
Those that carry spells are more costly and we
have fewer of them." The younger man looked
curiously at Wladex. "Why should an elf want
crossbows?"

"They are not for me alone. I am with a paladin and two knights and we are about to set off
into the badlands. We do not want to go un-
armed into those places, and although we have
swords and pikes they are little use against
floaters and other flying menaces." He made an
effort at a joke. "If they force a quarrel on us,
we want to be prepared."

The younger man laughed because it was
clearly expected of him, the elder managed a bit-
ter smile. "If you want them, you must pay legit-
imately. We do not accept enchanted coins of any
kind. If you try to pay with such things, we will
hex the weapons so that they will misfire."

"A prudent course," said Wladex as if he actually approved.

"Tell us how many crossbows you want, and
how soon," said the younger.

"Three, of course. One for each of the men. I will want twenty quarrels for each, half of the kind that will carry spells." He was glad to be getting down to business. "The men are good fighters and can handle powerful weapons."

"Of course," said the younger man. "Three crossbows. With levers or crank action?"

"Crank, I think," said Wladex. "The bows can be made stronger with cranks, can't they?" He knew the answer but wanted to find out if they would be truthful.

"Yes. But they take longer to reset," said the elder.

"Their force is twice that of the lever bows, providing there is no magical interference." The younger held up his finger as a sign of additional caution. "We cannot guarantee our weapons against magic, of course."

"Unless they are protected by magic," the elder added, smirking at Wladex. "But that is not our work here."

"No, indeed," said the younger. He contemplated Wladex for a short while. "Well? Are you willing to pay in gold, real gold?"

"I would not have come if I were not," said Wladex, his chin up in most un-elflike impudence. "I believe you would do best to show me what you have to offer before I hand over any gold."

The younger nodded. "Follow me," he said, pointing his way to the rear of the shop where a small, inconspicuous door opened into a room that was as impressive an arsenal as any Wladex had ever seen.

Pikes, lances, maces, mauls, cudgels, swords, dirks, poignards, daggers, battle axes, franciscas, spring-blades, balistas, slings, catapults, bows, many kinds of arrows, crossbows and quarrels were all hung along the walls. The quality of all was very good, a few would have qualified as works of art had they been designed for more pacific purposes. The owners of the shop went over to the crossbows, pointing out the variety they offered.

"This is our most powerful model, with sufficient impact to go through three full bales of cloth, or completely through a scevan if it is no farther away than twelve times your height," said the elder with justifiable pride as he indicated the crossbow with the crank draw. The weapon was heavy, its crank shining with polished brass, its butt carved with scenes of battle. The bow was almost as wide as Wladex's elvish arms stretched out, and the string was braided wire. "We have two of these," he told Wladex. "They are our finest creations."

"That is a beautiful weapon," said Wladex, already planning how he would have the knights use it. "I will take them both, and one of your second best. Which one is that?"

The younger man took a longer crossbow down from the wall. "This would be our second best," he said. "It does not fire quite so heavy a quarrel, nor does it fire quite as far, but it is a good weapon, nonetheless. For fending off floaters, or even a swegle, it will do the job."

"Excellent," said Wladex. He let himself begin to hope that his plan would succeed.

"Do you wish to take them with you?" asked the younger man, amused at the thought that an elf would want to carry such a heavy load.

"Yes. Crate them, with the quarrels I asked for, and I will leave your shop well pleased." He looked at the elder of the two. "What is your price? And do not make it high, for I am not inclined to haggle. Tell me at once what you will accept."

The younger man looked disappointed, but the elder grinned. "Nine gold fingers," he said promptly.

"Done," said Wladex, and produced the ingots demanded. "Subject them to any test you like. They will be true." He put his hands on his hips while the two men began a sorcerous series of tests on the gold.

"Very good," said the elder at last. "The gold is acceptable. If you will give us a little time to make a crate for you?"

"I am pleased to wait," said Wladex, and sat down on a muster drum to do just that.

Chapter 20

"BUT WHAT DO WE NEED CROSSBOWS FOR?" Brior demanded as he lifted the weapon to his shoulder and aimed at an imaginary spot on the far wall. He pulled the trigger and the string gave a satisfying *ping* as it snapped. "If I'd had a quarrel, it would have gone through two buildings, I think," he said as he put the nose of the bow down and began to work the crank again.

"We need crossbows because we have a very dangerous venture ahead of us," said Wladex. "It is going to be important that you have the most powerful weapons we can find."

"Magical ones," said Dusho. He was holding his crossbow with respect. "What do you expect us to face with this?"

"Reaver guards, for the most part," said Wladex. "You will have to keep them from firing at me while I go to retrieve the black pearls."

Stariat, who had not been paying much attention, was suddenly very alert. "You have discovered where they are?"

"I believe so," said Wladex. "I have been given a location that is so fiendish that it must be accurate. I learned it from one who would tell me if only to see me fail in my attempt to secure them." He began to pace. "This mentor is a great liar, but there is no reason he should have lied about this."

"Why?" asked Stariat. "If the place they are hidden is so remote, why risk telling you?" He was clearly in doubt.

"Because the hiding place isn't remote at all. It is so obvious that it takes my breath away for its splendid simplicity." Wladex paused to be sure he had their full attention. "The pearls are in caskets placed on the tops of the monoliths in the Great Square."

The three men took this in silently. Finally Dusho shook his head. "A cunning place. No one knows and yet everyone protects the pearls." He gestured his admiration.

"If that is true, how are we to get them?" asked Brior, his eyes huge.

"As to that, I have a plan," Wladex said. "It is very dangerous, and once we begin we must see it through to the end. The Laria is aware of our purpose here, and it will muster its forces against us. That should mean more reavers in the streets, if we are fortunate." He shook his head as he was pestered for more answers. "I have to go out again. I shall not be long, but I want you to prepare to leave while I am gone."

"But we have paid for—" Brior began, only to be cut off.

"That is part of the ruse," said Wladex, and went to the cart. He took a ruby, an emerald, and a diamond, each large enough to fit in his palm. These he tucked inside his wallet beside his dagger. "Dine downstairs. Say nothing of my absence or our coming departure. Most of all, do not mention these crossbows. Put them on the cart and cover them. Wait for me in readiness. I will explain as soon as I have returned." He gave them no more opportunity to question him further, but left their chamber and ran lightly down the stairs.

Aside from the color and angle of the shadows there was not much change in the streets since Wladex had set out for Thanor's the first time. Anticipating his watchers, he set out in a different direction than the one leading to Thanor's. When he finally changed direction, he did not go by the same route to that low-set door, nor did he bother to announce himself when he arrived. Assuming the guise of a zombie king in formal robes over his rotting flesh, he burst through the door, ready to confront Thanor, who still lay on his divan.

This sudden interruption brought him upright, spilling the drink in his pudgy hand. He looked around in shock. "Who? What?"

Satisfied that the power of the gems made his disguise impenetrable, Wladex advanced on the old mentor, his rusty sword raised. "You have brought this on yourself!" he cried in a voice like the scraping of ancient metal.

"How?" Thanor struggled to get upright. He clutched at the amulet hung around his neck and began the magical words to bind Wladex where he stood.

"You gave away the location of the black pearls!" Wladex accused, still advancing.

Already pasty, Thanor turned the color of old milk. "Where was the harm? How can anyone steal them? I told him only to taunt him. I didn't think it mattered that he knows; it will only serve to frustrate him." He was blathering, frightened because he had not been able to cast a spell in time to halt this dreadful visitor.

"But you told him the truth!" Wladex bellowed, hoping to have final confirmation that his information was correct.

"I said I meant no harm. It was only to incite him. He has no chance of getting the caskets. I told him the wrong monoliths," Thanor babbled. "Even if he tries he will find nothing but ashes."

Wladex raised his sword. "Traitor!" he shrieked, bearing down on Thanor, changing into himself at the last instant before impact. He heard Thanor's sob of dismay, and then he sank his teeth into the old mentor's neck, drinking up his blood vengefully, wanting Thanor to suffer for misleading him. When he was done, he put a spell on the body that would make reanimation impossible. "You deserve to stay dead," he told the corpse as it fell from the divan. He stood over his victim, adjusting his disguise back to that of the zombie king. He left the low door open when he departed.

On his way back to the Wizard's Rest, he changed his disguise twice and went a long way out of his way in order to throw any watchers off his trail. All the while he wondered how he would discover which of the monoliths actually held the black pearls. He supposed he would have to take the caskets from as many of the monoliths as he could. That was a difficulty he had not anticipated, and it made him angry as he thought about it. He had to admit that in Thanor's position he would have done the same thing, but it still infuriated him. He was almost sorry now that Thanor could not be restored to life so that he would have a chance to kill him again—more slowly.

The enterprise would be tricky enough, Wladex realized, as he came up to the rear of the Wizard's Rest. He slipped in by magic, as insubstantial as the shadow of a ghost, so no one noticed him when he went up to his small chamber, where he planned what they would have to do. Not knowing which monoliths held pearls was a setback, he had to admit that. It meant he would have to expose himself longer than he had originally planned.

His hands felt clammy as he considered how he would have to try all the monoliths except the ones Thanor mentioned. His mind raced as he considered ways he might conceal himself, and knew that in Dismas all such ploys were likely to fail; in a city built on illusion and deception, he would have to anticipate detection simply because misdirection and spells were common devices.

He was motionless for some time as his thoughts tumbled and changed. His mood went from dejection to elation and back again.

Finally he clapped his hands. It was worth the risk, he told himself, if his companions would agree to follow his plans. He had come up with the solution to the problem, if they were lucky, and he would do all that he could to see to it that they were. He knew that if the Laria thwarted them now, all his ambitions would be worth nothing. He would never take the place of the Laria as master of Delos. He did his best to convince himself this was not very important, and did not believe it for a moment.

A bit later he left his room and went to where his companions awaited him. He carried with him three amulets he had just prepared; they lay in the smallest pocket of his robe. Entering their chamber, he paused to peruse them, trying to discern their states of mind before he entrusted the amulets to them. He saw they were a bit nervous, and he could not deny they had reason. He looked at each of them in turn. "This is a desperate time," he said at last. "We have come too far to set our mission aside, but it is that very achievement that exposes us to more danger than we have ever known."

"We rise or we fall now; we accept that," said Stariat. "The Laria must act against us or be cast down."

"*And* be cast down," Brior corrected. "This is the opportunity we have been hoping for. Once we secure the black pearls, what can the Laria do to defeat us?"

"The Laria will have to use all its power," said Stariat. "If we manage the four jewels skillfully, the Laria will not prevail." For all his confidence, his voice shook.

"So the mentors have taught," said Dusho. "We will have to trust they are right."

Before the three could talk themselves into defeat, Wladex said, "I have a plan that I think has a good chance of working. It will take a little time to get into position, and I will need you to stay at your posts with your crossbows until we are sure that we have the pearls or we are overwhelmed."

"This is the fight we began when we pledged to support Ossato," said Stariat, strength coming back into his stance. "If we fail, we fail for all of Delos."

"Yes," said Brior. "This is the fight of a lifetime—of several lifetimes." He caressed the stock of his crossbow. "You have made it possible for us to undertake the greatest battle of all."

"Yes, yes," said Wladex, cutting him off. "And we had best plan for that battle as if all of Delos depended on our success, for it does. Either we succeed, or the Laria rules forever, for no one could again assemble the four jewels as we will have done once the black pearls are ours." He could feel the sweet sense of power welling in him, and he knew it would be so much better when it was absolute. He pointed to Stariat. "You will go out of the city, to the oasis in the east, the one with four springs. That is a place where the magic can be most powerful."

"Is that the oasis where the ancient city once stood? The one they say is haunted?" asked Brior, his face shining.

"Yes. I trust ghosts do not frighten you?" He saw Stariat shake his head. "The Laria blasted it soon after it became the ruling force on Delos. You, Stariat, will have our other jewels with you and you will protect them from all comers, no matter how fierce. That is a great deal to ask of you, but we are so few, and you are a paladin. You of all of us are the most prepared for such a fight. You will have to do it alone, for I will need Dusho and Brior to help me in my attempt to seize the caskets of pearls."

"How do you plan to do that?" Dusho pointed toward the window. "You cannot get near the Great Square, let alone the monoliths, without someone noticing. The reavers will stop you long before you can reach the caskets."

Wladex held up his hand. "Not if you keep the reavers pinned down. And not if I attack from above."

The three men stared at him in varying degrees of astonishment. Then finally Dusho laughed aloud. "Above. Oh, yes, certainly. You will use a levitation and a transportation spell to carry off the caskets. Very innovative."

"A spell could not raise those caskets, not the way they have been put in place," said Stariat, his face falling.

"No, no, no," said Wladex, glowering at the

men. "The only thing to be levitated and transported will be me, myself. I will be able to carry off the caskets. But I will need a place to take them, and quickly, which is why you, Stariat, must be at the oasis and you must fend off anything that tries to keep me away or attempts to seize our jewels." He drew his dagger from its sheath. "We must be prepared to do all that we must to hang onto what we have gotten this far."

"I can see that," said Dusho. "But what about the people of Dismas. You do not expect them to let you do this without protest, do you?"

"That is where you and Brior come in. You will fire the quarrels with immobility spells on them to keep the reavers from acting. The ordinary quarrels you will use for keeping any warriors from attacking me." He pointed to the crossbows. "Those are good enough to help you hold off a mob, if you have to."

Brior went a little pale. "What if the mob is more than the people of Dismas? What if the Laria unleashes monsters against us?"

"I almost expect it will," said Wladex without any sign of discomfort at the notion. "Once I have the pearls in hand, we will not have to worry about monsters." He longed for that moment just as he yearned for more blood. "Think of it. Once we have enough pearls to match what we have of the diamonds, emeralds, and rubies, there is no monster that we cannot defeat."

"Except perhaps the Laria," said Dusho quietly.

"Does that frighten you?" asked Wladex, his voice cutting.

"Shouldn't it?" Dusho responded, turning to face Wladex directly. "Godoh, you do not see what this means to us. You have enough magic to come through an attack with something left. But we—we will be as nothing, or less than nothing. A speck on the most remote mountain will be far more real than we." He spoke quietly, and although his eyes were bright, nothing about him showed faltering. "We must not deceive ourselves, even if we deceive all others on Delos. In self-deception lies our downfall."

"Yes," said Wladex. "You are right. Any deception the Laria will be able to turn against us, and use it to our ruin." He put the tips of his fingers together. "I hope we all can face the possibilities that Dusho—" He stopped. "You say that I could survive, and I reckon that I might be able to. But I would not want to. The hold the Laria has on Delos is terrible enough now. To see it grow would be intolerable." *I could not endure the humiliation of such a defeat,* he told himself. *I will triumph or I will be blotted out, as the three suns blot out anything else beyond them in the sky.*

Brior took hold of his sword. "Knights are not knights only to fight battles they are certain to win. There is no glory, no honor in easy triumphs. You cannot turn away from what may be the most important battle since the sun shattered. If you can abandon Godoh when Ossato and Casilta and Hornos did not turn aside then the Laria has beaten us already."

Stariat nodded somberly. "No one will leave before we have done. The Laria's rule will come to an end or we will be as dust."

Wladex very nearly felt pride in his companions at this. "You deserve the highest praise," he said at last. "If you fall, I will fall with you. But so that you will not, I have made protections for you all." He handed the amulets to each of the men. "Keep these with you. They will give strength to your weapons—swords, daggers, pikes, crossbows, whatever—and endurance to your bodies. If wounded, you will not bleed or have pain until the fighting is done. If you fight against many, your weapons will move much faster and be easy in your hands. If you confront monsters, the weapons will have the power to kill them and absorb their might. This cannot be so for long, but as long as the fight goes on, unless you face the Laria itself you should be proof against defeat."

Stariat held his amulet up to the light. "This is remarkable craft. Did you do this yourself?" The amulet glinted as it turned on its chain.

"Most certainly," said Wladex. "I would not trust you to the spells bought in Dismas. No, I have put all my knowledge and will into these amulets. Nothing of the Laria has touched them. No magic but mine is in them."

"Good enough," said Dusho, and slipped his over his head, tucking it inside his tunic. "No use showing this off to the world."

Brior did the same, but with a trace of regret. "It is a very beautiful amulet. One day I would like to let the world see it."

"Perhaps you shall," said Wladex, pleased that his offerings were being so well received. He could feel the magical link to his own amulet growing stronger. "Well, Stariat? Are we ready?"

"Yes," said Stariat. "We are."

Chapter 21

THEIR DEPARTURE WAS MARKED BY stealth. Wladex had conjured an invisibility spell that made them unseen, but they could still be heard and touched. They descended the stairs with great care, and once in the entry hall, they had to lift their cart high over their heads and stand close against the wall as four prosperous merchants arrived, enthusiastically demanding rooms and a place to gamble.

The street proved hardly less precarious, for they had to make their way through the crowds without attracting attention. Shoving and jostling were usual in Dismas, but not from men you could not see. To avoid the greatest crowds, the four went through a confusion of side streets and alleys until they reached the city gates, where in a brief, whispered conversation, Stariat was sent off with their cart and the disguised jewels.

"Two days I will wait," he whispered. "If nothing has happened, I will come looking for you."

"Make it three," said Wladex, waving out of habit, since his friendly gesture could not be seen. He stood with the two knights for a short while until they were fairly certain Stariat was some distance from the gates. Then Wladex pulled the two back into an alley. "You know where you must go. I will need until the green sun is overhead to prepare. Be in position by then or I will not be able to take the pearls."

"What if we run out of quarrels?" asked Brior.

"Don't," Wladex recommended. "You have enough. Remember to use the ones with the immobility spells first. Then you should be all right."

"Do you think they will notice us?" Brior was looking a bit nervous. "Won't they try to capture us? Or kill us?"

"Not if you immobilize them first. That is also why I want you to find vantage points in the Great Square, or at its edge." Wladex did his best to look encouraging. "If there are many people and confusion around you, they will be slow to fire weapons or spells and you will have the opportunity to immobilize them before you can be stopped." He knew this sounded good, and he wanted Brior to believe it.

"This is a good plan," said Dusho. "Especially if our opponents will do precisely what we want them to." He looked directly at Wladex. "But what if they don't? What if we are stopped or captured—what then? You will not be in any position to come to our aid, will you?"

"Well, no," said Wladex apologetically. "But

in the air, I will be far more vulnerable than you. If you act as soon as I appear, we should not be vulnerable. We will all have the advantage of surprise, which should be enough. If it isn't, then you will have to abandon your positions and go to Stariat at the oasis until we can think of some other means to obtain the pearls. You will have strengthened weapons and you can slip away into the crowd. I will not have that capability."

Dusho was not convinced. "And the Laria? If you come near the pearls, it will know. What if it should decide to—"

"The Laria will try to fight me before it does anything to you," said Wladex brusquely. "I am the one who has controlled the magic we have used. I am the one the Laria will attack."

Dusho nodded. "Very well. Then let us plan our positions, Brior." He glanced at Wladex again. "I don't know how you will strike from . . . where you say you will strike from, but we will do our part."

"May fortune favor us," said Wladex, saluting the two knights before he moved away into the crowd. He was looking for one particular stall where he knew the cloth made there was adapted to magical purposes. He did not hurry, and took a circuitous path to the stall, taking care to be sure no one was watching him. When he arrived at his destination, he found the old weaver sitting amid his tapestries, seemingly indifferent to the passers-by. As Wladex approached, the old man's face broke into a smile.

"You want something from this place, don't

you?" His inquiry was a matter of form, for he clearly knew the answer to his question.

"Yes, master weaver, I do," said Wladex. He made a deep and respectful bow to show his sincerity.

"An elf is seeking to buy a tapestry from me," he remarked to no one in particular. "Very well. We will see that this elf has what he desires." The first tapestry he indicated showed a splendid vision of the Ten Cities before the Laria blasted all but four to ruins. They were glorious, turretted and domed, glistening in the light of all three suns, each one a vast and lovely jewel. "This is a fair sight. But you do not want this one, I think." The second he produced was very large, depicting the exploits of seventh High Lord Fause the Glorious in the Troll Wars. The details were sharp and the whole of the story shone out of the fabric as if it could be brought to life. "A fine tale, but not what you want, is it? You have something more unusual in mind." He pointed to two medium-sized works of the famous legendary subject of night, with an unthinkably dark sky filled with many-colored lights no larger than a fist, some encompassed by broad and shining rings, some with sprays of light around them, a few looming near, most seeming small or distant. "These may serve your purpose."

Wladex grinned. "You are perspicacious, master weaver," he said. "You discern my needs well. What price for those magnificent tapestries?"

The master weaver stroked the dark blue and

spangled tapestries as if he were touching a beloved child. "These are worth more than anyone can pay. But I will let you have them for a gem the size of my thumb," he said.

"Done," Wladex said, producing one of the shards of ruby he had taken from the cart. "This is finest quality. Perhaps it is not as fine as your work, but you will not find better on Delos."

"It is a fine stone," said the master weaver as he turned it over in his hand. "It will do." He pointed to the tapestries. "They are my finest work. I knew they would have to go to someone seeking them for a great purpose."

"And do you know what that purpose is?" Wladex asked, doing his best to sound at ease.

"If I did, I would not speak of it," said the master weaver. He began to roll up the two tapestries, laying one inside the other. "Use them well, elf. They are the pride of my loom."

Wladex ducked his head. "I am humbled by your generosity," he said, not exactly meaning it. "You have done magnificent work." It was perfect enough to hold his spells for as long as he would need them. "Is there a leather worker near you, one whose work is to exacting standards?"

"Livice, in the next street, does superior work," said the master weaver as he handed the rolled tapestries to Wladex.

They were lighter than he had thought they would be, which was all to the good. He rested them across his shoulders like a yoke and set out for the next street. His dessicated vampire heart was almost joyous as he made his way to the leatherworker Livice. He looked over the goods, remarking, "I have some large and awkward boxes I will have to carry. I need some kind of harness that will hold them."

Livice pointed out two of his best harnesses, saying many merchants used them. "They are satisfied with them."

"No doubt," said Wladex. "Still, I think the boxes are larger than those will accommodate." He paused. "Have you nothing a little larger?"

"If you were not an elf, I might have," said Livice. "They are made of sweglehide, and take sturdy men with broad shoulders to carry."

"Let me see them," said Wladex, and waited restlessly as Livice went to the rear of his shop and brought out two massive bags. Slung over Wladex's shoulders they would almost drag on the ground. He studied them and said, "How much?"

"Four gold fingers. I can't part with them for less. Sweglehide isn't easily come by." He held out his hand. "It is a reasonable price."

"If you think so," said Wladex, not wanting to bargain, although the price was high. He pulled out the gold and handed it to Livice. "There."

"How are you going to carry all that," Livice asked as Wladex started out of his shop, "if you have a long way to go and a heavy load?"

"I will manage," said Wladex, adding with a chuckle, "Perhaps I'll fly."

This amused Livice, who waved him away as he pocketed his money. "You may need to."

Wladex hurried into the crowd, keeping his elf

shape because of what he carried. He zigged and zagged his way to one of the older quarters of the city, where many of the ancient houses were deserted and in tumbled ruins, too far gone for even the most treacherous thieves and killers to hide. Here he found himself a place under the eaves of a listing building where he could perform the rites he needed.

Setting the jewels at the points of the compass, he spread out the tapestries and lay down between them, his arms outstretched, the swegle-hide bags over his shoulders. He began to recite his transformation spell, this time into a form that was new to him, and to Delos. Gradually the tapestries fused to his arms, two of his fingers elongated, his feet changed to talons, and his body shifted, becoming longer and lighter. Finally he made himself a tail out of some of his robe. When this was done, he got to his feet, an act that proved difficult due to his cumbersome wings. Satisfied that he could manage this new form, he toddled out of the tumbledown house into the narrow street, then began to climb onto the crumbled walls so that he would be able to take off. If anyone saw him, he was unaware of it.

He drifted over the city walls, trying to learn to use his wings and tail accurately. When he was confident he could, he turned back toward Dismas and headed directly for the monoliths in the Great Square, hoping that Dusho and Brior would do their parts. He had said nothing of changing his shape, but surely they would know this was he.

A few of the people in the streets noticed him drifting overhead, casting two shadows as he went. Those who looked up either shouted in alarm or simply stared.

"This is the time to strike," Wladex said, hoping that the two knights would do as he wished. He saw a few of the reavers on the battlements reach for their longbows, preparing to fire. Wladex braced himself to evade the arrows, but then sighed as he saw the guards freeze in place as a shining quarrel landed in their midst. With any luck the same thing would be happening to the guards behind him. He did not take the time to turn to see, but flew on toward the Great Square.

Looking down on the monoliths, he saw that each was surmounted by a casket. He remembered that Thanor had deliberately told him the wrong monoliths, so he paid no attention to the second, fifth, or seventh. He began with the nearest, the eighth, opening the casket with his taloned feet. There was only a pile of sand in the casket, so he flew on to the ninth. Here he found three pearls, and with some difficulty he managed to load them into one of his bags. He ignored the shouting below him. If only Dusho or Brior would fire an immobilizing quarrel into the crowd! Flying on to the tenth monolith, he found more sand. At the first, sand again, but five pearls at the third.

An arrow zinged past him, almost nicking his wing. Wladex almost dropped the pearl he was wrestling into his bag, but rose a little higher, wanting to get beyond the range of arrows as much as he could. The fourth monolith had two more pearls, and Wladex managed to secure them both while dodging arrows. It was only a matter of time until one of the mentors or mages tried to bring him down with spells. He knew he had to get away quickly, for although he had protected himself with spells of his own, staying aloft was draining his magical reserves. He tried the sixth monolith and found a black pearl larger than his head. This was too heavy and too large for even his huge talons to encompass. As he tried to lift it, it slipped and fell into the square below.

The shouts of outrage and fury that had risen to Wladex were replaced by screams of excitement, horror, and greed as the people in the Great Square fell on the black pearl as it shattered. None of them paid any attention to Wladex.

Taking advantage of the distraction, Wladex spread his wings and headed for the walls of the city. He moved slowly, for the weight of the pearls forced him to fight to stay in the air and he could not soar as he had hoped. He told himself that this was worth it, to have so many of the black pearls—more and larger than he had hoped. He wobbled over the walls and headed out toward the oasis. He could see merchants below pointing up, and a babble of voices reached him like a distant storm. He smiled, glad his efforts had succeeded. In a short while he would have all four jewels and then he would be able to cast out the Laria and take its place. This was what he had wanted, had striven for, but until this moment had not actually thought he could achieve. He waggled his wings in victory, proud of himself as never before.

He had a momentary thought for Brior and Dusho. He hoped they would get away, and not simply because he needed them for his attack on the Laria. They had done as he had ordered and he did not want them to give him away, as he was sure they must do if they were captured. These morose thoughts threatened to overwhelm him as he flew on. *Perhaps*, he thought, *I should double back to see if the knights have left the city*. But if he did that, others might follow him, and that would mean he would be at risk again. It was hard enough carrying the pearls as far as the oasis without adding to the distance. He continued on, thinking he might be wise to land and change back into his elfin form, but that would mean lugging the pearls, which would be more exhausting than flying and much slower. *No*, he decided, *better to remain in the air*. When he reached the oasis, he could change back.

Wladex scanned the horizon and saw a line of clouds in the distance, their underbellies purple and shot with lightning. He knew it would be prudent to keep an eye on that distant storm, for his flight was hard enough without battling winds and driving rain. He did his best to increase his speed, growing more enervated with every flap of his tapestry wings. As soon as he came down he would have to find some blood. It was tempting to make Stariat his target, but the paladin was still more useful alive than as fodder, so he began to look for merchants or lone travelers on the road below. He could swoop down, he decided, and take a victim with his talons. He might have to remain on the ground while he drank, but after that, he would be back in the air once again. Scanning the road ahead, he saw it was disappointingly empty.

A playful breeze slipped by, like a mrem sniffing after prey. Wladex adjusted his tail and rode out the mild buffeting, letting the wind fill his wings so he could rise higher. He rocked gently on the next gust, beginning to enjoy himself. Far ahead he could see the green fringe of the oasis. In another hour or two he would be there, and then he could begin his conjurations that would result in the end of the Laria and mark his own ascendance to power. The nearness of this achievement made him intoxicated with his own accomplishment; he flapped higher into the air as if to show how great his deed would be.

Then he noticed the storm had moved closer, that its winds were picking up, and that all among the roiling clouds, the indistinct shapes of forcelords and force elementals could be seen, moving inexorably in Wladex's direction.

Chapter 22

WLADEX FLAILED AT THE WIND, HIS WINGS stretched and aching as the power of the storm grew, fueled by elementals and cyclones, all apparently competing for the honor of battering Wladex out of the sky. Only the pearls protected him from the worst of the tempest's fury, and that protection was limited by the nature of the air, for the pearls could not create a stability where none was possible. No lightning singed Wladex, though he was thrown about like a leaf on a flooding stream. He could not see the ground, nor could he tell which direction he was being tossed. He could not draw his sword to fight, for his wing-modified hands could not clutch the hilt, nor could he bring up his talons to seize the weapon. He began reciting spells, all of them aimed at getting him safely back to the ground. The howling winds and the crackle of thunder all but drowned out his chanting, so that it took him some considerable time to finish reciting the first spell. As he began the second, he heard a massive voice boom at him through the storm.

"Foolish mortal. You cannot hope to hurt me, vampire lord though you are. You struggle in vain. I will crush you. I will extinguish you. I will obliterate you."

Doing his best not to listen, Wladex continued with his chanting. He was shaken at the enormity of the voice, which he was convinced beyond all doubt was that of the Laria. The huge presence lent wrath to the winds, so that Wladex was struck with sand and stinging hail as he was flung about the sky. He felt one of his wings rip, and was resigned to falling to the ground. But to his astonishment, he was let down with little more than a bump; the black pearls had preserved him, though they could not stop the storm.

The cyclones danced around him like crazed dervishes, sand and small pebbles scouring the air. Wladex lay flat on his face, changing himself back into his vampire lord form so that he would not have to lose strength maintaining wings and talons that were now useless to him. Once or twice he attempted to raise his head, and was given a face full of sand for his efforts. He put his hands to his eyes so that he could try to determine which sun was shining beyond the storm and where it was in the heavens, but the tumultuous clouds blocked all but the most feeble, diffuse light. Wladex continued his spells to quiet the weather, and gradually the worst of the gale abated, becoming a hard-blowing wind under sullen clouds.

Sitting up, Wladex took stock of himself. He saw that the tapestries that had been his wings were in tatters, the representation of mythic night nothing more than scraps. He sighed, sad that such fine works as those had been sacrificed. He rolled up what was left of them and put the roll across his shoulders. Then, adjusting his sacks, he started out in what he hoped was the right direction to find the oasis. It would take him a long time to get to it, even if he was going toward it. But sitting alone in the badlands seemed too much like defeat, and so he decided it was better to try to be moving. "Besides," he said aloud, wanting to hear something other than the distant moan of the wind, "if I wait here, who knows what the Laria might send to fight me. This way I will not be wholly at its mercy." He felt a bit better for saying that.

He had gone a considerable distance when his hunger began to increase again, gnawing at him incessantly so that soon he found it difficult to think of anything that did not include his need for nourishment. He realized he would have to find prey soon, or his famished state would overcome him entirely. A short distance ahead there was an outcropping of rocks, ones that might contain animals large enough to take the edge off his need. He moved more quickly, telling himself at least he would be able to rest, and when he woke, he might be able to calculate where he was. He almost stumbled in his haste to reach the rocks, and as he arrived at the first scattering of stones, he dropped to his knees, almost worn out.

Then he heard a slithering sound not far away, not loud, but enough to catch and hold his attention. He lay still, listening keenly, and finally heard the soft chittering that told him Yngling were inhabiting the rocks. Encouraged, he pushed onto his knees, willing himself to go forward but not to rush. A stealthy approach was what was needed, or so he told himself. He slunk along the curve of the rocks, and found himself peering at a troop of the small creatures. With a lupine cry he was on them, ravening them until they were nothing more than bloodied bits of fur and bone, and his hunger was diminished enough that he could rest in the shade of the largest rocks, not truly replete, but satisfied.

He awoke as the green sun was heaving itself into the eastern sky. He did not know how long he had been asleep, nor how long the storm had blown him about the sky, but he determined to discover both these things as quickly as possible. In spite of the burden of his bags of pearls, he climbed onto the highest rock and squinted across the badlands, seeing nothing but desolation. Discouraged, he sat down, trying not to be disheartened. He had come this far, and he would not permit anything to stop him from achieving his goal. He would find the oasis he was seeking, he would find Stariat and Brior and Dusho. They would use the four jewels to defeat the Laria. As if he were restoring himself from another death, Wladex began to repeat, "I will come back. I will come back. I will come back." Until he began to believe it.

By the time the green sun was overhead, casting its red shadows like puddles of blood beneath the rocks, Wladex had struck upon an idea he thought would help him out of his predicament. He still had a few small bits of ruby, diamond, and emerald in his shredded clothing, enough that if he put a finding spell on them, the bits of precious stones should lead him to where the larger stones were. It was a difficult spell, and one that could easily be disrupted, but it was the only thing he could think of to take him to where the three men were. He told himself they might have left the oasis, and so looking for it would not necessarily bring him to where he wanted to be. It was better to take a chance with this more ephemeral spell. He kept repeating the words and gradually he felt something tugging, ever so slightly, at him. This had to be the finding spell, he assured himself, and he trudged off, keeping to the path where the pull was the strongest.

He went on until the green sun had set and the blue sun was halfway up the sky, and then he looked for a resting place where he could gather his strength and look for food. His head was aching, his shoulders were stiff as old wood, his back felt as if a swegle had trod on it, his knees seemed filled with broken glass, and his feet hurt as if he'd trod on hot coals. All this and a return of his hunger made it difficult for him to heed the subtle promptings of the finding spell. He saw a small village in the distance, hardly more than half a dozen shacks thrown together around scraggly patches of worn out fields. There was a small well in the middle of the village, and a few men out working encouraged Wladex, in his elf guise, to approach the place.

An old woman sat near the well. She was weaving rough cloth on a lap-held loom, and hardly stopped the movement of the shuttle as Wladex came nearer.

"Good day to you, lady," said Wladex, making himself as polite as possible.

"To you, too, stranger," she replied looking him over with sharp, black eyes.

"May I have a cup of water and a place to rest a while? I have been walking a long way—"

"You certainly look it," said the old woman, bestirring herself to point to the community cup; it was dented and rusty, and ordinarily Wladex would not have touched it. Now he took it gratefully and filled it from the old bucket that he hauled up from the depths of the well.

"Cold and sweet," said Wladex. "You are fortunate." He filled the cup a second time and drank eagerly, all the while yearning for blood.

"That's a matter for doubt. The well keeps us here, but it doesn't give us enough water to thrive." She sent her shuttle along her loom again. "Where are you coming from, elf?"

"From Dismas," he said, having no reason to lie.

She laughed. "Dismas! You have come a great distance. Where are you bound?"

"I am trying to find three companions. We . . . we were separated by a storm, and I have not yet found them again." He patted his bedraggled tunic. Dust came off it in small clouds. He coughed a little. "I have been trying to locate them."

"Magically?" asked the old woman.

"Yes." He achieved a self-effacing grin. "I am not so worn from traveling that I cannot make an effort to find them."

"Very sensible of you, no doubt," said the old woman without a sign of interest. She pointed to one of the shacks. "That is the only house in this village with a sleep-room to spare. We ask no money for it. What good is money here? But if you will work a spell for us when you wake, we will be well paid."

"It would honor me to do this for you," said Wladex, bowing deeply. "And I hope you will be made fortunate for your generosity." He cocked his chin in the direction of the house the old woman had pointed out. "Whom should I speak to about the sleep-room?"

"That is my house, and you have spoken to me," said the old woman with a nasty chuckle. "Go inside. There are three rooms off the entry. You may use the one on the left side of the door. It was painted blue, once, but it has faded. The others are yellow and brown."

"Thank you," said Wladex with a sincerity

that was rare in him. He almost regretted that he would have to take her blood when he left.

"Should your companions arrive, shall I have them wake you?" the old woman asked as Wladex started toward her house.

"My companions will probably not come here. But if they do, they are a paladin and two knights. They will wake me themselves." He dragged himself the last short distance to the house and all but fell across the threshold. As his eyes adjusted to the dim light, he saw a table and chair next to a shuttered window, and the three doors. He opened the one on the left and saw an unusually large bed covered in a hand-woven blanket. Simple as it was, it was as inviting as the finest beds in the grandest houses in Dismas or Terris. He put his sacks on the bed to serve as a pillow, pulled off his boots, and climbed up onto the bed to rest. As he drifted off, he could still feel the finding spell like a soundless hum in the bits of jewels he carried.

He did not know how long he had been asleep, but he woke from a dream in which a floater had entangled him in its tendrils and was slowly crushing the air from his lungs. He tried to take a deep breath and discovered this was impossible—the blanket was wrapped around him like a shroud and was tightening slowly but steadily. Wladex tried to pull his arm free in order to fight the blanket, but the fibers proved too tough. He tried to roll off the bed, but was held inexorably in place as the blanket continued to increase its purchase on him.

"No," said Wladex, and tried to remember a spell to break free. But too much of his power had gone to the finding spell and to maintaining his elfin shape. In an abrupt decision, he ceased his disguise—he was angry enough now that he did not care if these contemptible villagers saw him as he was. They would pay for trying such a scheme upon him. No doubt this was one of the places that preyed on unwary travelers, robbing and killing them, and disposing of them in the badlands. "They have the wrong traveler," he muttered as the blanket fell away, turning to patches of lint as it did. Wladex got up, slipped on his boots, adjusting them to his much larger vampire feet as he did. Then he took his dagger from his belt and crouched down behind the bed, readying himself to face the villagers when they came to find him. At least, he thought, he would leave here well fed. That would repay him for the cowardly attempt they made on his life.

The red sun day dragged on, and finally there was a sound near the front of the flimsy house, the soft tread of stealthy feet.

In his hiding place, Wladex tightened his hand on his dagger and prepared to fight. He was looking forward to the battle and the surprise he would give the villagers.

The front door creaked open, accompanied by breathless whispers. Then the villagers—Wladex reckoned there were four or five of them—advanced on the faded blue door, preparing to end the life of their guest. Someone tapped on the door as if to find out if Wladex could respond, and when this effort was greeted with silence, they slid the door open wide enough to look in.

"What?" exclaimed one of the villagers, a raw-boned yokel with few teeth and a mangled hand.

"Where is he?" another demanded.

The old woman shrieked aloud. "Where is my blanket? What has that elf done with it?" She rushed into the room. "Where is it?"

"How could he have got out?" asked a fourth, and a fifth repeated the question as if to make it more clear.

Wladex rose and advanced on the villagers. "I didn't get out," he said.

Curses met him, along with pitchforks. The taller men tried to force Wladex back from them with scythes and sickles, but their efforts were uncoordinated, and they only got in one another's way.

"This is almost too easy," said Wladex as he reached for the nearest of the men, seized his head, and in a single turn, broke his neck. He dropped the body, intending to drain it as soon as he was through with the rest.

The man with the ruined hand struck fire into the torch he carried, thrusting it toward Wladex as he muttered obscenities.

This was more than farm implements, and it held Wladex back for a short while. He weaved and dodged as one of the villagers tried to get close enough to the bed to snatch Wladex's bags. "You will not," Wladex hissed, and lunged at the would-be thief, pulling him over the bed and snapping his spine at the same time.

The old woman hurled a large metal bowl at Wladex, aiming to hit him in the head. Wladex fended it off with a raised arm. She squealed and shrank back, all her courage going out of her.

"I haven't done anything to you, yet," he shouted at the old woman. "Cringe when you have reason." The torch was beginning to bother him and he decided it was time to be rid of it. In a single ruthless motion, he swept out with his dagger, stabbing the tall man in the fleshy part of his side.

The man yowled, bent double and dropped the torch on the bed where it began to smolder in spite of the pumping cascade of blood pulsing out of the man's horrible wound. He collapsed onto the bed, next to the guttering torch.

Wladex struck out with the dagger again, and sliced into the arm of one of the other men, who clapped his hand to the injury and bolted from the room. Wladex made a third stab, and nicked the cheek of the smallest of the men.

The attackers—those that could—fled from the room, a few of them screaming. One of them threw a sickle in Wladex's direction; it landed with a metallic thud an arm's length from Wladex. The old woman was the last to go, and she left with dire imprecations flung at the vampire lord.

He watched them go, then set about dousing the flames before he began to feed on the two dead men. He knew he had to make the most of the time; the villagers would be back soon, and this time they would be prepared.

Chapter 23

WLADEX DID NOT HAVE LONG. THE VILLAG-
ers were back before he had finished draining
the first of the dead men. He managed an amiable curse as he hurried to load his bags onto his
shoulders. No point in bothering with a disguise
spell—not yet. He pulled the first man he had
killed upright, and, after taking a little blood
from him, Wladex held him as a shield as he
started toward the door.

The smell and the heat stopped him. The fools
were actually trying to burn down the building!
He knew he could not go out through the door
without running into a fiery trap. "Morons!" he
shouted. Was he to be stopped from bringing
down the Laria by a pack of ignorant farmers?
Bad enough that he had had to let one man bleed
to death and could make full use of only one of
the other two. The outrage that filled him gave
him strength. He swung around and began to
kick at the weathered wall behind him. Outside
he heard the farmers shouting, and a few mo-

ments later, the wall he had kicked began to char. They were trying to keep him inside the house. "Buffoons!"

A scrambling above him warned him that someone had climbed to the roof, and soon the broken shingles would be ablaze. From outside, a ragged cheer rose among the villagers.

"You will not do this!" Wladex roared. He lifted one of the bags containing the smallest of the black pearls and began to recite a transportation spell; it wasn't very strong and could only carry him as far as the eye could see, but it was better than staying in the village. At least he would be far enough away that no one would be able to follow him. He coughed as he conjured and his eyes began to smart from the heat and smoke. Flames appeared, lapping at the door.

The spell finally took hold just as the ceiling beams began to blacken, bits of fire winking in the darkness. For an instant the air shook, and then Wladex was a long distance from the village; he could see the smoke rising on the horizon behind him. The spell had carried him and his bags as far as it could, leaving him in desolation as the red sun set. Resigned, he reinforced the finding spell and began to walk in the direction it pulled him.

In the afternoon of the green sun, he passed the wreckage of an ancient city. He paused to look at it, wondering which of the ten it had been, or if it was older than that, dating to a time before the sun shattered, before magic came to

Delos. He was tired but not as worn out as he had been before he reached the village. He was beginning to fear the storm had carried him a much greater distance than he had first supposed. It seemed to him he had been walking to the northwest for a very long time, and that he should have reached the oasis he sought long before now. Looking at the demolished city, he began to worry that the Laria might have struck already, blasting the remaining cities of Delos before he could confront it. The very idea kept him moving. If the Laria had wrought more ruin, he—Wladex—would claim vengeance on behalf of all Delos.

The black pearls seemed to be growing warmer, and that indicated to Wladex that he was nearing the other jewels. The bits of emerald, ruby, and diamond he still retained also felt hot to the touch, reinforcing his certainty that he was nearing the treasure he and his companions had secured. It troubled him that he saw no oasis in the distance, which implied that the jewels, as well as Dusho, Brior, and Stariat had moved on from the place they were to meet. Wladex made himself stop fretting, for he could not believe that the three men would simply make off with the jewels. More likely, he thought, they had set out in search of him—if they were aware he was still alive. They might have been captured, too. That was a nasty possibility, but one he could not wholly dismiss. "Better to think they are looking for me," he whispered. As if in response, the black pearls grew warmer still.

Topping a rise, Wladex saw more badlands ahead of him, but the jewels he carried indicated he should be nearing his companions. He scowled. The thought arose again: what if the Laria was deceiving him, deliberately luring him away from the men and the stones he was seeking? He uttered a few terse oaths and looked about, and only then did he see a thin plume of dust rising in the middle distance, hardly noticeable against the monochrome landscape. As the pearls grew hotter and the shards of gems he carried all but vibrated, Wladex started toward the little procession. He remembered to assume his elf form before he got too close, a necessary adjustment that slowed him down a bit.

The three men were moving very slowly, dragging the cart as if it held the weight of mountains on its frame. Dusho was limping and Stariat had a bandage around his head with a red stain over his right eye. Only Brior seemed unharmed, but he walked with the mindless steadiness of utter fatigue.

As Wladex approached, Stariat caught sight of him and shouted a greeting. "Godoh! Is that you?"

"Yes," Wladex called back, and walked faster. He was amazed at how pleased he was to see these three men again, and not simply because they had his jewels with them. "I have been searching for you."

"We had to fight our way out of Dismas," said Dusho, glad of an excuse to stop walking. "They followed us to the oasis, and we barely managed to escape. If that storm hadn't come up, we might not have been so lucky."

"That storm blew me—oh, a great distance," said Wladex.

"How great a distance?" asked Brior, who shaded his eyes with his hand in order to stare up into the sky. "It took hours and hours to pass us."

"I don't know how great a distance," said Wladex testily. "I had no way to measure."

"But you found us," said Dusho, a note of disbelief in his words. "How is that possible?" His face showed the strain of favoring one leg for so long.

"I have the black pearls," said Wladex at once. "And I still have a few bits of diamond, ruby, and emerald left; there is enough to hold a finding spell. I have been following that spell since the storm dropped me."

"And you weren't killed," Stariat marveled. "Few would have survived, but you did."

"I have the black pearls," Wladex repeated. "They shielded me from the worst of the tempest, and kept me from falling to my death when the storm abated." He studied the men. "You look as if you have been in as fierce a storm as I was."

"The reavers fought hard," said Stariat. "They may be rogues, but they have a great love of battle." He touched the bandage over his eye. "I didn't have the chance to use a healing spell before we made our escape, and since then, we

have been making our way through the badlands, none of us with energy to spare."

"We cannot go back to that oasis," said Dusho
solemnly. "They will be waiting for us if we try.
If that is the only place the four jewels may be
used to destroy the Laria, we may have achieved
much in vain."

The other two men looked downcast; Wladex
could tell they had been speaking of this among
themselves and had lost heart because of what
they decided. He made himself stand straight.
"Nothing of the sort. We know the Laria crushed
the Ten Cities in a single blow. I would think
that any of the ruins would do, for the concentration of the Laria's power must still be in those
places." He was uncertain if this was true, but it
was plausible enough that he did not think he
was being untruthful.

"But how shall we find these cities if they were
reduced to rubble?" Brior could not hide his disheartened state of mind. "I cannot fathom how
much magic we would need."

"Exactly!" Wladex cried as he took the bags of
pearls from his shoulders and laid them on the
cart. "We have more magic here than anyone has
controlled since the cities were razed. None of
us knows how mighty these jewels are, but we
know that the Laria fears them being together."

As if in agreement, the jewels on the cart made
a low, humming sound.

Brior was shocked. "What does that signify?"

"That the jewels have forces within them that
we cannot imagine," said Wladex with deep sat-

isfaction. Everything he had endured had been worth it. He admitted to himself now that he had feared that after so long a time apart, the four jewels would not have the harmony to work together, or that some spell cast in the meantime would have blocked their united power. When he ruled Delos, he would make sure such spells were in place so that no adventurers could come against him. He patted the cart. "We have the power to bring down the Laria right here."

"If your spells are strong enough to master them," said Stariat quietly.

"Of that I have no fear," said Wladex, not wanting to boast, but unable to resist the urge. "I have trained for many years to do this thing. It will come to pass, of that I am convinced."

"If the Laria does not stop us before then," said Dusho. "Three men and an elf, if you will pardon my mentioning it, is hardly an army."

"But we do not need an army," Wladex said emphatically. "We have the four jewels, in sufficient concentration, and so we have the might to move suns." He held up his hand. "I know I have told you this before, but none of you were able to have faith enough to be sure this was so. Well, I tell you again, with the jewels as my witness, that we have triumph within our grasp. Only a failure of purpose will keep us from achieving the goal of our mission." He regarded the three men. "Once we reach one of the blasted cities, we can begin our attack."

"Assuming the Laria permits us to reach a blasted city, and assuming the city can still serve to focus the four jewels," said Dusho. "You speak as if we have no more reason to consider the Laria, but as a target. I wish I had your conviction, Godoh, I do."

"If you lack the conviction, it may be that you will defeat yourself," said Stariat, obviously renewing their debate. "If you cannot imagine the possibility of failure, you will be far more apt to succeed."

"But any reasonable man must be aware that this undertaking, while noble in purpose and laudable in end, is not likely to be done without high cost," said Dusho in his most sensible manner. "It would be folly to go into so difficult a fight as the one we face and not be aware of these things. I would hesitate to follow any leader who was unable to see the many dangers ahead."

"See the dangers, yes," said Brior, taking advantage of the moment to interject his point. "But in seeing them, we will prepare to fight them. The Laria is a monumental force, and it commands monsters of every kind. This we know. And we must prepare to face them—"

Before each man could become more entrenched in his position, Wladex interrupted. "We would be reckless to think that we will not have to persevere against heavy, unknown opponents. Yet we must have faith in our final victory, or we will be likely to succumb to the fears our prudence will instill in us. If we come to a ruined city that has lost all its power, then we will go on to another one until we have what we seek."

He patted the cart. "The protection we have here must be equal to anything the Laria can send against us. The four jewels are the greatest weapon Delos has had since the sun shattered." He pointed off to the north-northeast. "We have a long way to go, wherever we are going."

The three men agreed, putting aside their differences for the time being. As they moved off, Brior said, "I hope you can conjure a meal for us soon. We have been on short rations for a full green sun day."

"Let us see what we find ahead," said Wladex, who knew he would begin to hunger before the next sunset. "If you watch for signs of life, we may not have to make food by magic."

Again the men accepted his assurances, and continued to move along through the wastelands. There was a sharp wind blowing, colder than it ought to have been, and after a few hours, Stariat said, as if confessing to an inexcusable weakness, "I need a cloak."

The other two chimed in with the same complaint. Wladex looked at them and knew he had to do something to protect them. "In the bags, along with the pearls, there are a few bits of tapestry. I think I can turn them into cloaks for you, if you do not object to such garments." He knew what their answers would be.

"That's fine with me," said Brior. "Anything to get warm again. You'd think with two suns overhead we would be sweltering out here, but not in this wind."

"How did it turn so cold?" asked Dusho, not expecting an answer.

"You know the answer to that," said Wladex. "The Laria is hunting for us, snuffling the wind to find us, making the wind cold to force us to give ourselves away with fires. If the suns heat us, it must make more of an effort to find us." He looked about uneasily, anticipating another storm.

As he was handed the bits of tapestry, he recited spells over them, creating first a cloak that was black but for sprinkled bits of brilliant color like dust, then a cloak that was swathed with sprays of light against black, and finally a cloak with four large orbs on it—one brilliant gold, the other three smaller and silvery. "Think of it," Wladex said as he handed out the cloaks, "we may yet live to see night again."

The implications of this held the men silent as they donned their cloaks. Finally Stariat said, "Whatever night may be, it would be a great thing to see it."

"Do you think there are elementals on our trail?" Brior inquired, unable to think of any observation about so momentous an event as night, and trying unsuccessfully to sound indifferent to the answer.

"Elementals, scevan, even nits are tools for the Laria," Wladex reminded them. "We cannot ignore any of them."

"Then how are we to sleep?" Dusho sounded annoyed. His limp was worse.

"We sleep in shifts," said Wladex, smiling as

the notion occurred to him. "Yes," he went on as his thoughts became clearer. "That is what you do. One of you will sleep on the cart, his sleep-tent opened over him, and the rest of us will go on. When the sleeper wakes, another will take his place, and so on as we travel. We will eat when all are awake," He gave a long, thoughtful look at Dusho. "You should be first, I think, for you have the most need of rest. The jewels will help you to heal."

"Then Stariat should be first to sleep," Brior protested.

"No," said Wladex. "Stariat has been injured on his head, but he can walk; he may be in pain, but it is not enough to hinder him. Dusho is limping. He will have to improve if he is to be able to help us pull the cart."

"Wladex is right," said Stariat. "I would do the same in his position." He did his best to smile, and ended up looking pained. "But I will be glad to rest my head when my turn comes."

"We will arrange that as soon as Dusho is rested," said Wladex, watching as Dusho unpacked his sleep-tent and improvised a rigging for it on the cart. "Very good. Make sure you keep wrapped in the cloak, in case the wind gets colder."

"That I will," said Dusho, climbing awkwardly into the cart and huddling down among the jewels.

"Come, Brior, Stariat. Let us be underway," said Wladex as soon as Dusho closed the flap on his tent. "We gain nothing standing here."

"True," said Brior, and took his place by one of the shafts of the cart. Stariat took the other and they began to move, slowly at first, but gathering speed until they were walking at a good pace.

"This is excellent," Wladex approved, shivering in the bite of the wind. They trudged onward, and the wind battered at them as they went.

Chapter 24

AT FIRST IT LOOKED LIKE NOTHING SO much as a line of time-worn buttes. Only when Wladex and his companions drew closer could they see that these were not the skeletons of rocks, but of buildings. They had been abandoned, even as ruins, long ago, and no trace of men remained in them. Only the wind strummed eerie music from the twisted, empty spires with its gelid fingers.

"Which of the Ten Cities was this?" asked Dusho, who was much restored after two long rests on the cart.

"Who knows?" Brior responded, staring at the empty spaces between what had long ago been turrets. "There is nothing to tell us."

"There might be, if we search for it," said Wladex, who was disappointed that he felt no magical emanations from the place. That so vast a place could not offer them any might at all was more disappointing than not finding the city. He did his best to conceal his dejection. "Who knows what might lie under the sands?"

"Whatever we find might be dangerous, mightn't it?" Brior asked, his hand on his sword as he watched the sand slide, almost as if it was a living thing, driven by the wind and marked by the shadows of the towers.

"Does anything live here?" Dusho asked Wladex uneasily. "I feel as if we are being watched."

"So do I," said Stariat, who had just emerged from the sleep-tent on the cart. "I felt it yesterday, but here it is much stronger."

"But what could be watching us?" Brior looked around as if he expected to catch a monster or two lurking among the wind-eroded pylons. "Should we be worried?"

"If we are being watched, yes," said Dusho. "No matter who is watching us. If it is only a half-grown nit, it can be used by the Laria." He stared directly at Wladex. "Isn't that right?"

"Yes," said Wladex, wondering why Dusho had been so direct with him. "And it would be wise for us to take care in our traveling, for we do not know if the Laria is monitoring our progress, or merely spying on us from time to time." He noticed that Dusho looked a bit more accepting, but his eyes glittered. "Do you think I have overlooked something?"

Dusho shrugged. "In a case like this, it is hard to tell," he said, being deliberately ambiguous. He pointed off among the titanic ruins. "Look there. That place must have been as large as all of Fuego in its time, and it is only one of hundreds."

"Yes," said Wladex, allowing the subject to

change. "There were many more men in those days, and hardly any monsters. The Laria has done all this."

"So the legends say," Dusho agreed. "And who am I to doubt the legends."

If Brior was aware of the tension building between Wladex and Dusho, he gave no sign of it. "All Delos must have been an amazing place, having great cities and grand roads and lush fields stretching to the horizon—and night." His face grew wistful. "If we succeed, we may one day have all that again."

"If we succeed," said Stariat. "It is a magnificent burden, our undertaking. We have come very far, and we must continue to be dedicated. If we fail in our resolve, we might as well throw in our lot with the Laria and turn rogue, for we will have earned that for ourselves." He put his hands together, fingers interlaced. "We must be like this"—he held up his hands—"dedication and action functioning as the same thing."

"A paladin would say that," Dusho declared. "Brior and I are knights, and our preference is action." He gave a long sigh. "I am disappointed that we have come so far and found so little of use to us. This place is a reminder of all we have lost. Looking at it, I find it hard to imagine that we might be able to accomplish what the people of this city could not."

"What kinds of men abandon such a city as that? Surely they could have defended it?" Brior asked with uncharacteristic indignation. "If they would leave this city to avoid a fight, they hardly deserved to have it."

"You don't know what happened here," Dusho said sharply. "They might have done the right thing."

"How? Look at those towers." Brior flung his hand in the direction of the city's spires. "If men will fight to defend Astra, they should have done more for so fine a place as this was."

"But they might not have known what they were fighting," said Wladex. "The Laria may have been newly strong then, and it might have taken this place by storm."

"Or there could have been something else that drove them away," said Dusho. "Sickness or storms, or—"

"The legend says it sent larines into the cities, and everyone went mad," Brior reminded them.

"But no one has seen a larine since," said Dusho. "Why was it so much worse than any other monster? A ghoul or a skeleton, or a dragon is devastating enough—what was it about the larines?"

"They sowed dissension," said Wladex, remembering the stories told by ancient vampires. "They made everyone distrust his neighbor, his family, his friend, so that all the men fled this city, battling against one another as their terrors and hatred grew." He looked down at the shifting sands. "Some vestige of the larines must be here. Listen to how we are bickering. If we remain long, we will begin to accuse one another of dire acts and despicable motives, and then the Laria will win."

"You are a cynical fellow, Godoh," said Brior. "With all we have done, how can you think we would succumb to anything of the sort?"

"Anything of the sort?" Stariat challenged. "You are beginning to—" What he thought they were beginning to do was never said, for a myriad of small creatures came scuttling out of the sand, hurrying toward the little group. They were of changeable shapes—some looked like flat, animated flowers, some were like scaly rodents, others had ruffles and frills along their sides.

"What—?" Dusho exclaimed.

"Larines!" shouted Stariat, although he had never seen one before.

"Don't let them touch you," Wladex ordered with unexpected calm. "They are dangerous."

Now the larines swarmed around the cart, keeping a short distance from it, milling in what seemed to be distress.

"The jewels are holding them at bay," said Stariat, and very nearly smiled. "They cannot reach us."

"But they can poison the air," said Wladex. "We must kill them, or they will instill anger and doubt in all of us." He drew his sword and brought it down on a small knot of larines. A thin shriek went up as he impaled three of the creatures on his blade. "Get a mace. That will be best."

"We have one," said Dusho, pulling it off the

cart. "There are more of those things coming." He pointed to where the sand was seething, more like a river in a flood than sand. "There must be thousands of them—tens of thousands."

"We cannot pound them all to death," said Brior, taking a lance from their weapons. "How are we to—"

"Do not let yourself doubt," Wladex ordered them sharply. "We will be at one another's throats if you do."

Dusho was already bashing at the larines, swearing in the worst possible terms he knew as he crushed the small, skittering creatures. A terrible stench rose from the dead ones as if they were filled with corruption. "I can't stand the smell," he complained as he dispatched another half-dozen.

"Nor can I," Stariat admitted as he used the flat of his sword to mash the loathsome things. "Shouldn't we depart? There is nothing here for us."

"Just these hideous larines," said Dusho, who was doing his best to make a joke of their predicament. "That's hardly enough to make it worthwhile staying here."

"But they are all around us," said Brior. "How are we to escape them?"

"We can rush through them," said Stariat, smacking more of the disgusting pests.

"Or we can move slowly, fighting them off until we are beyond their place," said Wladex. "If we hurry, we may excite them to a more concerted attack." He told himself that was what he would do if he had command of the larines. They were very useful, and less destructive than most of the monsters the Laria sent against people.

"I think Godoh's right," said Dusho. "I think we'd manage better if we take it slow. I get the feeling these things can get nasty if they're disturbed." He killed a few more and wiped his forehead with the edge of his cloak. "That smell makes my eyes sting."

"Whatever we are going to do, we had better do it soon," said Stariat, pointing some distance away to another wave of larines.

"How many are there?" Brior cried out, sounding as if his nerve could fail him. "Will they ever stop coming?"

"Now you know how the city became empty," Wladex said dryly. "We must go now, or the jewels will be in danger." He did not add that the source of the danger would be the four of them. "Move very slowly. Stariat in advance; I'll bring up the rear. Dusho and Brior, pull the cart. Do not move faster than a walk."

"So *you* say," Dusho responded, and struck at the larines again.

"That smell is making me sick," said Brior, blinking as if against a very bright light.

"Don't speak of it," Stariat warned as he began to walk, smacking the ground ahead of him as he went.

"How far do we have to go until we are free of these larines?" Brior asked, kicking a swirling bunch of them into a mass of others. The largest of the larines was no bigger than his foot, but he felt as if he had jammed his toe into a boulder. "What are they made of?"

"Dissension, malice, anger, meanness, confusion, ill-will, resentment," Wladex said as he ticked these things off on his fingers. "For a beginning. Work against them and you increase their strength." He was walking backward, his sword held so he could hit with the flat of the blade. "The more we fight them, the more persistent they become."

"That does not please me," said Stariat, using a sweeping motion to clear his way through the creatures.

"No; it shouldn't please any of us," Wladex said, hoping to keep the men from being overwhelmed by the poisonous presence of the larines. "They will keep testing our weaknesses."

Brior gave a cry of dismay. "Ahead. There are millions of them."

"There are a great many," said Stariat, doing his best to remain calm. "Perhaps we should turn aside? The track is narrow, but they might not follow us over such steep terrain."

Wladex was by no means convinced, but he said, "It may be worth a try."

"Think. We can move away from these things by going up the slope. How can they follow us?" Brior looked hopeful at this suggestion as he brought his heel down on a larine that had gotten too close to him.

"Be careful," Wladex warned. "They cling."

He wasn't absolutely sure of this, but he recalled the old vampire saying that larines could hold onto their victims until every fiber of the victim's being was permeated with fear and wrath. "Don't let them—"

Dusho pried one of the little monsters off his leg, batting it away with the handle of his mace. "Tenacious. I might admire that if circumstances were different."

"No doubt," said Stariat, making for the track up the slope. "Keep moving."

Brior sighed. "It is just such a craven thing, to run from small beasts like these."

"If it were one beast, or ten, that might be so," said Wladex. "But there are hordes of them, and they are all heading toward us." The second wave was almost upon them, and Wladex began to mutter a spell to increase their area of protection.

"You are a prudent elf," said Dusho, mocking slightly as the effect of the larines became stronger. "Prudence is a better word than craven."

"Dusho!" said Stariat sharply. "You know better than to say that."

"You're a paladin. You have to take a lofty tone," said Dusho. "You'll have to forgive an ordinary knight like me for my views."

"Stop it," said Brior, stopping in his tracks. "You do not speak for me, Dusho. You can think as you like, but I have my own opinions. I don't need you to voice them for me."

Again Wladex stopped the growing acrimony.

"We must keep moving. You can see for yourselves the trouble these things are causing us." He pointed to the steeper part of the road, some hundred paces ahead. "Once we are there, it may be safe to pause. But here, we will shortly be surrounded by the larines, and then we will lose all we have endured so much to get."

"True enough," said Stariat. "Come. It's not so far to go. Move." His order was sharper than any he had given before. "The larines are trying to get ahead of us."

"Look at them go," said Brior, almost admiringly. "They are determined."

"They are also dangerous," said Wladex, shoving the cart forward. "I have enlarged our area of protection so they cannot get onto us. But they have a magical power from the Laria that will wear ours down if we linger. Dusho. Brior."

The two knights reluctantly resumed their task, but now they watched each other warily, as if neither trusted the other to do as he was told. They made their way up the slope, the chittering mass of larines growing denser with every step they took.

Wladex kept brandishing his sword from the rear of the cart, calling curses down on the larines. He despised the mass of them, the odor of them, their mindless, evil power. He would have to change them when he ruled. He might be rid of them entirely, but he could see their usefulness. As the road grew steeper, the larines began to falter, and Wladex sensed a little lessening of their malign presence. "Keep on. Keep on," he urged his companions.

The track grew steeper still, and the larines no longer streamed along beside them, but kept behind them, falling back as the men climbed the hillside.

"It looks like we're getting away," said Brior, taking a moment to glance behind him. "They must cover half the ground between here and the ruined city."

"At least," said Stariat, who stood at the narrowest part of the road. "By the look of it, there's a narrow valley up ahead. It curves around to the left, so I don't know what may lie within it." He made this observation with caution, but also with a degree of relief. "I don't think they can follow us now."

"Probably not," said Wladex, who had the agitated sensation that their deliverance was not what it seemed. He tried to dismiss this as the residue of the emotions generated by the larines, and almost believed it. "We'll have to go this way, in any case. Just stay alert."

"Are you expecting more larines?" Dusho inquired, overly polite.

"I don't know what I am expecting. That's the trouble." Wladex made a sign for them to be quiet as they went more deeply into the valley.

Its walls rose up around them like tremendous cupped hands. There were small shrubs and bushes clinging to the sides, and along the rim were a few, scraggly trees bent and twisted by the wind. The valley continued to narrow as they went forward, and the shadows of it lay long and deep.

Then Wladex realized what was happening. "The larines weren't attacking us," he announced, unable to keep the horror from his voice. "They were herding us!"

Chapter 25

"THERE IS SOMETHING WRONG HERE," SAID Stariat a bit later as they continued on into the valley. No sunlight reached them now; they walked in perpetual shadow. "There." He pointed to the stream that ran along the path they followed. "Don't you see it?"

"What about it?" asked Dusho. He was looking a trifle abashed in response to the impact the larines had had on him.

"It is flowing toward the end of the valley, ahead. Not away from it." He frowned. "I have been watching it to be certain."

"Why is this wrong?" Dusho kept on. "It isn't going uphill; this is all fairly flat. The stream is following the valley floor. Streams do that. It could go into an underground channel and cut through the rocks. Or the valley could be the bed of an ancient lake. It looks like one," he added, pointing to the bowl-like sides. "It drained away to some other place. What is wrong with that?"

"Nothing, if that is the real explanation," said Stariat.

Wladex shared Stariat's apprehension. "The paladin is right," he told the three. "Something is wrong here. I don't yet know what that may be, but I can feel it around me, and I know that it is increasing."

"The jewels will protect us," said Brior, who had been reluctant to speak at all, for fear some lingering ill effects of the larines would bring him into trouble with the others.

"Unless the jewels are what the Laria is seeking," said Wladex. "These are very dangerous to it."

"You are certain it is the Laria that is doing this?" Dusho did his best to sound skeptical, and failed.

"What else controls the larines?" Wladex asked. "We have taken the path they forced us on, and now we are where the Laria wants us to be." He made an angry gesture, directed as much at himself as at the Laria. "I should have been more alert. I should have seen what the Laria was doing."

Stariat looked grim. "If you're right, then this place is—"

"A grave," said Dusho. "And the four jewels will fall into the control of the Laria. That will make its power absolute and all we have done will be to aid the very thing we came to stop." Despair was building in him, and it echoed in his voice.

"How can you say that?" Brior protested. "If

we fear the jewels may be taken by the Laria, we must destroy them."

"How?" Dusho demanded.

Wladex stopped the two of them, holding his hand up in mock supplication. "Knights. Do not do the Laria's work for it. If we must face the Laria here, then we must use the jewels to weaken or destroy it. Since we are not in a place that focuses the four jewels, this will be difficult, but it is not impossible. At least we can break its power in some way, which is less than we want, but more than Delos has had for millennia. That is a worthy goal in itself." This was so far from the truth, he was angry at himself for saying such dishonest things, though he knew it was necessary. He pointed to the other side of the stream. "Now we must be careful what we say."

The three men looked, Brior shocked, the other two surprised, for a creature they had never seen before was pacing the opposite bank, keeping even with them.

"What is it?" Brior asked. "It looks something like a scevan, but it is not a scevan. It's bigger, and it has . . . It looks a bit like a gigantic Yngling and is not one, not with those teeth and those forelimbs. And those things at its shoulder are like the tendrils of a floater."

"This is the Laria's place, and everything in it comes from the Laria," said Wladex. "There will be creatures here that can be found nowhere else on Delos."

"Nor would any other place want them," said Dusho.

"And you think it can hear what we say," said Brior, puzzled by the thought.

"I think we must assume that it can. It is one of the Laria's creations, and therefore will do its bidding. Including listening to us." Wladex wanted to take a throwing axe and use it on the creature, but he knew he could be courting trouble if he did.

"True enough," said Stariat, looking at the creature. "I wonder how many of them there are?"

"Not as many as there are larines, I'd reckon," said Wladex. "In this place, we must be careful. We know nothing of what we may find. Those . . . things may be only the beginning." He patted the jewels on the cart. "This is what they want, and what we must protect."

"Do you believe that's possible?" Dusho's face revealed the depth of his doubts more than his voice did.

"So long as we have the jewels, it is," said Wladex.

On the other side of the stream, there were now two of the creatures, and they watched the men with eyes like marbles.

"Are they tracking us?" Brior asked a little later as they continued on into the canyon.

"They appear to be," said Wladex.

"What if we turned around and went back the way we came?" Dusho suggested. "The larines won't come up the mountain."

Wladex shook his head. "I don't think that would be a very good idea. We don't know what other new creatures the Laria might conjure up—"

"We don't know that no matter which way we go," Dusho stated. "Wouldn't the other way be safer?"

Wladex glanced back over his shoulder and saw half a dozen of the scevan-like monsters a short distance behind them. "I don't think that's a very good idea," he said quietly.

His companions took turns looking back, and each one in turn acknowledged the presence of the monsters; Brior actually shuddered.

"Do we challenge them?" Stariat suggested but without any force of conviction. "Shouldn't we do something before we're completely boxed in? Shouldn't we look for a place to make a stand?"

"I think they are choosing that for us," said Wladex dryly as the canyon ahead of them stopped with the shrub-covered face of ancient rock. "We can't go much farther."

The three men stared at the rocks, their faces set as they recognized their predicament. They all halted, and the monsters across the creek and behind them stopped as well, waiting with the patience of victory.

"This isn't a good thing," said Dusho very quietly.

"No, it isn't," Stariat agreed. "But we can still fight." He rested his hand on the hilt of his sword. "We will have to keep them off while we try for a way out."

"Can't we use a transportation spell?" Brior implored.

"We could, if we knew what the Laria was doing overhead, or at the rim of this canyon. There could be greater trouble there than here. In the air, the cart and its contents are far more vulnerable than on the ground." Wladex scowled, his thoughts racing, but coming to no happy notions. "If only we knew how thick this rock face is. We might be able to use these stones to blast our way through it." He offered a ghastly smile. "The creatures are moving."

The two across the stream were preparing to jump. The pack behind them began to close in, the long tendrils at the shoulders uncoiling and beginning to snake into the air.

"Do we fight them?" Brior asked, as if he could not think how. His confusion was as much from exhaustion as unfamiliarity with the monsters.

"Of course we fight them," said Wladex, drawing a pike from among their weapons. "Get ready. They're going to rush us."

As he said this, a few of the tendrils came striking through the air, flicking out with terrible precision, leaving welts on Dusho's shoulder and Stariat's arm.

"What—?" Dusho cried out as his arm went numb.

Wladex surmised the trouble at once; he thrust a shard of emerald inside Dusho's tunic. "Keep this near the cut," he ordered as he prepared to use his pike. He clambered atop the cart, using his position to look over the attacking monsters.

"There are about fifteen of them. Make sure your blows count."

Just as he said this, Brior howled as a lash landed on his face, leaving a bloody track along his left cheek and over his eye. Blood streamed out of the wound as Brior clapped one hand over the injury. "I can't see!" He sounded panicky, and began to swing his sword in wide arcs.

"Your other eye is fine," Wladex shouted to him. "Use it, and keep turning your head, so they can't come at you on your left. I'll try to get some protection to you as soon as I can."

This stern order seemed to steady Brior, for he took a more solid stance and began to cut at the air at the level of the tendrils.

"They're almost on us," said Stariat very calmly. He was poised and ready, meeting the creatures hurtling at him with a double, expert cut that left both creatures rolling back into the stream, great slashes in their chests.

Wladex used his pike to snare the tendrils of one of the creatures and, pulling it toward him as if fighting a dangerous creature of the sea, he hauled the monster onto the cart and cut off its head with a short sword.

Dusho had managed to chop the tendrils from a pair of the monsters, and was going for a head blow with his mace. He fought with the kind of automatic fury that had earned him a reputation for effectiveness in battle. As he bashed in the skull of one of the monsters, he kicked it away, sending it tumbling down into the stream.

Even though his face hurt and his vision was

impaired, Brior continued to fight. He cut the legs out from under three of the beasts, shouting for Stariat to finish them off as he cut at the tendrils striking around him. "Kill them!" He continued to lunge at the attacking creatures, ignoring his pain.

This courage inspired Stariat and Dusho, who battled the creatures with renewed fury while Wladex put his best efforts into snagging and cutting the tendrils before they could damage his comrades any further. The monsters came on relentlessly, one even managing to get onto the cart before Wladex could kill him and kick the body into the stream, which was now rising a little, gurgling around the bodies of the monsters that were clogging its course.

In a last, maddened rush by the creatures, Brior was hurt again, this time by fangs that left a gash in his thigh that made him howl with torment. He sagged back against the cart as Wladex piked the last of the monsters.

Dusho tugged on Wladex's tunic. "Get jewels for him. Quickly. He's losing blood fast." He went to hold Brior upright.

"Better to bring him up here," said Wladex, making a quick decision. "He will do better lying down, and the jewels will lend him healing."

"Why not just use a healing spell?" Stariat demanded. He had bad scrapes on his knuckles and a bit of weal on his arm, but he had come through the fight with relatively little damage.

"In this place, I don't know what the Laria might do with the spell," Wladex admitted.

"There could be bad results if I used more than the jewels. Besides, they are more potent than most spells." He helped as Dusho wrestled Brior onto the cart. "He is badly hurt."

"That's what I've been telling you," said Dusho, watching apprehensively as Wladex did what he could to ease Brior around the jewels. "Will he get better?"

"If the jewels cannot heal him, nothing can," said Wladex grimly, knowing it was the truth. He got off the cart carefully, taking care not to unsettle the wounded knight. "If he can sleep undisturbed for a full sun, I should think he will improve."

"How can he have that?" Dusho asked, his temper controlling him. "Here we are, boxed in, cliffs on three sides of us, and the Laria's beasts on the fourth. How can he have an opportunity to recover when we have no idea what the Laria is going to send against us next?" He paced down to the edge of the stream and kicked at the bodies of the monsters they had just killed. A few of the corpses floated free, and, caught in the current, disappeared down a cleft in the base of the cliff where the stream flowed.

Stariat was watching him, not quite curious enough to join him. "What is that?"

"Seems to be an underground channel," said Dusho, not very much interested in it.

"Is it large?" Wladex stopped adjusting the cover over the jewels and Brior.

"Large enough for one of those creatures to go through," said Dusho with a shrug, and then his expression changed. "It might go through the rocks—that's what you're thinking."

"Yes," said Wladex.

"And we could use that for escape," said Dusho with the first sign of optimism since they entered the canyon.

"That is not so sure a thing," said Wladex, disliking having to dash his hopes. "But there might be a way to find out."

"What would that be?" asked Stariat, who was beginning to be interested as well.

"It is tricky," Wladex allowed. "But it just might tell us what we need to know." He looked from Stariat to Dusho. "Will you haul one of those bodies onto the shore for me?"

Dusho was startled by this request, but he did as Wladex bade him. The waterlogged carcass was heavy, and it took more strength than Dusho had anticipated to bring the creature onto the bank. "What do you want to do with it?"

Wladex came down to the dead monster. "I want to attach something to it. I can put a small spell on it." He did not say more, for fear of being overheard. He began very softly to make the fur of the beast sensitive to direct sunlight of any color, and to the duration the sunlight struck the coat. Satisfied, he cut off a length of the dust-colored fur and stuffed it into one of his many pockets. "That's all. You can put him back in the stream again."

"You think you will learn something from that?" Dusho asked, lugging the body back to the water once more.

"I hope I will learn something useful, yes." *Whether or not the Laria heard that,* Wladex thought, *it will find out nothing it can use against us.*

"What about food?" asked Dusho. "There are leaves enough to use for conjuration."

"Yes, but these are also the Laria's. Who knows what might become of us if we ate anything magicked from them? I have a few bits of dried meat left, and I can enlarge them, but I would not take a chance on things growing here." Wladex climbed the bank to the cart again. "I wouldn't drink the water, either. It could be dangerous." He patted one of the water casks where the diamonds were concealed. "There is enough in here to serve our needs for now."

Stariat looked annoyed, but he nodded. "I hate to say it, but those are all sensible precautions." He glanced at the face of the canyon wall ahead of them. "We'll see a little sunlight in a while, but it won't last long."

"It seems strange to be without sunlight," said Dusho.

Wladex nodded. "Almost like night must be." He might have said more but the bit of fur in his pocket was suddenly warm.

Chapter 26

THEY SAID LITTLE DURING THEIR MEAL, which was made more enjoyable by an hour or so of light from the red sun. The floor of the canyon fell into shadow after that, the line of sunlight creeping brightly up the eastern side of the canyon. Higher up the walls, some of the brush bent in the wind, but aside from an eerie, echoing moan, no air stirred where Wladex and his companions sat beside the chuckling water of the stream. The canyon was once again undisturbed. All the bodies of the scevan-Yngling creatures had washed away and the whole scene was one of apparent peace.

"I wish we could get out of here," said Dusho as he set up his sleep-tent. "I feel as if we're doing nothing here, just making ourselves better targets."

"I've noticed something up on the rim," said Stariat quietly. "I don't know what it is, but it's been pacing back and forth along the west side." He pointed unobviously. "In case we're being observed."

Wladex managed a casual glance at the canyon rim and saw something move, a lithe, long shape, serpent-like, but not a serpent. "The Laria is inventing new monsters for us, I think," he said very quietly. "It's testing us."

"I don't like it," said Dusho. "This place is a trap. All they have to do is start dislodging rocks and we're finished."

"No, we're not," said Wladex. "I can't do much in the way of spells, but I can extend the shield over the jewels to include us, at least for a while." He smiled a little. "You can sleep without worry."

Dusho glared at the canyon walls. "Maybe," he said.

Stariat gave Wladex a searching stare. "Do you think that's safe? Mightn't you put the Laria on alert, doing that?"

"I doubt it," said Wladex. "The Laria must expect something of the sort. It is aware of our mission. It should expect us to have a new plan. I know I would in its place." He had an instant of private amusement from his own remark. "I don't think it would be worth the Laria's efforts to try to break the shield I've put on our cart. If we were able to leave here, that might be different." His shoulders lifted in an exaggerated sigh. "We're not going far, not for now." He patted his pocket where the fur from the dead scevan-Yngling lay. It had remained warm, meaning the body he had taken it from had been in direct sunlight for a while. "We'll have to come up with a plan before the Laria sends more monsters to put us to the test." He leaned back, looking up at the eastern rim of the canyon. "Better keep a watch on both sides. We don't want to be surprised."

"No," Stariat agreed. He waited a short time, then said, "Do you really think Brior is going to recover? He looked pretty badly hurt."

"The stones will heal him if he isn't disturbed," said Wladex with a greater show of confidence than he felt. "We'll see how he is doing when Dusho wakens. By then Brior's wound should be closed."

"It was a bad bite," said Stariat, his words hinting at more.

"And we know nothing of the bites of such creatures because we have never encountered them before," Wladex finished for him. "That is what the Laria is counting on, I suspect." He stifled a yawn. "Dusho, you go ahead and sleep. Stariat and I will work out who is to stand watch first."

"You should rest," said Stariat, apparently untroubled by his injuries. "You look worn out. You've been doing so much magic, you're exhausted."

"I am tired," Wladex said, meaning something different than Stariat did. "Very well. I will curl up under the cart. There's room enough for me there, and I can respond quickly if anything happens." The one thing he would not be able to do was to return to his own shape, which was mildly inconvenient, but a small consideration, given their current circumstances. He rose and went to the cart. "Call me if you need me, and wake me when it's your turn to sleep."

"I will," said Stariat, and began to circle around the cart and sleep-tent, a lone sentry on patrol.

With the sound of Stariat's regular footsteps for comfort, Wladex curled up beneath the cart, one of his tapestry cloaks around him. He was beginning to feel the daze of fatigue and did not know when he drifted off to sleep. The next thing he was aware of, Stariat was shaking his shoulder and whispering "Godoh" fiercely. Wladex edged out from under the cart and sat up. "What is it?"

"The thing on the rim," Stariat said, pointing upward. "I've been watching it. It's . . . growing larger."

"How do you mean, growing larger?" Wladex had the peculiar sensation that made him wonder if he were still dreaming.

"I think the Laria is making changes," said Stariat. "I've been watching it since the green sun began to shine, and I've noticed that it's different."

"Tell me how different it is," said Wladex, surprised to hear Stariat sound so upset. "What did you notice first?"

"The head seems larger. It *has* a head now, something like a dragon's, but longer, and with—I don't know. The back of the skull is—" He stopped, making a gesture in an effort to illustrate what he had seen.

"When did you see this?" Wladex asked.

"I told you, since the green sun began to shine—two or three hours," Stariat answered.

"You're sure it isn't just some other creature, a new monster the Laria has invented for us?" Wladex got to his feet and shrugged out of his cloak.

"No, not entirely." It was plain that Stariat was rattled. He made an effort to compose himself. "But while I've been standing sentry, I have been keeping an eye on the rim of the canyon. If the Laria has conjured up a new monster, it did it when I could not see, and that would mean it was made in a very short time. No, I think the Laria has been modifying what it had put up there." He took a long breath. "It's been watching us."

"The Laria or the creature?" Wladex asked, peering upward. There certainly was something up there, longer and more massive than what Wladex had seen before he went to sleep.

"Possibly both," said Stariat. "I'm afraid we will have to face it. I saw it testing the rocks a short while ago, as if it intended to climb down."

"Down these walls?" Wladex laughed once in disbelief. "I don't think that would be likely for a creature that size." Still, he was more wary as he squinted at the flicker of movement he saw at the edge of the canyon.

Stariat cocked his chin toward Dusho's sleeptent. "Should we wake him? We may have to be ready to fight in a very little time."

"So we might," said Wladex. "All right. I don't like having to do this, but, as you say, we may have to fight soon." He had no desire to battle another monster just now, and not in this trap of a canyon. "Be careful how you plan. We don't want to give ourselves away."

"True," said Stariat, and went to Dusho's sleep-tent to lift the flap and call his name.

Dusho emerged, still rumpled from his bedroll. He rubbed his face as if to bring himself awake. "What's the trouble now?"

"There's trouble up on the rim. Or it looks like trouble." Stariat pointed to the long reptilian head hanging over the edge of the canyon. The snout was long, the mouth filled with teeth, and the back of the head had a fan of bone that stood out like a gigantic ruff. The rest of the creature wasn't visible, though there was a dull shine around it, as if the suns' light struck burnished scales.

Dusho muttered obscenities as he stared up. "When did that thing show up?"

"More than an hour ago," said Stariat.

"Looks like it wants to come down," said Dusho. "What are we going to do about it?"

"That depends on if there is only one of it, and how large it is," said Wladex. "We can fight one such monster. Two is another matter."

"How big do you think it is?" Dusho studied the monster's head. "If the body is proportional, then we've got a huge creature to deal with."

"So we might," said Wladex, who had already assumed the body matched the head. "It would help if we knew how many legs it has, and how sharp its claws are."

"It looks like it might have started out as a gigantic Lizcanth," said Dusho. "Nasty beasts, Lizcanth."

"This one appears not to stand upright," said Stariat.

"Maybe, and maybe not," said Dusho. "It could be lying down in order to conceal itself." He glanced at Wladex. "What do you think, Godoh?"

"I think we could be deceived into taking actions that would harm us. If that creature began as a Lizcanth, then it most surely could stand, and that would make fighting it much more difficult." Wladex hated to admit such vulnerability, but he could not lie to these men.

"And Brior?" Stariat asked. "Is he able to fight?"

"Not yet," said Wladex. He had not yet checked on the knight, but he knew from the sound of his breathing that Brior was not strong enough to wake yet. "Another sunset and he will be stronger."

"Do you think that creature will wait that long?" Dusho asked in a tone of voice that provided his own opinion.

"I don't think we can afford to assume it will," said Wladex quietly. "I think we must plan to fight it—very soon." He sighed. "If only we still had the spell-holding quarrels for the crossbow. We do have one of them left."

Stariat grinned suddenly. "We have small bits of jewels, not much bigger than fingers. We could fire those with the crossbow." His enthusiasm was so genuine that Wladex and Dusho grinned with him.

"How many shards do we have?" Wladex asked.

"Perhaps five or six of everything but the pearls," said Stariat, going toward the cart. "If you will remove the spell from the stones, we'll soon see what we can salvage. We should be able to hold that monster off a while."

"What good will that do?" Dusho asked, no trace of anger in his words, but no sign of hope, either. "It will attack us eventually."

"But by then Brior may be more able to fight," said Stariat. "That will give us a better chance against the monster, and against the Laria."

Wladex nodded. "Making new monsters is tiring for the Laria, and distracting. The longer it has to maintain new forms, the greater chance we have to discover its weakness. If we can stand against that Lizcanth-thing for an hour or so, the Laria will have to divert much of its consciousness to the fight, and that may provide the opportunity we seek."

"The thing might also kill us, and then the Laria will have control over the four jewels," said Stariat, his face grim.

"We have to protect the four jewels, no matter what," said Wladex. "If we don't, then all we have fought for is lost."

"Yes, we know," said Dusho. He pointed down to the stream. "Can this give us a way out?"

Wladex shrugged cautiously. "Perhaps. The

water does emerge into the open not far from the wall of this cliff. But it may be in another canyon, or it may—" He stopped. "It is getting through the rock that is the trouble. The current is swift, and if the channel is too narrow, well, it would be a hard way to die."

"And fighting that monster would be easy?" Stariat shook his head. "Can you make a spell that would protect you going through the rocks?"

Until now this possibility had not suggested itself to Wladex. He scowled in thought, his ambition mounting as high as it had fallen. "Tell me," he said quietly, "have either of you any Imur-worm silk about you?" Of all the silk on Delos, Imur-worm had the most magical properties. "I have a few scraps, but they are not enough for what is needed here."

Stariat smiled. "My leggings are woven with it."

"So that is why you do not bother with armor," said Dusho, and Wladex had to bite back a similar observation—Ossato the mage knew about Stariat's lack of fighting armor, Godoh did not. "It never occurred to me."

"It never occurs to most people," said Stariat as he bent down to unwind the lacings over his leggings. "There are nine arm's lengths of it for each leg. I'll let you have half, and I'll rewrap with what is left. What are you planning to do with them?"

Wladex studied his hands. "I can make safety bubbles out of them. One for each of us. They will serve to protect us, give us air and pass us through the channel in the rocks, that is, if the channel isn't too long." This last was the part that bothered him.

"Do you think the bubble would be enough to get you—you and Dusho and Brior—and the jewels, beyond this canyon?" Stariat's eyes were very bright and he almost bristled with determination.

"Yes," said Wladex slowly. "Yes. And one for you as well." He added this in an emphatic tone, as if he did not know what Stariat intended.

Stariat laughed. "I'll find my own way out, thank you." He looked toward the cart. "I'll need a fist-size jewel, one of each. I want you to fuse them to the blade of my sword. You can do that, can't you?"

"Yes," said Wladex carefully. "But that makes the blade hard to handle. It isn't just the weight, it's all the magical power."

"Good!" Stariat clapped his hand onto Wladex's shoulder. "Very good. That's what paladins are trained to do. I never thought I'd have a chance like this. But now—" He went back to unwrapping his leggings.

"That thing is a brand new piece of the Laria!" Dusho exclaimed. "If you go up against it, you'll be killed."

Stariat continued his task. "I know. But I'll weaken it and then you can finish it off." He saw Dusho's exasperation. "Don't you see, this is the best fight I will ever have in my life?"

"Good thing, too, since you won't live through it," grumbled Dusho.

"That's why it's so important you escape with the jewels. You'll have to survive, and long enough to get the jewels to a focal point where they can be used to destroy the Laria. That's what we've set out to do from the first. I don't mind that I won't live to see it happen, but I would mind if you would not do your part." He tossed the unwound legging to Wladex. "Make your bubbles, elf. I'll redo this for my fight." And he started loosening the fabric on his left leg.

Wladex took the cloth and cut it into three equal sections. "Each of us will have to carry a full set of jewels with him. That way, if one of us doesn't make it, the other two will be able to go on." He didn't have to say he was referring to Brior, who still lay in a stupor on the cart.

"Get the bubbles ready and I'll start loading," said Dusho in a flat voice. He glanced at Stariat. "You sure you don't want help?"

"That would be a waste," said Stariat. "I can manage on my own." He paused. "Thanks," he added.

On the rim of the canyon the monster was growing restless, beginning to slap its tail back and forth like a whip.

As he put the jewels on the cart into selected piles, Wladex separated out fist-size jewels for Stariat. Now that the disguise was off them, the rubies and emeralds shone like miniature suns. Selecting the largest water cask, he took out half a dozen diamonds, and put one of the proper size with the emerald, ruby, and pearl. "When you're ready, Stariat." He thought that when he ruled in the Laria's place he would have to be very careful of men like Stariat. He had no intention of letting heroes seek him out for destruction, and Stariat was reminding him of how dedicated paladins could be.

Stariat approached, his leggings retied, his sword out of its scabbard. "What do I have to do?"

"Hold your sword out flat. Keep it steady," said Wladex, and carefully laid the jewels along the blade. Then he began the spell that would make the jewels part of the shining metal, and give it power enough to strike at the heart of any monster the Laria could create. The sword glowed, and then the jewels merged with it.

Stariat raised the radiant blade. "I'm ready," he declared. "Prepare the bubbles."

"Very well," said Wladex, and turned his attention to that task.

Chapter 27

BRIOR WAS GROGGY AS DUSHO BUNDLED him into the bubble Wladex had conjured for him. He did not grasp the importance of what was happening, and the sight of the reptilian monster on the canyon rim made him cringe. "Why are we doing this?" he asked Wladex for the third time.

"So we can fight the Laria. You remember that?" Wladex was nearly out of patience with the young knight, wounded or not. "The bubble will protect you and the jewels you carry. All you have to do is let the stream carry you. Don't attempt to steer the bubble or you might hurt yourself." *And damage the jewels*, he added to himself.

Brior nodded several times but it was apparent he still did not understand. He blinked as Dusho closed the bubble and rolled him down toward the stream.

"You next," Dusho said to Wladex. "I can use the jewels to close mine." He was purposefully avoiding looking at the side of the canyon where Stariat was climbing, making his way up through the brush toward the massive creature on the rim. The enormous monster had reared up half its length, revealing a huge, scaly body and taloned limbs.

"I hate abandoning the cart," said Wladex, who was not looking forward to lugging the jewels across the badlands. He had been fighting off hunger for half the day, and now it niggled at his thoughts, as persistent as a pain in his foot. It would be some time yet before he could feed, a realization that made him want to be off.

"We haven't room for it, and Stariat can't use it," said Dusho bluntly. "It's just a cart. It was useful, now it's not. Get into the bubble."

"If you think that's best," said Wladex, not wanting to sound too eager. He had no wish to see any of the battle between Stariat and the Laria's monster. It would be brutal and ultimately deadly for Stariat. But if that was what Stariat wanted, Wladex would be the last to deny him.

"I think it is best, yes. I also think you should hurry." Dusho held the flap of the bubble up. "Brior's already in the water. He'll be in the current shortly."

There was a thunderous yowl from the canyon rim and a flash of movement as Stariat hauled himself to his feet a short distance behind the tremendous creature. The sunlight gleamed off the blade of Stariat's sword as he made his first swing.

"You're right," said Wladex, and slipped into

his bubble, sealing the magical silk with a touch of the nearest pearl. He felt the bubble begin to roll down the bank and into the stream. He was aware of a series of high, trumpeting howls, but the sound was muffled by the bubble, and then lost in the burble of the stream as the current took hold of the bubble, tossing it toward the small cleft in the face of the cliff.

Wladex knew it was unnecessary, but he found himself holding his breath as the bubble was sucked deep into the water. The creek plunged into darkness, swirling through a narrow, twisting passage cut through the rock. The bubble tossed and writhed along with the swirling water. Wladex pressed tightly to the stones in his bubble, taking courage from their presence.

Ahead where a second stream joined the one in which Wladex rode, a waterfall roared, and Wladex did his best not to cry aloud as his bubble went over the wall into a deep pool. He had a glimpse of Brior's bubble some distance ahead of him, and then the river took a sharp bend, and Brior was once again lost to sight. The river continued on through vast, fantastic caverns, with stalactites and stalagmites joining to make colossal pillars that were lit only by the shine from the bubble. In one of the caverns, Wladex thought he saw strange creatures hanging from the ceilings, vast, scaled wings extended. These creatures were unknown to him. He decided that when he ended the Laria's hold on Delos and secured it for himself, he would explore to discover how many monsters the Laria had created in its long hold over the planet. But the bubble continued on and the caverns were lost to sight.

The walls closed in again, forming a tunnel that wriggled through the rocks, the water gathering speed. Wladex could feel the bubble jounce against the walls of the channel, and he braced himself for injuries that never came.

Finally, far ahead, he saw a bit of light, a wedge of brightness that grew steadily larger as Wladex's bubble hurtled toward it. The relief Wladex felt was much greater than he wanted to admit. His hunger hit him again like a blow, and unwise though it was, he found himself thinking about Brior, so weak and confused. He could provide the nourishment Wladex needed. He tried to calculate how far behind Dusho might be, and could not decide if he would have time to take what he needed.

Sunlight angled in from above as the river cut through a cleft on the far side of the cliff face. The steep walls made the water flow faster, and Wladex wondered how far they would have to go before it would be safe to come ashore, or how he would manage that maneuver. Overhead the green sun was setting and the blue sun was rising. Wladex had never enjoyed seeing them more than he did at that hazardous moment.

The cleft gave way to a series of rapids. The ride was as fast as it was perilous. Once the huge pearls in Wladex's bubble bounced sharply into his shins as the bubble was tossed by a standing boulder into a whirlpool. The danger was over as swiftly as it had begun, and Wladex was once again careening down the rapids, the bubble riding the frothing water with an ease that Wladex found reassuring. He shifted his position so that he could get a better look at what lay ahead.

The river grew wider and its frantic pace slowed. It still moved quickly, but there was no longer a headlong plummet to its flow. Now Wladex had the opportunity to look beyond the water, and what he saw entranced him. The banks were lined with tall trees, like an oasis, but larger and less stark. There were meadows in which creatures he had never seen before grazed. The only thing missing was men.

"This is the Laria's haven," said Wladex with a certainty that made him glower. That the Laria should keep so pleasant a place to itself while the rest of Delos scratched and suffered in the desert. Even a vampire lord saw the injustice in that. "This must be in the heart of the badlands," he said a bit later as the river made a lazy bend past ancient ruins that must surely have been a city, eons ago.

Ahead, Brior's bubble was bobbing toward the shore, making for the land as if under some power of its own.

"The jewels know there is a focal point here," said Wladex to himself, and felt a kind of nudge from the jewels in his bubble. He glanced behind him but did not see Dusho's bubble yet. Wladex felt a surge of emotion that combined his hunger with the nearness of triumph; it had eluded him for too long and now he was going to have it— he was entitled to it. He willed his bubble to reach the shore quickly, welcoming the scrape of sand and pebbles beneath the silken cocoon. Opening the flap, he stepped out into knee-deep water. It wasn't difficult to drag his bubble out of the river and to beach it a short way up the bank. Satisfied the jewels were safe, he went in search of Brior.

The bubble was still closed, although it rested against a fallen log in a backwash of the river. Wladex could see Brior inside, still wan, his eyes half-closed. As he bent down to haul the bubble ashore, Wladex saw Brior blink slowly, but he made no other effort to get out of the bubble.

"Come on," said Wladex as he tapped the flap of the bubble. "Get out. We're here."

"Here?" Brior repeated, sounding like a very young child. "What place is here?"

"I don't know. The jewels brought us here." He held out his hand. "Come on," he repeated. "I'll help you up."

Brior was unsteady, wobbling as he took a step, and then dropped to his knees. "Sorry. I can't . . ."

Wladex sighed in aggravation, and then fell on Brior, hurriedly draining the blood from him. The knight collapsed without a sound, and lay sprawled at the edge of the river. Making sure he had Brior's bubble and its jewels, Wladex kicked the dead knight back into the river, shoving him toward the part where the water ran deepest. The strength from his feeding was exhilarating, and he found himself eager to keep on with the mission. He watched to make sure Brior's body was gone, then he went back to the bank to wait for Dusho to arrive. He occupied himself with inventing a credible story to account for Brior's death. He had just put the finishing touches on the tale when he spotted Dusho's bubble coming down the river. Wading into the water, he prepared to snare the bubble as it approached.

Dusho caught sight of Wladex, and made a gesture of recognition as his bubble swung in toward the shore. He opened the flap as soon as Wladex was within reach, then got out of the bubble and pulled it toward the shore.

"Stariat?" Wladex asked as they reached the pebbled sandbar where the other two bubbles lay, now looking like disgarded blankets with strange shapes within them.

It took a moment for Dusho to answer. "The Laria overwhelmed him, Stariat charged right for the monster's heart, his sword held true." He sat down on the bank, staring into the distance. "The blow was to the heart, and the monster was felled by it. But then, Stariat was . . . was absorbed into the monster's body." He shook his head. "I have never seen anything like it."

"What do you think caused that?" Wladex asked, trying not to sound too eager, for he knew the power of the four jewels was greater than any but the Laria's.

Dusho shrugged, his eyes narrowing. "The monster was dead. That was beyond doubt. The jewels may have—I don't know—worked their magic on the monster, going into the body. I think the jewels forced themselves to be assimilated, and that weakened the Laria." He looked about. "Where's Brior? Is he all right?"

Wladex shook his head sadly. "Brior's bubble was here when I arrived, but I could not find him. The bubble was against that log," he said, pointing to the dead tree stretching out into the river. "The bubble was open, but I could not find Brior. I'm afraid he wasn't recovered enough to fight the current." He paused, then went on. "He made sure the jewels were safe."

"It's hard to lose a hero like Brior," said Dusho quietly.

"It's hard to lose a hero like Stariat," said Wladex.

"Stariat's different. He decided to make his attack. He knew he was up against impossible odds, but he chose to do it," said Dusho. "Poor Brior died by accident. That seems worse to me."

"I see your point," said Wladex. "But that doesn't lessen their loss, not of either one."

Dusho nodded. "For an elf, Godoh, you understand knights," he said. "We'd better start making slings for those jewels. We should start looking for the focal point where we can use them." He patted Wladex on the shoulder. "This is going to be hard."

"Possibly. But I think the place we are seeking isn't far away. The jewels have been warm, and if I give them a finding spell, they should guide us directly to the strongest focal point on all Delos." He went over to the two bubbles that had carried him and Brior to this place. "The bubbles can be changed to slings, I think."

"A good idea," said Dusho. "I wish I knew how far we're going to have to go. A little way could be hard."

"So it might," agreed Wladex. "But this is so beautiful." An unpleasant thought struck him. "We'll have to hope this isn't an illusion, another trap created by the Laria to throw us off the track."

"Could that be?" Dusho asked. He was piling up the jewels. They made an impressive mound about as high as his shoulder and half his height in diameter. "Would the Laria do such a thing?"

"It could," Wladex said. "But with the jewels here it isn't likely. But we'll have to be on the alert. The Laria must know where we are, and it will not want us to find the focal point we seek."

"It hasn't wanted that all along, and we have come this far," said Dusho. "Those slings will be useful." This mild prodding caught Wladex's full attention.

"I'll make the shape-changing spell. It's a good thing the silk holds magic as well as it does." He began to recite the words that would make the silk take another form. He could feel a kind of warmth come from the jewels. "They are very powerful."

"That was the point of finding them," said Dusho bluntly. "And now we have them. It is time to complete our mission." His face was somber and he stood beside the jewels as if he were a monument to stalwartness.

"That will be . . . a fitting tribute to our companions," said Wladex, having a hard time keeping from smiling. At last he would have what he sought. He would rule all Delos in the Laria's place. With the four jewels to give him power, no force would be strong enough to oppose him.

"Yes," said Dusho quietly. "It will be a fitting tribute to all of them: Ossato, Hornos, Casilta, Stariat, and Brior. Their memories will be held in highest honor for all time to come." He looked at Wladex. "You and I, Godoh, have the obligation to them to see this mission through to the end."

"I agree," said Wladex, and held out the newly shaped slings. "This goes over your shoulder, so that you have sacks hanging down in the front and the back. Between the two of us, and with this silk, we should be able to carry them all."

"Then let us load up," said Dusho. "The sooner we head off, the sooner we will get where we are going." He did his best to look optimistic, and almost achieved it.

Wladex murmured the finding spell, slipped the silk over his head, and began to load up his slings. "Make sure we divide all the jewels equally between us. That way, if one of us falls, the other will have stones enough to do what has to be done." He did not say that he had no intention of falling himself, and that if he did, he would will himself back to life and join Dusho to end their mission.

"A sensible precaution," said Dusho, handing

an emerald brick to Wladex. "Which direction shall we go?"

"The way the jewels pull us," said Wladex. "And be careful. The power is apt to attract monsters."

"I will be careful," said Dusho, and finished loading his slings before helping Wladex with his. "I didn't know elves were so strong."

"We can be, if the circumstances are right," said Wladex as they began walking, following the bank of the river until the fields widened, lushly verdant, and they could strike out to the northwest.

"Who would have thought there was such a place left on Delos, and in the heart of the badlands? The merchants never come this far to the center of the land," said Dusho when they had been going along for a while. The ancient ruins were behind them, and the beautiful, empty grasslands lay ahead.

"The badlands hide it," said Wladex.

"The badlands hide many things," Dusho agreed. "The badlands, and the Laria."

Wladex adjusted the sling support on his shoulders. "A good thing these jewels are here to protect us."

"Do you think they will?" Dusho looked about again, his movements jerky with nervousness.

"They have thus far, and they are stronger than anything used against the Laria." As Wladex said it, he hoped again that it was true; he had never felt so exposed as he did on this pleasant, wide, grassy plain.

Dusho nodded. "I don't know what I should look for." This admission explained his edginess.

"Look for creatures you have never seen before. Like those," Wladex said, pointing ahead at great lumbering shapes—swegles, but bigger than anything Wladex had ever seen before.

"Yes," said Dusho, glaring. "And they're coming our way."

Chapter 28

THE HERD OF SWEGLES HAD BROKEN INTO a clumsy run and had wheeled to charge Wladex and Dusho. The thunder of their hooves was so loud that Wladex could barely make himself heard over it. "We must make a shield. Stay still." He raised one of the diamonds into the air and recited a spell quickly.

"Do you think it will work?" Dusho asked, his hand on the hilt of his sword.

As if in answer, the swegles turned aside, blundering away toward the distant river. Their sounds died quickly, more as if they had vanished than gone elsewhere.

"The jewels did that?" Dusho marveled.

"The jewels and the spell they powered. We must be alert," said Wladex again. "The swegles are huge, but the larines are small. Who knows what the Laria will invent for us next."

"I wish we'd brought one of those things down while we had the chance. I'd have liked a swegle steak." Dusho shrugged. "We'll tend to that later. I can manage to go hungry a while longer."

"Good enough," said Wladex, his hands on the stones again. "We keep to the northwest, I think." He resumed walking.

"Do you think it would be worth the risk to use a transportation spell?" asked Dusho a little later.

"There's too much in peril, now that we are nearing our goal," said Wladex, his reservation genuine. "I don't think we should make ourselves so obvious, and waste the power of the jewels when it may not be necessary." He pointed into the distance. "There is something out there, near the horizon. I think that's where the jewels are taking us." He gestured confidently. "I'll keep us shielded as we go."

"All right," said Dusho, unwilling to argue with Wladex. "But make sure nothing goes wrong with that shield."

"Of course," said Wladex. The last thing he wanted was to have to exhaust the power of the jewels when their goal was within reach.

As they went on, the grasslands lost their greenness, becoming dry, then parched, then blasted, as empty as most of the country they had passed through on Delos. Their journey was enlivened by a parade of monsters, some hideous, some strange, some almost pitiful, such as a great beast with a soft-skulled head and flexible arms that seemed more a creature of the water than the air. Wladex told Dusho to ignore them all, as he would the chimeras of a dream. "They are the things the Laria plays with—its toys."

Dusho shook his head. "No wonder men are unable to win against the Laria."

"We are going to change that," Wladex reminded him, thinking how much he was exhilarated by what they had seen. He would have to create more diversity among his monsters when he ruled in the Laria's place.

By the next sunset, a twisting pillar of flame rose ahead of them, spinning toward them, leaving a swath of scorched earth in the dust wherever it went. Lightning crackled from it, and the baleful light of the flames made the sunlight lurid.

"It's trying to block our path," said Dusho, halting to size up the pillar of fire.

"And to lessen the power of the jewels," said Wladex with a sharp stare at the Laria's latest horror. "But it is a beacon. It would not be in our path if we were not going the right way."

"Do we fight it?" Dusho asked, sounding both eager and apprehensive.

"Not unless we must," said Wladex. "We need to save as much of the jewels' force as we can. The shield should protect us." He studied the pillar as it swayed, seductive as a dancer, never getting much closer to them, but not diminishing, either. "If you are not too tired, we should walk on. That city is where we are bound, I am certain of it."

Dusho put his hand to his eyes. "It is a long way off still. That pillar of fire could make us—"

But Wladex would not listen to any words of discouragement. "The pillar of fire is the Laria's creation. If it comes directly to us, then we will have to use the jewels to destroy it. As long as it cannot touch us, we have nothing to fear." He was not being completely truthful, but he saw no reason to tell Dusho that if he had to choose between defending the knight or the jewels, he would defend the jewels. "Keep walking."

"What if the focal point isn't in that ancient city? What then?" Dusho eyed the pillar of fire anxiously.

"Then we will go on until we find what is," said Wladex. "We have come this far. We must finish the task we have sworn to undertake."

"And we will," said Dusho, watching the pillar of fire out of the corner of his eye.

They were near enough to the city now to see its ruined walls, still shining as if they had been made of glass. *What were these ancient places built of, that they glistened even in ruins?* Wladex thought. He noticed that this city had not been as large as the one where they had been chased off by larines. Its towers did not rise as high, nor were they as massive, and yet this place had a grace to it the other had lacked, and a ravaged beauty that held Wladex's attention. They saw more and more of its details as they grew nearer. They were less than an hour's walk when they noticed a wide ditch ran around the ruins, crossed by tumbled lines of shining bricks. "It must have been surrounded by water, and had bridges," Wladex surmised. "Why else should those—"

"No outer walls, though," said Dusho, who was also staring. "It wasn't built for defense."

"If it had the four jewels, it did not need any more defense," said Wladex.

"Until the Laria," said Dusho. "What force it must have needed to blast those towers to pieces."

"Yes," said Wladex. "And now a greater force will defeat it."

The pillar of fire, which had moved off into the badlands, now came undulating back, circling the ruins at the outer edge of the ditch. As Wladex and Dusho went on, a second pillar of fire rose in the empty sky.

"They're keeping their distance," Dusho said. "So long as they do—"

"So long as they do, we have no reason to heed them," Wladex finished, although he disliked the swirling flames.

"Just so." Dusho nodded and pressed on, all traces of hunger and thirst gone from his features now that victory was near.

The wide ditch was deeper than it appeared, and crossing it took longer than either Wladex or Dusho had anticipated. As they scrambled up the inner bank, they saw the crumbled buildings in the street were intermixed with bits of bone, not all of it as ancient as the city.

In their slings, the jewels were humming, quivering as if alive. The air around them seemed close, thickened, as if the jewels caused a change in it. Each building they passed glowed from a light that was not the sun.

"Where are they taking us?" Dusho asked, his voice hushed.

"I think that is where we are going," Wladex said, indicating a rounded tower ahead of them. The top of the building had melted away, and part of its side sagged, unbroken but bent.

As if in agreement, the jewels vibrated more vigorously. The diamonds shone more brightly, the red and green of the rubies and emeralds became more vivid, the luster of the pearls was deeper.

"That's our destination," said Wladex, grinning.

Dusho frowned. "It's too easy. After all we've gone through, this is too easy."

"We have the jewels to protect us, and the spell to shield us," said Wladex confidently. "This shows you how much the four jewels can do." He was walking faster, picking his way through the rubble and shards of bone with certainty.

"There are three pillars of fire now," Dusho said, hitching his shoulder in the direction of the new blazing column.

Wladex was unimpressed. "They have not entered this city. If the Laria were strong enough to send them against us, it would have done it before we got this far."

"Perhaps," said Dusho. "But you yourself have said that when things are easy it is because they are traps."

This reminder annoyed Wladex, who stopped long enough to put his hands on his hips. "You don't realize what we have here," he said, meaning the jewels. "This is what will bring the Laria to an end. The Laria knows it."

"Then why doesn't it attack?" Dusho asked, and answered his question for himself. "It's marshaling its strength. It is preparing to strike with all the force it commands."

"And so are we," said Wladex. "That the Laria has not been harrying us tells me that we have the greater power here, with the four jewels." He reached out and tugged at Dusho's sleeve. "The sooner we get to that melted tower, the sooner we can dispatch the Laria."

Dusho fell in slightly behind Wladex. "I don't like it, Godoh. The Laria hears everything we say. It knows where we are going, and why."

"Fine," said Wladex brusquely. "It would be too foolish to survive if it did not." He saw the tower was now directly ahead. "We'll be inside shortly."

"Unless something happens," said Dusho as he kept pace with Wladex.

There was less rubble and more slag here, as if the walls of the tower had flowed, molten, through the streets. There were fewer bones, and those that remained here were so old it was impossible to know what they had been. The surface underfoot was slippery, so every step had to be made cautiously, a task that became more difficult as the glass began to rise toward the gaping hole in the side of the ruined building.

"Five pillars of fire," Dusho reported as he struggled not to slide back down the glassy incline.

Wladex chuckled. "The Laria is worried. Not without cause." He entered the blasted opening, sighing with pleasure. "Now we must find where we are to put the four jewels." He noticed a staircase, many of the treads missing, leading up the curve of the walls. The stones in his sling strove to rise. "We go up there."

"Very well," said Dusho, doing his best to conceal his growing tension. "You should be able to climb to the next level." He pointed to the partially broken ceiling which revealed another floor.

"You're going to climb, too," said Wladex. "You can't stay down here. I . . . We may need the jewels you carry to give our weapon its full strength."

"If you insist," said Dusho, and prepared to follow Wladex up the rickety stairs. "Hang onto the rail," he recommended. "You wouldn't want to fall."

Wladex took the advice, picking his way carefully up toward the level above. The jewels in his sling were elated, their humming now more of a throb. As he reached the floor of the upper level, he felt the air change again, as if something made up of nightmares and horror were coalescing out of nothing. Finally, he told himself, the Laria is making itself known to me. He swung around, prepared to confront unimaginable hideousness and saw instead Stariat, sitting on the edge of a large, circular device, his sword out, and a smile on his face. Wladex halted, taken aback.

"Wladex," said Stariat, in a voice that vibrated on the air. "You finally got here."

"Stariat," Wladex said cautiously, realizing the paladin had used his real name. "You survived?"

"In a manner of speaking. I'm here." He raised a hand in greeting to Dusho. "So you have been spared."

Dusho looked dumbfounded. "Stariat? Stariat? But you were dead."

"And I was restored." He rose, moving his sword in a menacing way. "By the Laria."

At this Wladex stood very still. "The Laria sent you to stop us?"

"Actually," said Stariat, "the Laria combined with me to stop you." The sword sliced through the air, spitting sparks and flames as it went. "You have come a long way, but not quite far enough." Ill-defined and ghastly shapes were moving in the air now, following the path of Stariat's sword. "In a way I am grateful to you, Wladex. Had you not beguiled me with your promises of destroying the Laria, I might not have known what power is, and how good it is to have it." The sword moved again, leaving a trail of fire on the air.

Dusho had not moved since he caught sight of Stariat, but now he lunged forward. "You aren't Stariat!" he shouted. "You're one of those!" He pointed to the clear wall beyond which two pillars of fire coiled. "You just look like Stariat."

"Oh, I am much more than that," said Stariat, growing much larger so that he took up half the space on this level. His sword hissed as he struck at Dusho.

As if wakened from a terrible dream, Dusho shouted to Wladex. "Put the four jewels in place. I'll hold it off as long as I can." With this vow, he parried the murderous thrust from Stariat, his sword glowing hot as it touched the paladin's.

Wladex needed no more encouragement. He hurried to the circular device and looked down on it. The ancient writing seemed to writhe as he looked at it, so he ignored it as he did his best to ignore the cloudy monsters hovering in the air. "Emerald, emerald, emerald," he muttered as he drew one from the sling and set it down on the surface of the device; the stone slipped easily into a groove and nestled there as if it were alive and finally home.

Stariat howled, and slammed his sword at Wladex. Dusho managed to beat the blade aside with his own, but not before the left side of his face was burned and a white swath appeared in his hair.

"Four pillars!" Dusho cried in warning as he chopped at Stariat's legs, forgetting the magical silk that made his leggings into armor; his sword clanged as if against stone, and Dusho staggered back.

The second emerald was in place, and then a third. Wladex pulled out the diamonds next and concentrated on putting them in position. The sound in the air around him was like the wailing of millions of destroyed lives, accented by two notes, one so high it made Wladex's skull hurt, the other so low that the ground trembled with it. Two diamonds fit into place, and he was reaching for a third when Stariat's sword bit deeply into his shoulder. Wladex dropped the diamond in his hand and cursed vehemently.

"Keep going!" Dusho yelled as he took a jewel from his sling and threw it at Stariat's face.

Shrieking with rage, Stariat drew back. The air became denser, little glints of flame spangling around Stariat. Dusho pulled another jewel from his sling and prepared to throw it.

Wladex would not give up, not when his goal was so near. He gritted his teeth against the pain, for he did not want to stop to do a healing spell, not with the forces of the Laria all around him. He dragged another diamond from his sling and put it in place on the device. Then he began on the rubies. These were more difficult, for the agony of his wound made thought and action difficult, and the atmosphere in the huge glass chamber was thick. Slowly he set the rubies down while Dusho continued to hold Stariat off with a barrage of gems.

"Hurry!" Dusho shouted. "I am getting low!"

Stariat laughed again, and grew larger. He no longer looked like the paladin who had braved so much with them. His head was snouted like a scevan's and his body was more like a gargoyle than a man. He extended his huge, leathery wings, the talons raised for gripping, his clawed feet scratching for purchase on the glass floor.

Wladex put the last of the rubies into place and reached for the largest of the black pearls. His head swam and for an instant he feared he had undertaken too much. Then his pride soared and he set the pearl into position. He felt the swick of air as Stariat's talon just missed his head.

"Godoh!" Dusho cried. "Finish it!"

In a daze of agony, Wladex put the last pearl into position, then sagged against the device. How he would make the monsters of the Laria pay for this as soon as he was in power! He began to read the old words carved on the flat of the device.

Now there were a dozen pillars of fire hovering just outside this tower as if watching and listening.

Dusho dropped to his knees as he threw the last jewel—a black pearl, striking Stariat in the middle of his forehead just as the device began to glow.

Wladex clung to the rim of the device as it trembled, shimmered, shattered, and cracked. In the rush of air and fire that followed, Wladex was flung from the glass tower just as it smashed to myriad bits.

Epilogue

THE AIR OVERHEAD WAS CLEAR, THE BLUE
sun near setting, the red sun well-risen. A slight
breeze stirred the sand on which Wladex lay. He
was dimly aware that the Laria was gone, that
the four jewels had broken its power forever. He
could just recall being flung, enveloped in
flames, out of the tower before it collapsed.

Then why was he lying here? Why had he not
gained the Laria's power? Wasn't that what the
mission had been about? Wasn't that what was
supposed to happen? He summoned all his consciousness and realized he was not much more
than a smear of ashes in the middle of the badlands. He thought he heard the sound of water
far away, rushing toward him.

But that was impossible, he decided.

The wind picked up, stroking the ashes.

"I will be back again. I will be back again. I
will be back again," Wladex recited in a voice he
no longer possessed.

The Laria was gone. Now it was his turn.

"I will be back again."

Now the wind was stronger, and the ashes began to blend with the sands.

"I . . . will . . ."

Liberated from the hold of the Laria, the water was coming nearer, rushing in a glorious flood across the badlands.

". . . I . . ."

Wind and water carried him away.